IT TAKES A MURDER

Anu Kumar has a degree in history from Delhi University and has also specialised in human resources management at the XLRI School of Business. She writes for children as well as for older readers, and her short stories have appeared in various magazines and anthologies. *It Takes a Murder* is her third novel for older readers after *Letters for Paul* (Mapin, 2006) and *The Dollmakers' Island* (Gyaana, 2010). She lives in Singapore with her husband and four-year-old daughter.

IT TAKES A MURDER

Anu Kumar

First published in 2012 by Hachette India
(Registered name: Hachette Book Publishing India Pvt. Ltd)
An Hachette UK company
www.hachetteindia.com

Copyright © Anu Kumar 2012

Anu Kumar asserts the moral right to be identified
as the author of this work

All rights reserved. No part of the publication may be reproduced, stored in a retrieval system (including but not limited to computers, disks, external drives, electronic or digital devices, e-readers, websites), or transmitted in any form or by any means (including but not limited to cyclostyling, photocopying, docutech or other reprographic reproductions, mechanical, recording, electronic, digital versions) without the prior written permission of the publisher, nor be otherwise circulated in any form of binding or cover other than that in which it is published and without a similar condition being imposed on the subsequent purchaser.

This is a work of fiction. Any resemblance to real persons, living or dead, or actual events or locales is purely coincidental.

ISBN 978-93-5009-494-5

Hachette Book Publishing India Pvt. Ltd
4th/5th Floors, Corporate Centre,
Plot no. 94, Sector 44, Gurgaon 122003, India

Typeset in Arno Pro 12/14.65
by InoSoft Systems Noida

Printed and bound in India
by
Gopsons Papers Ltd, Noida

*For Ajay Kumar
and Vatsala Kaul Banerjee
for being there when it mattered*

Part I

1984
The Man on the Boulder

That night when Maddy called, it was her first in six months. Six months, twenty-three days, I remember such things. She said she had just been nominated for an award, and was informing me. 'They might do a story on me, and could get in touch with you. You are the first person I mentioned.' And only I heard the aloneness in that statement, though she said it in the practised offhand way she had learnt to use on me. *I am leaving*, the three words she had said just before she did. If she had raised it by several notches, it would have sounded like 'Get out, you...', someone else's last words to me. Maddy would never know how much she looked like him either.

I wanted to tell her of the song that played just then on a cell phone. It was from Maddy's latest serial and someone hummed it as he strolled by that part of the river that had always been mine. Someone who looked familiar but I knew Kerketta had been dead for as many years or more that Maddy had left Brooks Town, and because one can't talk of ghosts, even about seeing them, especially over a long distance telephone call, I leaned against the old comforting walls by the river, and let Maddy's happy laughter wash over me.

'Aren't you happy?' she asked. 'You aren't laughing.'

I was but it was my own ghost laughter that I hoped no one heard. In a big city, a lovely young woman who has never looked her age could be allowed her eccentricities but here I was, by myself, growing old and slowly losing the ability to charm people. I didn't want to be bundled away into an asylum. People muttering to themselves as I left: a laughing, old hag.

'Best actor.' And she added in an undertone, 'For television.'

'That's okay. All your mother had been was an actor on stage. A school stage.'

'I can't hear you,' she said, irritated.

'I am happy for you, my dear,' I said instead.

And she laughed, the laughter taking me back many years ago. Her laughter that flew in the sky and that the wind carried back to me, to the sound of her bicycle bell. In my mind, those sounds are intermingled. A memory that also works as a time marker. This and what would happen soon after.

The Maddy of the present filled my ears, she said to me then, 'I told them about you, the teacher of dramatics, my first influence.'

I laughed finally at what she said, and it came out a sob. She said mock-reprovingly, 'You must have a laughter suitable for the occasion. And you taught dramatics, you say. Don't you have any other kind of laughter?'

I remembered a time 25 years ago, and how she had laughed then. I would never forget it. That was a year people of a certain age remember. The year a prime minister was gunned down by her own guards, and for the first time we saw and heard about it all on TV.

I was almost as old as Maddy is now, though she never told her right age to anyone – the understandable vanities of a movie star. Or a wannabe movie star, though she was doing very well on television, even winning awards then. I've never understood why mothers cannot be frank about their own children.

That year for a very short period, we cycled to school together. I never knew it would be so short – one's happiest moments usually are. There was Kerketta too, and we rode to school making a grand threesome. The entire town, or most of it out on the streets in those early mornings of that year, stopped to watch us. I always fell behind in no time. Maddy rode her bicycle at great speed, taking the Brooks Hill road at a rush. Then one day a circular traffic stand came up, and a few days later a traffic constable followed.

It was the year Jaspal Singh left school because of the knife fight he got into with Mahesh. Maddy and her eleven-year-old heart loved both though I never told her this and she thought I never knew.

And also the year someone from the past returned and sat on the boulder we passed every day till Maddy, who had never seen him before, told him to get lost.

Maddy rode fast and always gave Kerketta a hard time. From a long way off, I could hear her bicycle bell, loud and clear, and Kerketta's frantic shouts, as he tried hard to keep the road clear. *Girl on cycle. Clear road, clear road.* Kerketta's eyes wide in alarm, his voice quivering, and I can still hear Maddy laugh as she rode on, mimicking him with wild unconcern. Sometimes she let him catch up with her and they would have one of their conversations that I was never really curious about. Then with a whoosh she would dash ahead, cycle uncaring past everything that stood and watched. I was glad when the traffic stand came up.

I followed sedately dismounting as I took the hill and as befitting my age. I was 37 but never mind how old I was, I was at that age when people make you feel old. I could take dismissals like Kerketta's knowing gaze, but not someone's outright ignoring, the quick glance, the judging look-over that was really a brush-off. Every morning, I would look at myself in the mirror, fingering lines and counting days and years. It is a terrible thing, being forced to grow old before your time. The world was digging my grave and forcing me to look on. And I fought back. And it was this year that I would begin this lying game about my age; with every advancing year, my age would correspondingly fall two or three equivalent notches.

So that morning, with these thoughts running inside me, and all of us running late, I saw him. Again. The first moment he was just a man sitting on a boulder. The very next, I knew he had reappeared, sitting on that boulder the way he would in the days that followed, the place just where Brooks Hill sloped to the village below. It was the way he sat and I knew someone who had sat like that, still and watchful, looking down at another valley as it unrolled around him, where the powdery snow alternated with patches of dry green grass. Five years and more since he had last appeared in Brooks Town. Soumen's absences were like a marker too.

Past the boulder on which he sat, the road to school ran on. It held onto the very edge of the hill, pushed there by the tall eucalyptus trees that Robert had planted. When the wind blew hard, it seemed the hill would kick the road off its perilous perch.

Maddy was a dancing blob ahead and I, struggling up the uneven hill road, was already short of breath, the sweat gathering in beads on my face, stamping itself on my back. No one else that I wanted could see me, or want to see me then but that man from the past sat there, with that fixed look he always had, and he was looking at me. I didn't mind that, it was his being there I minded.

He hadn't changed, only looked a bit older and much the worse for wear. Half his face was hidden by a cap but there was still that deeply cut pointed chin, the thin lips ready to curve into a wry smile and those narrowed eyes that saw everything. And he was still very thin.

Now he had a rexine bag with a striped, scratchy look. He wore stonewashed jeans and strapped sandals, stuff you get from the smuggling routes all the way to China. He sat there as I passed, his head turned to follow my every move. Just as he had that day, the year Maddy was born. Just as he had those many years ago when he first came to this town. A lazy-eyed, crinkled stare, holding onto a smile that never came.

At dinner, because Maddy was quiet, I told her about the man.

'What did he look like?' she asked. Her voice eased the silence away, for that moment.

'I don't know, I didn't see his face.' I lied, for I didn't want to invite more questions then. I had to find out why he was here again, after so many years. The last time he was here, only I had been witness to the fight he had then had with Gautam Singh Dogra, in the night's late hours, in the perfect pitch-black setting the riverbank provided.

'And you say he stared at you?' Her question held mocking disbelief.

But what did I expect? These are things I could not tell anyone, and it was safer that eleven-year-old Maddy heard it. So I didn't tell her how I had almost gone up to him, wanting to touch his chin, as I had done that time. Had twelve years turned the snow on his chin into an old man's stubble? And was it white or were my eyes beginning to fool me too?

Instead I told her of the jeans he wore and that made her talk of the new pair Jaspal Singh had worn to school that day. Jaspal was Maddy's senior but was in my special drama class and his father, Manjit Singh, owned two cloth stores in the city. I had learnt only recently of the letter the senior Singh had written to Sister Rose demanding an end to these drama classes. This is the kind of thing that encourages licentious behaviour, he had written and Sister had obligingly showed me, smoothening its crinkled edges to make sure I missed not a word. I could imagine him pushing his long beard away as he wrote that, the steel bangle on his wrist punctuating the righteous indignation he felt.

'My god,' I said disbelieving, 'he's actually spelled that word right.' But like many others Manjit Singh hated the drama classes while I thought he was uncultured and uncouth, and a bad influence on his son. 'We will have to convince him how useful these classes can be,' I said. I should have been pleading, more ingratiating, and got Sister Rose on my side. But I was my assured devious self, and already planning to have Jaspal as hero in all my plays. The ones I would direct and control and no one could stop me.

Jaspal's stonewashed jeans, the ones Maddy was so impressed with, had been shipped from Bangkok; his father went every month to Calcutta for his consignment of imported clothes and the Lucky Cloth store always had the latest in fashion. It was from him that our neighbour, Parida the police commissioner, got his batik shirts that were the latest fashion in Bangkok and Singapore. It made those places seem nearer than they actually were in Maddy's Oxford School Atlas.

Maddy adored him for the things he had, and always kept an eye out for his bicycle every morning. He did not take the hill road but the village road at the very bottom. I always noticed him too, but that day I was distracted for the man was sitting just where he had been the previous day, only he was smoking, the thin grey strands of smoke like his own flyaway hair that would never be tamed by any cap.

Slowing down, I asked him, 'You didn't reply to my letter that time?'

'I see Dogra's still around,' he said instead. And so it had to be him, the same laid-back voice and words that came soft in the wind. It reminded me of a mountain breeze, dry leaves flying away and timelessness.

'Why are you here?'

But again he didn't reply and then Kerketta was riding back to see if I was okay. What took you so long, I wanted to snap. That day they had been too far ahead to notice me. Maddy had already reached school and perhaps that day won the race against Jaspal.

'Leave my daughter alone, if that's what you are here for.' That was the last thing I told the man. 'There's nothing about the past that should touch her.'

And his laughter was low and gravelly as if a volcano rumbled inside him. 'You still talk like one of your heroines.'

The village road to school was an old dirt track, flattened by generations of cyclists and villagers on foot. Still it wasn't trustworthy. One carefully negotiated the unexpected rocky outcrop, the pothole, and sometimes an untidy knotted pair of chillies and lemon left behind by someone in hope that an unwary cyclist would ride into it and draw the evil eye. Every morning we would see them riding down. Jaspal Singh bent forward, his bottom raised above his seat, as he gave himself a clear lead over his brothers and younger cousins, all of whom were in the same school, each class having one representative of the Singh family. We always heard their laughter, the merry ringing of bells, wavering in the breeze. One day, when Maddy was sick and had missed school, she said those bicycle bells rang still in her mind. I have never laughed at anything she has said as I did that day.

And for several weeks those months after summer, the man sat at the same place. On that boulder painted white and green, in his stonewashed jeans, watching me in the manner he had done before. His rexine bag on the boulder by him, and that tear I noticed, a straight line along his right knee, which was reassuring.

'You still haven't got a steady job.'

He looked away, and shrugged.

'You must be getting old now. Have you saved anything?'

He turned to look at me, looked where Maddy was riding away fast. And grinned, that reckless, hard to place smile. 'Then you must surely know why I am here.'

'You won't get anything. No one knows.'

I raised my voice so that Kerketta whose pace had slowed though he still kept an eye on Maddy, could hear. 'No work, sitting here all day, good for nothing.'

'You are still the memsahib, I see.'

I could feel his eyes on my back as I rode away. I felt Kerketta's curious stare as I rode up to him.

I tried to forget him the rest of the way to school, past the curving hill road and the parish building built like a big European chalet with its red thatched roof, its climbing driveway and the rooster weathervane that never worked. There were smaller houses all the way down to the village road, houses that had sneaked a toehold into the hard hill rock and were now sinking into the hill.

If only his return did not worry me. Only he knew about my past, that visit to Shimla I had made the year Maddy was born, only he, looking at Maddy, could tell just why I had been there.

That year I finally admitted to myself I was old, with the feeling a woman has when she knows that she will never be looked at in a special or particular way, a time when you find yourself wishing that your past sins also become of little consequence.

But who sets these rules and why is one expected to live by them? And if only he would stare, look, not do anything that threatened the life I had. The only life I had a chance of living now. I thought these thoughts as I moved from class to class as the crafts instructor. For I refused to be called a needlework teacher. You can take other classes too now, Mrs Hyde, said Sister Rose gently. With the curriculum getting harder, it's best we leave drama classes for the junior classes. So I would no longer have Jaspal Singh as my hero. Perhaps it was the agitation that made my eyes water, the thread wavered before my eyes, making the needle's eye ever smaller and always farther away, and I spent more of my time looking across the red quadrangle to where the senior classrooms were.

The students weren't bothered, most did their own thing anyway. Only if the noise got too much, I would rap on the table and the hum would dim to a low murmur. Who notices a needlework teacher anyway? Someone who doubles as a fill-in teacher during absences. I wore my long skirts, my frilled tops and left my hair loose reminding everyone that till last year the plays had drawn huge crowds, as big a crowd as a small town would permit.

My hair flew into my eyes and so I must have seen the scene, which Maddy would later describe to me over dinner, through my tears. How Jaspal Singh had taken off his shirt to show everyone the knife he carried as his religion commanded.

Still she couldn't fill in what I had seen for myself, the haziness induced by the tears just made it more real. She described how he had locked the door to the cupboard that stood at the far end of the classroom after a group of very scared girls had seen it open, and the one armed skeleton half-dangling out of it. When no other boy had volunteered, Jaspal had gone up to it, slammed the door shut, then fixed the press lock that kept the skeleton in place.

'He will come and get you at night, Jaspal,' someone warned. And the fright returned to Maddy's laugh when she told me.

The girls had screamed sweet Jesus, crossed themselves.

But Jaspal had magnificently placed his hand on his hip and said he was armed. I can fight that thing. He shrugged.

Show us, Jaspal, show us.

He turned away from them, so that, across the quadrangle, he was looking at me instead. His shirt slipped off his shoulders, the girls turned their heads away and I held my breath, brushed the hair away from my face and looked on. A taunting smile slowly grew on his face, as I looked my fill at his fine, broad shoulders, the delicate collar bones, and his fine smooth chest. And the gazelle neck, the hair that appeared, and the manner it vanished into the buttons towards his navel.

The girls opened their eyes only when another murmur swept through the class. Jaspal Singh held up a short pointed knife in his hand, one with a serrated wooden handle. In his other hand, he juggled its sheath made like a cattle horn, grey black in colour. Around his shoulder was the thin leather belt he wore under his shirt.

I can defend myself from anything with this, he said, lifting it high so it caught the flickering tubelight that was always on.

That night, I asked Maddy more about the knife, we giggled and I was the one pretending to. I wanted to see it and Maddy offered to borrow his knife from him. Playful pacts that on occasion held us together, for all too brief moments.

Then she asked for no reason about the man on the boulder. 'Kerketta also said he talks to you.'

'He's still there and he does stare at me.'

She stared at me too, then. Looking at me like everyone seemed to, those days. As if she too had suddenly noticed me, after all these years. As if I was a lizard crawling out of the woodwork.

She laughed and after a while said, 'He must be mad.'

That night I heard her preparing for bed next door, and I looked out of my window, letting my gaze run along the river to stop at the only other light still on. A golden bulb shone in Gautam Singh Dogra's study. Perhaps he was still writing another letter to the government. I turned away, twisting my lips. He should have let me write his letters, but he had not even replied to my offer.

Someone smoked on the riverbank, a red dot of light danced carelessly and I hoped the gate was closed. Maddy switched off her tape recorder then, and everything plunged into quiet, and I could then think again of the straight, smooth look of Jaspal Singh's shoulders as his shirt slipped away. The few tendrils of hair that had slipped out of his patka and curled around his neck. And the angry welt of the belt as it lay tight against his skin. Did he sleep with the belt and the knife in it? It had been so long since I had a long, dreamless sleep. I no longer had to go look out of the window and count the last lights before putting mine off.

It had been some while too when I had last thought of a man, any man.

I walked close to the window, as I undressed. Unbuttoned my kurta and pulled it off over my head. The lamp behind me showed me up against the wall, and the red light pointed straight at me. It was almost like I was daring him to come up the gate, walk up the garden path.

The next day, Maddy wasn't in a mood to talk. I saw her crush the gravel under her wheels, work up a cloud of dust as she rode up. The man who had stood smoking by the river last night sat on the boulder, and I saw her turning her wheel towards him.

Just get lost, will you?

You've nothing better than sit here and stare.

Good for nothing.

She repeated the words, loudly, stopping at every word. I felt an ice-cold hand crawl up my heart and leave me shrivelled and frightened. It was the fear that accompanies the loss of a secret. And my voice rang out just as she started up again.

Leave my mother alone

Those words, the fact that she said *my mother* did not register. Only the tone of her voice did.

And that's why I said what I did next.

'That's enough Maddy. Real ladies don't do that.'

She stopped, and I remember the hurt look on her face. But I could not tell her anything more. It was the first time she had come to my, her mother's, defence. I would weep later when I thought over it again. The two of us, stood together at that moment, defiant, looking at the man, a few steps below, who slowly and very deliberately took off his cap. I saw his hair was now cut close to his scalp, and his face covered with thick worry lines.

I saw his eyes move, his stare shifted and I saw Maddy straighten her bicycle wheel slowly, saw too from the corner of my eye the whirl of the multi-coloured ribbon that formed the hub of Kerketta's cycle. I heard the distinct creak of his wheel as he neared. The man had heard it before me.

Leave my daughter alone, I said finally.

And then there was Kerketta's voice. Madam, what happened? Did he say something to Babyji? Why did you both stop? What happened?

I turned away, and Maddy rode off. Kerketta got off his cycle and did something unexpected. Hey, you. Got no work or what? Troubling Baby here. Go away, go. Or else.

He bent down and picked up some stray pebbles on the road. But he had no need to throw them. There was already a slither, the sound of pebbles skittering and falling over each other like children chasing each other down a slide and I saw him go. He wobbled down the hill, bouncing a little, moving side by side, as he took the declivity, like a small pebble himself.

There was one last time he turned around and I saw his inscrutable face, his face thin and pinched, those staring eyes of his, giving nothing away.

There I sent him away… now he won't trouble you.

And Kerketta tossed away the pebbles, rubbed his hands, straightened his crumpled shirt. Then he twirled the ends of his moustache, and assured me again.

He won't come back. Sent him away.

I laughed a low, throaty laugh and said, 'Oh he will be back. He always is.' Kerketta looked hurt, for I hadn't thanked him.

I won't need Jaspal's knife any more, I said later that night. That's no knife but a kirpan, she said contemptuously. Besides, he doesn't show it around any more, I don't know whether he's carrying it.

But I knew better. He had seen me stare at him that day and

in his adolescent conceit, Jaspal now took a precious delight in flicking open the top few buttons of his shirt, each time we crossed each other in the school corridor. It was done in so sudden a manner that to anyone else it would have appeared an accident. He looked at me too, the way no one else did, his eyes running lazily over me, and I wished my skirt would fly up just a little bit. For my part I saw through his half-buttoned shirt, the belt that held his knife, and the thin hair that sprang on his chest, and his taunting, self-assured smile and not once did I look away.

He says it's not for general display.

What? I distractedly returned to the conversation, the dinner table, the food before us.

You've become hard of hearing, I can't repeat everything for you.

Oh the cruelties the young inflict! Perhaps that was why Jaspal was tormenting me. Maddy must have seen my sudden tears for she said, in a gruff, more conciliatory tone, it's a kirpan. And he says he can't take it out just for showing off. It is to be used for important occasions...

Like?

Like when religion has to be defended or when someone insults the Sikhs. He is one, you know.

I nodded, though Maddy had expected me not to understand. But then it was the time when everyone knew what Jaspal meant. The patka he and the others like him wore on the head was often the butt of cruel, merciless teasing. And now Jaspal and his younger cousins who were scattered in different classes had begun to mind. Before the knife made its appearance, Maddy, her classmates too, had no compunctions addressing his short patka by a variety of other names. And I had seen for myself the paper planes that were directed to it from the back rows.

'And it's a kirpan,' Jaspal Singh had begun insisting on this as well. No, he said. It was not a knife. Not even a sword. It was a kirpan. A holy weapon.

It was of course to lead up to the fight that I came to know about much later. Maddy was asked to repeat it in the staff room for the fight was over her. And by the time I asked her again for the story when we were home, she was already bored, and so, as always, I filled in the scenes even she couldn't describe.

'Where is a thing like that available?' Someone asked Jaspal Singh a very unwise question about his beloved kirpan.

Jaspal Singh pulled the offending boy up by his collar, and shouted into his face. 'It's a kirpan, damn you. It isn't a common weapon that is available everywhere.'

It was easy for me to imagine a scene such as this. I had watched mesmerized, similar scenes in over a dozen Hindi films that had once been telecast every week at the club. Scenes where the hero takes the villain to task, but yet in this instance, it was unexpected. Jaspal opening his shirt, throwing it away. Standing there, towering over Mahesh, the boy who had dared take him on, and asked him that question. Mahesh was Maddy's friend too, but even then, everything about his physical appearance held portents to his becoming a fat, paunchy sweet-seller like his father, doomed to spend a life behind a sweet shop counter. It turned out that, like Maddy, he always had other ideas about himself.

I had seen Mahesh around the house often and now there was Maddy, shouting up in his defence, trying to prise him away from Jaspal's grasp. And Mahesh shrieked, his face purple with impotent fury. Let me go, you egg-headed surd.

The boys grappled with each other, pulling at each other's shirts, but Jaspal was easily the stronger, the taller of the two and he had soon pinned the other boy to the ground. The circle around them widened, they kicked, rolled on the ground, hit out at each other, we heard their harsh breathing and the sound of the kirpan every time it scraped the ground.

I will kill you...

But the other boy could never finish for it was just then that the senior teacher arrived. Get back to your classes, he said, and you, follow me to the principal's office. He meant Maddy, and she made up the laggard third, behind Jaspal, his shirt now unbuttoned and disarranged, and Mahesh. Everyone saw her reach for Mahesh's hand, maybe she was trying to make Jaspal jealous and perhaps it was this that started people talking till I could take no more.

Of course the principal had a word about it with me. Your ward, Mrs Hyde, she really is most recalcitrant. Please talk some sense into her.

I had no idea then it was Maddy they had been fighting over. The other teachers seemed to understand. They thought I found the news hard to take. 'We think our children never grow up, leave their innocence behind.'

But that wasn't the truth. Maddy was 11, and people were making me feel older than I was. I was responsible for Maddy, and then there were the totally irresponsible feelings I still had. How could I ever tell anyone of those? The man on the boulder would have listened, and not said anything. But he might have laughed.

Jaspal never apologized for his behaviour, he was told he could come back the next year if he did. His father wouldn't hear of it. All the donations, madam, he screamed at the principal. You are forgetting all the donations. And it was Mahesh, not Jaspal, who returned to school the very next week.

By then, everyone believed that the decision to suspend Jaspal Singh had been a correct one. It was the news on TV, at once audacious and frightening, that made us believe. Those people who wanted a new Khalistan where Punjab was, who so far, had only killed selected people, using their AK-47s and their motorbikes, had gone and hijacked a plane to Pakistan. This made things far worse. The news embarrassed everyone who heard it; as if they could almost see Zia, Pakistan's dictator president, with the funny hairstyle and big front teeth laughing with barely suppressed mockery. Everyone hoped he would laugh so hard that the parting in his hair right at the centre would crack, splitting him open.

'Those Khalistani terrorists are getting too daring.' First it was the commissioner, Mr Parida, who said so and then everyone else at the club began saying it. 'The weapons they are moving around with,' everyone said, 'and the impunity with which they kill. Really, things have gone too far now.'

'How could they be allowed to carry those kirpans into the plane?' Asha Dogra, who taught history, sweet and always bewildered, asked again and again.

Commissioner Parida said we should follow those Israelis. 'They send their army in whenever there is any ins... ins...'

'Instruction,' I supplied the word but of course no one looked my way.

'No...' Parida heard and shook his head. 'No, not that.' He clapped himself on the head, smiled apologetically and I could no longer hold myself back.

'Instigation.'

A split second later, I saw relief on his face. 'Insti-gashun.' And he was embarrassed, looking away from me. 'Instiga-sun,' he repeated. 'You know, when those hijackers took the plane to Africa, they sent soldiers in.'

Brooks Town had always been far from everything but now all that was happening, up in the north, in Delhi and in Punjab, seemed too close and in danger of becoming very real. We never saw Jaspal Singh on his bicycle again, but his father's new Maruti was visible too often, coloured red, and streaked with golden stickers on every side, that made people pull over and stare. No one had ever seen a car so very small and so quiet too. Manjit Singh's Maruti was the first one of its kind in Brooks Town.

That K word began to be mentioned all the time, on the nine o'clock national programme and in the front pages of newspapers. We heard every day of things the Khalistanis now did on a daily basis. *Shot dead two people in Gurdaspur. Shot a schoolteacher in Amritsar. Issued a warning to any Sikh not wearing the turban.* They also spoke of a man called Bhindranwale, and the television showed him standing on the terrace of the Golden Temple, the gold of its spires glistening in the sun, one foot on the parapet, like a terrible dire warning to anyone who went against him.

He wore a blue turban wrapped tight around his head and a long flowing saffron kurta. He had big yellowing teeth, bushy eyebrows and eyes that mocked everything, even the prime minister.

'They are really getting bold,' I heard the commissioner say over and over again. The only words he could bring up time and again. Nothing like this had happened before. Was this why Jaspal had given himself such airs? On TV, the numbers of the dead were only increasing. From 2-3 people killed, it had now become 9-10, once an entire busload of people was offloaded. And then there was only a line of dead bodies lying on the highway, arranged in orderly fashion, covered in white cloth, waiting for the important people who would come to commiserate over such unnecessary deaths.

The fear was hard to answer in a town where the spectre of violence had manifested itself only when two boys pummelled each other to the ground over a girl, barely an adolescent herself. The man on the boulder had disappeared, the empty boulder now simmered like a blank menace, and I had reached that stage in my life, when easy answers were fast disappearing.

It would be the last summer that I would belong to any place, be someone, my own person. Because from now on, there is always a blip in the rush of my memories, like I am flipping over fast and quick through a much familiar photo album, turning the pages over, letting the pictures fall back in place in their plastic casing but somehow they never return in the same order as when I first found them.

What I remember next are those early days of winter that year, and the principal's announcement in the staff room, one Wednesday afternoon.

We are closing early. Please wait for all your students to leave. Not a single child should be allowed to leave alone.

We looked at each other, nervous. What had happened? It was 31 October, and there was only an hour or so for the final bell to go. But the principal had swept out of the staff room, tossing us a too quick, nervous smile. And the servants, orderlies, drivers and others who came to pick their wards up, told us what had happened.

Indira Gandhi ko mar dala. Her own bodyguards. They sat on the ringed platform around the trees, by the driveway, everyone in deep shock, telling us in a daze what had happened.

Don't believe them. I heard myself telling Maddy, hoping somehow it wasn't true. Servants will believe anything, they get scared at the slightest whiff of a rumour. They spread those rumours of the dam bursting last monsoon.

But it was I who burst into tears even as I spoke, embarrassing Maddy thoroughly. If I told her, she would never understand. I had seen Mrs G the year Maddy was born and since then she had become so very familiar to me, though Maddy had seen her on more occasions on television. But even before television, she was already someone known in so many ways. We knew about her family, her father, her sons and even her grandchildren. We knew the domestic gossip too, of how she had driven out her widowed daughter-in-law, forced her guards to search her luggage. I cried for all this and more. But Maddy looked so very woebegone at the news, at my crying and I suppose I had let her down then.

On the road, as we walked home, towing our bicycles along, people were still talking. 'We do not know the details. She was taken to the hospital after her bodyguards shot her.'

What does the radio say? I stopped a passing cyclist, ignoring Maddy's glare.

He unfurled the antenna even higher. Apart from static that buzzed and bubbled we caught the mournful strains of Bismillah Khan's shehnai that always played during momentous occasions, whether it was a marriage or something more grave, like death announcements on television and radio. I wept more.

The silence had spread itself like a shroud over the town. At home, the afternoon was interminable, the silence sharp against the windows. It was hard to be alone and at the Paridas', everyone was angry. Mrs Parida beat with her hands on the windows, the futile anger that sees no resolution.

The school was closed for a few days.

'It's a precaution,' said Mr Parida as Mrs Parida waited for her son, Ashok, to return from his hostel too.

The procession happened a few afternoons later, the day the school reopened. We heard it come nearer and nearer every passing moment as we waited at the crossing. The traffic guy had already had his hand up a long time. Maddy chafed, pressing the little used ring into service repeatedly. The traffic policeman smiled apologetically, and gestured, a few minutes only. The shouting that preceded the procession was clearer now, I could hear the refrain at the end of every slogan. The afternoon never let up, instead it seeped into everything around. Kerketta pushed his bicycle ahead and I followed him. Anything to stir the afternoon up.

It's a procession of the Punjabi log, said Kerketta.

And then I saw the Matador, a three-legged tempo now thrust into a position of importance. Marigold garlands curtained all its sides, leaving space on the front window next to the driver, for a photo of the smiling Mrs Gandhi. And holding onto the photo, clinging to the Matador's sides, and the open doors and windows, were assorted men. The Matador had metamorphosed into a many-headed, many-limbed creature, that thrust its hands out in desperation, shouting her name and the name of the country.

Kerketta shook his head, and his fist at them. *Trying to be sorry after all they did.*

I stared as the procession passed, as did everyone else, unsure, hostile, not doing anything. The Matador moved slowly across the road. I saw the driver, his hands tight on the wheel, stiff in fear and in his own importance. I noticed the odd manner the light fell on his face, the way he moved his head, and I couldn't look away. And then Kerketta broke into a loud laugh as he understood.

'Trying to disguise themselves,' he chortled. 'As if removing a turban, cutting off hair will do away with the guilt... of murder,' he said, angry now, his fingers bunched into a fist.

All of them in that procession looked that way. That clean band across the forehead and the chin, areas of skin now exposed, places where the hair had been hurriedly cut away, now giving them a blotchy look. There were more people laughing at them now, loudly and raucously and it only grew as each one nudged the other next to him.

The men in the Matador and those on cycles following raised their arms and shouted slogans in praise of Mrs G and the country, albeit more feebly than before. *Indira Gandhi ki jai. Bharat mata ki jai.*

Kerketta hadn't stopped laughing, but some seriousness had returned among the bystanders. They were talking in low whispers, shaking their heads, looking skywards, a few crossing themselves repeatedly.

I cycled away and Kerketta remained, talking to his newly made friends, explaining to them, all over again, the circumstances of Mrs Gandhi's murder. Things were settling down slowly. We had seen on TV, the new prime minister being sworn in. He was 40, an age when a woman begins to think herself old, yet people said he was young. I read the newspapers daily now, reading what he had done and said. I felt I had an authority to decide about him, make my own mind up unlike in the case with his mother, who had been too powerful to ever figure in my thoughts or in my reasoning.

I turned left and pedalled away, hoping to get away from Kerketta, from the noise, from everything. I rode on, blinking away the sun. My shoe had caught against the metal chain of the cycle which let out a painful screech and then unravelled, and I, straining over and over again to pedal on, failed miserably.

The buckle of my shoe was fixed to the chain and I was forced to get off. Maddy wasn't anywhere, perhaps she was already home. I bent, working to reattach the chain when I saw Jaspal ride up. The sun was bright and everything glistened.

Jaspal rode towards me, looking altogether different. His hair, without his turban, had a middle parting, and it gave him, with his oval face and full pink lips, a surprisingly womanish look. I smiled at him trying to hide my blackened hands.

He stopped his bicycle, leaned over, one foot on the ground and said, 'I saw you laughing at me… Miss.'

His voice had a sneer in it.

'Laughing…,' my self-consciousness had returned. Was he seeing me as I was? Dirty, perspiring, buckle-broken? 'No, I wasn't. They were.' And I pointed in the other direction.

'I saw you…' he said, 'on the hill, I had left behind my camera… and went back to get it… I saw you clearly… and watching you laugh, they all laughed too. You are a teacher, you could have told them…'

He pushed at my cycle and it fell against me. 'You dressed-up bitch with that bastard daughter. Remember your own lines: Laugh at others and see the stones hurled back at you.'

'No, no, you are mixing metaphors,' I made to say but he let go my bike roughly and the handle jerked against my stomach and threw me off balance. My right foot caught in the spokes and last of all, it was my hand that scraped itself on the road as I braced for the fall. My carefully done up work on the cycle was thoroughly spoiled. The buckle had slipped and my shoe too was now irreparably spoilt. But these thoughts were eaten away by the flash of pain that rose through me, filled my eyes and I saw Jaspal Singh run his fingers through his hair before he pedalled away fast.

He cycled away, the strap of his camera trailing along the ground in a mocking farewell.

I walked home alone, stopping to lift the bicycle chain that slipped often, and trailed behind me on the road. Kerketta was waiting for me at the crossing. He saw me and crossed himself.

What happened...? You fell?

No, got hit...

Who... his hands fell away from the bicycle and it teetered before he reached it in time.

I don't know... someone chased me.

My god...

He gave me a lift then, and the two of us made quite a picture. Me, lurching on his backseat and he riding gingerly, holding himself awkwardly forward, both of us careful to keep that inch of distance between us. He tried to make conversation, turning his head, so I saw the poky hair in his nose and he must have caught the sweat on my skin.

My bicycle left behind with a roadside vendor with Kerketta's promise to pick it up later, looked as forlorn as everything else, once the slogans faded and died away.

'I forgot. The procession held things up. I had to give Dogra his medicine.'

I thought I hadn't heard him right. 'Medicine? What for?'

But we had just turned the corner to where home was and my eyes fell on his pocket that bulged open invitingly. Inside I saw his bunch of many keys. Kerketta worked as a gardener in other houses too, those that lined the river, and so he had the keys to the riverside gates. It was this key ring that I now easily plucked out. I had no idea why I did so then. But it would be one of those small, little thought-out acts that would assume consequence later.

I insisted on getting off at the gate. I dragged myself home, hobbling up the driveway, feeling the heat rise from the gravel, the torn strap of my shoe flipping back and forth, buckle-less, Kerketta's keys heaving in my pocket. More than the shoe, it was the keys I held on to tightly, my sweaty hand clammy over them, afraid their giveaway jangling would draw attention.

'My God... how could it happen?' asked the Paridas when my ankle swelled up alarmingly, it was to leave me with a permanent hobble. This and my now always watery eyesight made people dismiss me out of turn and for no reason.

'At least the rest of me is unaffected,' I remember telling them.

'You are lucky,' the commissioner said, 'the procession was peaceful. There was every chance that it could have turned violent. That might have happened had there not been plainclothes policemen marching along.'

The commissioner boasted about it, as he spoke on the phone to his colleagues in other cities. Nothing serious happened here, he said. And he looked significantly at me as he said, 'No, there was only a damaged shoe,' and laughed heartily at his joke.

Mrs P in turn smiled her tight smile and only said, Of course, nothing would happen here. Does anything ever?

The shoe remained with me. Brown, chalked with dust, its strap flapping like a loose strand of hair. The shoe no longer looked like something I had ever worn. Its sole was grimy, its once sharp end had dulled and the dust and the street grime had carved out fine brown lines for themselves.

It was the year I knew that things would never be the way I wanted them to be. And I had always tried to shape life to myself. It never worked that way, the drama classes would never be. That is why I choose to remember things my own way, starting from a time five years before the murder of Gautam Dogra.

Five Lears Later, February, 1989
The Murder

FIVE YEARS LATER, IT WAS Asha Dogra who turned 40. It was the year her father was murdered. Only I knew she was 45, older than me, and I knew this from the horse's mouth or in this case, the murdered man's mouth. She was only a bit less vague about her age than the newspapers; a couple of which placed her at around 30, and mentioned her as the only daughter of Gautam Singh Dogra, murdered by a rickshaw puller in a cold-blooded, premeditated act. It was a romance that shocked everyone. What was stranger was that no one had known about it in a town that knew even before it was official the love story of the two schoolteachers, Subrat Mukherjee and Agamoni Gupta. Only after the deed was done, the murder committed, a man left for dead, did the stories emerge. Of the rickshaw wallah who for no reason had taken it on himself to ferry Asha home from school every day, who brought magazines for her, and who in time her father, Gautam Singh Dogra had come to detest. It was a murder of hidden desires, thwarted love and deep unabated hatred such as the kind Gautam Singh Dogra felt for Daya Sharan, the rickshaw wallah, a hatred that could only have one result – death.

How could she ever get involved with a man like that? This was the question everyone asked, after the murderer had been arrested. And while the murder weapon was yet to be found, Commissioner Parida assured it was only a matter of time. A motive matters more than the actual weapon.

'Solving a mystery is like linking together all loose ends, you see. There is a method,' he said.

Still, all methods failed to account for any rational explanation as to why Asha had chosen to fall in love with a rickshaw puller, one who had already been in jail for another murder.

The afternoon of the murder she had been perfectly normal. Disagreeing with me when I asked her mildly enough as we sat in the school staff room if Subrat Mukherjee needed to be told that Agamoni's marriage had already been decided and that she could even be married before the year end. In the perfectly arranged way, her parents had set their hearts on. But Asha pursed her lips and twin frown lines rose on her forehead. I knew then: a woman who knows she is getting old can fall in terrible wrong love; a woman who is old can refuse to let go of a terribly wrong love.

'We should not be thinking this way,' she said to my question, looking disapproving. 'Her marriage is something perfectly natural, and there is no proof about their feelings for each other.'

In the staff room I doodled on my pad, letting people think I was working on a new design, when all the time I was working on a new story. The story of the 'Boy on the Boulder' had recently appeared in *Eve's Weekly*, though of course I had used a different name. I was afraid the part where he spies on the considerably older teacher as she undresses for him by a bedroom window would certainly set off a scandal. I had not shown it to Maddy either. How could I be drawn to someone, a boy Maddy's age? She would never forgive me and I wasn't one for taking chances, anyway.

'No,' Asha's voice sliced into my reverie again. 'We don't have an iota of suspicion of what they feel. This is all needless speculation.'

When she was harsh, she sounded so like her father. Gautam Singh Dogra's phone hello was like a slow dozing road roller grazing over a difficult road. A voice that would no more allow for romance, not in his life nor his daughter's.

I was reminded of that harshness in Asha's voice when, a month later, Agamoni did get married. The next auspicious day when a marriage could happen was more than a year away and no one, least of all Agamoni's parents, wanted the delay. Subrat did not attend, he was away. We learnt later that this was only the first of many trips he would make to Calcutta to meet a travel agent. Before the year ended, he would have left for Indonesia.

If Asha knew the two events were related, as indeed they were, she did not show it. In fact, there was everything about her that suggested no place for romance, which was why she managed to carry on the subterfuge for so long. In her life and in the other lives she had a part in.

Already a frown line cut deep across her forehead, twin lines streaked down either side of her nose and her hair divided by a middle parting as thick as the river Mahanadi in spate, was a suspicious orange brown in colour. It was Maddy, during the time she was still around, who told me about the henna Asha religiously applied every Sunday, why she never emerged from her house on Sundays.

'Sundays she bakes cakes,' I had retorted. Asha Dogra's cakes were famous. She could make cakes out of anything, of the usual stuff, carrots, even bananas too spoilt to be eaten otherwise. 'So?' Maddy had replied, 'You are being illogical. She can bake cakes and still have mehndi on her head. You just need to wrap it up with a plastic cover to see it doesn't drip.'

Maddy got her information from her friend Indira, who in turn got her information from her father, who owned most of the rickshaws in Brooks Town. The rickshaw wallahs rented them from him and in turn supplied him with information – all about the clients they ferried, and where they stayed, what they had spoken about, etc. It was said that he lowered the rent in some instances only in exchange for good information that he then passed on to Usman Obeidullah, otherwise called Sheikh Abdullah, who used it to blackmail them.

So when Indira supplied information, you could safely bet that it was reliable. Whatever news that came to her father or that he gathered, always managed to get to Indira. In that house crowded with her siblings, and there were four of them, there was no conversation that could remain a secret. And that was how Maddy and then I knew about Asha, her magazines, all the issues of *Femina*, *Women's Era* and *Eve's Weekly*, that the rickshaw puller Daya Sharan got for her from the railway station.

In the beginning, Asha had bought the magazines herself, on her way back from school. The rickshaw she travelled in was one that came from the stable of Mohammad Taj Uddin, fashionably shortened to M Taj on his visiting cards. Then when he was late by as much as an hour or more, this same rickshaw puller gave his report to M Taj insisting he had foolproof reasons for his delay.

'Had to go some way off, sir.'

Really, said Mohammad Taj Uddin, making the appropriate entries in the register.

The rickshaw puller was late because he had to go out of his way, towards the station. He shrugged, what can you do when passengers become too demanding, especially women. They tell you to go one way and then change their minds. Not understanding the consequences this could have. You had to stop, ignore the furious stares from nearby rickshaw pullers, the honking of other horns for car drivers loved to show off their power. The station was way to one side, the road leading there was terrible, never repaired and the sewage tank near it stank to high heaven.

But he stumbled over his explanation. Taj sahib was a moody man; you could never tell what offended him.

You are an idiot, Taj sahib kept saying and Daya, the rickshaw puller, had to agree. It was his poverty, and forgetfulness, deliberately willed, that made him stupid. Fate had made him a rickshaw puller, when he would rather still be cultivating his own plot of land near the Mahanadi, the land he had forfeited when the dam came up. Of course, the government said they had paid his father. A sum of ten thousand rupees, they said, pointing to their register. Yes, he remembered looking on painfully, his eyes narrowed, trying to follow the officer's smooth, polished finger with the red stone embedded in his ring. It is as you say, he agreed dully. His father had got the money, ten thousand in all, in cash, one new bundle with the notes all stapled together. And the piece of land he loved so much was no longer his.

'You ask your father what he has done with it,' said the big officer. 'Don't think the government has time to go on making false entries, to try and cheat the poor?' The way he said that word, poor, made him feel more wretched and ashamed.

He went home, dragging his feet, hoping his feet would stamp themselves into the ground and confirm his existence. Where is the money? he asked his father. The old man was as usual lying on the cot, complaining. Day and night, they heard his voice drone on and wished he would stop. And then that day, he, Daya, had stopped it. He did not know what had come over him. He remembered only after the deed was done, the pillow in his hands that felt so heavy then that he had to drop it, and he fell to his knees, his head in his hands.

He did not remember what happened over the next few days. He had been sitting under the peepul tree while the elders debated over what was to be done with him. He did not have the money to pay for the penance ceremony they advised. You have a spirit in you and there is your father's spirit who is very angry because he was called away so unexpectedly. Two spirits can be difficult to handle and so the penance has to be heavy. Five hundred rupees in all, said Dharma Majhi, the mukhia. Even that was too much and that was why he was almost glad when the police came to pick him up.

He did not know why his wife ran after the bullock cart, that child in her arms, wailing, bemoaning her fate. The others stood around waiting in utter silence. And then she too had stopped running, beyond the point where she had never gone before. The barbed wire fence the government had put up and the tall electricity poles that had come up more than ten years ago.

Taj sahib's irritated look interrupted Daya's reverie. 'Can't you give a straight answer? You are late; I just want to know why. Why do you think so much?'

'Because you will not understand, sir,' he wanted to say. Because all my thoughts begin from other thoughts and I am still trying to understand those.

'You are late, she made you go way off, and so did she pay the normal fare?' Taj persisted with his queries.

'She invited me in for water,' he lied now. That was why he was even more late.

Taj sahib threw his head back and laughed. 'Daya, you say the funniest things. You mean to tell me she has taken a fancy to you.'

It puzzled him when the sahib laughed like this. But at least he wasn't so irritated when he said, 'Look Daya, I give you one more warning. Don't waste my time on your socializing, do it when you are free, all right?'

He did not understand but nodded his head. 'Forcing me to deduct your salary every time,' Taj said, counting out notes for Daya, 'I am giving you less than usual, 25, not 35 all right? You people must learn the value of time. You are now working for me, not in some village, still plowing your fields with your ugly buffaloes, understand?'

Daya said nothing, walked out with the notes in his hand. He had the five rupees the teacher had given him.

'Need to go towards the station side,' she had giggled, a soft noise like that water tap that never worked properly. It made him feel uncomfortable and nice too. These big people never smiled at him. In fact, they only saw the back of his head, the muscles straining on his back and the sweat that left a dark stain on his lungi and the seat. Twice before she had taken that long route home, to go to that station where the newspaper boy handed her those magazines that she quickly folded and put inside her bag.

She would be much happier after that. From the mirror on his handlebar, he would see her taking those magazines out, together, then one by one, flip through their pages, the smile fixed on her face. Then she would look up and ask him to put the hood up. It was that moment when he had got off, his arms pulling at the plastic sheet at the back, that they must have smelt each other. Her sweet perfume mingling with her gum-smelling sweat and his own sweat, raw and thick that draped his body like a second skin. She raised her hanky to her nose and quickly put it down again. 'Sorry, for making this longer trip. Must have upset your schedule.'

She spoke differently too, faster. And she said her sorry three times. The last time she was giggling again. But what could he say? No one had ever spoken to him that way; he could not follow when people spoke so fast.

She paid him the usual fare when she reached home. An older looking gentleman stood at the door, his hair violently disturbed, all askew, a frown stamped on his face, and the lines radiating out from his angry old man blue eyes. And she was arranging her hair, patting her bag with those fancy magazines in it. It would be a scene reenacted every time he brought her home.

'Late today?' He growled through the open door. He was looking at Daya as he asked that. There was a time when most people's stare would go past him as if he did not exist, but now it lingered, pinned and devoured. A look aimed to maim and shrivel, Daya had looked away.

'Some work in school,' she said nervous, jumping down from the rickshaw.

'You are always late this time of the month,' he said. But instead of replying, she gave Daya a bit more money, taking her time, talking over her shoulder to the man, who stood at the door, frowning still. Daya did not dare look him in the face. He ran his hand aimlessly across his handlebars, the mirrors. He stood, waiting to be dismissed, knowing that if she was late as her father accused her of, he too must be late. And then he felt the brush of her hand against his own, and saw too the wretched contrast of their skins – his dark and calloused hand against her fairer one, with those brown black blotches.

Go now, she mouthed the words at him and he left only then. He had not gone home since he had miraculously found himself free. He had saved around 560 rupees in his tin box already. It could have been 580 rupees but for the fact that he was never compensated for the detours he took. Whatever extra the teacher paid him was just a bit more but then Taj Sahib cut more than half, so in fact he knew he lost more in the end. He was like a piece of cloth at the tailor's. One never knew how they managed to make things always short, snipping from here, and there, allowing them to make their usual excuses. The sleeves would always be a bit short and the trousers would be way up the ankles.

It was the next month that Daya made his offer to the lady. 'Memsahib instead of you going all the way, maybe I can get them for you, when I am going station side?'

The arrangement suited her. But he was racked with doubts soon enough. The vendor only looked at him strangely every time he turned up, the other rickshaw pullers laughed and asked why he was giving himself fancy ideas, and they knew he couldn't read anyway. And then the teacher as usual took advantage of his kindness.

'Just drive, drive around anywhere,' she said one afternoon, after school. He took her to the one place he thought she preferred. The station. But she did not get down. Instead somewhere they passed an ice-cream vendor and she bought them a cone each. He had to eat his quickly because he did not dare stop the rickshaw to lick his way through the cone. So he took his in two gulps, wondering why people made such a fuss about the thing when it was cold and hurt the teeth and melted much too fast. But it left a delicious coolness inside his mouth and that smell around his lips that he kept licking in a short-lived remembered pleasure.

She made him drive in circles then, so that the neat straight lines of his usual routes were forgotten. He cycled past the agricultural campus, the petrol pump, the new missionary school, the cemetery, the house with the Englishman's grave, and then the deer park, reentering the city through the street cut through its side. This happened at least once a week. Sometimes, as they did a complete run of the city, she would on a whim ask him to plunge down some nameless, shadowy lane or the other. Take a right from here, she would say at the Modipara chowk, or here at the police reserve lines with the forbidding prison building that reminded him of another prison he never told her about. His thoughts were chained to himself and it seemed to him like she was escaping from someone or just playing a fantasy in her mind.

'Are you looking for someone?' he asked finally one day. It was not fair, for she was still paying him the usual fare from school to her house and back.

'Or maybe you have forgotten the address.'

She threw her head back and laughed. He watched her, smiling uncertainly. She laughed like a man, her head thrown back, the teeth large and yellowy on her face but the sound washed over him, it was kind and amused. She was not offended.

'Sometimes one need not ride to go anywhere. The fun is in the ride.'

But she would be serious too, asking him at moments, 'Are you getting late?'

'No, it's my duty,' he shook his head, he was half standing up from his seat, pedalling with an effort. It was a hot, humid day and he was sweating furiously. He could tell he smelled too. He did not want to inflict her with it. Besides, his rickshaw had got used to her. The way she sat in the middle so that her weight was spread evenly and shouldered by both wheels. That way he did not have to brake hurriedly when potholes or speed breakers arrived on the road, he knew she would not complain, as some passengers did. It was their fault if they were jostled and jolted unpleasantly, not his, the problem was most people did not know how to sit properly.

'No, but are you late?'

'It does not matter, not much,' he insisted.

'You have to be back at a certain time?'

He shrugged, 'Yes, but the master understands. Sometimes there could be urgent work. Or a passenger who has a long way to go.'

'Does he say anything?' She sounded anxious and he could hear her voice closer, as if she was speaking into his hair. The wind he whipped up and whistled around them both. His panting and her breathless words were mingled in it.

He nodded and then the floodgates of his complaints were released. 'Taj sahib, he is moody, one never knows. He can make fun of you and you realize only later that he is mocking you. It helps when his son is near, you can…'

'Taj sahib, yes his daughter, I know her from school.'

They nodded in mutual understanding. He had taken Taj sahib's two daughters out once, to the dance classes. He had waited for them too, smoking his bidi when Taj sahib had marched in, son in tow. The music came to a sudden standstill, and then he had seen the girls being marched out, their father shouting to whoever was within reach. My daughters will not become dancing girls. Never. Over my dead body and not even after that.

The four of them had returned home in his rickshaw. There was only the creaking of his wheels. The quiet was so sharp he had not dared draw breath. Yet he could sense the anger building up in the father. And the raw fear that reached him from the girls.

'I teach her…' she said again.

'Both his daughters?'

'Only one.' She wanted to talk. Her voice was flat and sometimes she stumbled, as she thought of a simpler way of telling him things. But it did not matter to him. He heard people talk behind his back, over his head. Openly, effusively, because for them he did not exist. But he could follow, and now he remembered, bits and pieces. If she wanted he could tell her about them too, all the people he had ferried in his rickshaw. A man who wanted to buy a television and kept scolding his wife for spending money on other things. Another woman who kept talking about the trouble with the daughter-in-law, who had no children yet. The servant boy who rode like a king in his rickshaw, with money he had unexpectedly received. But she wasn't the one for stories.

It was the other memsahib, the light-haired one who had listened to him, when he had taken her to the knife sharpener's shop in the old city. She had that hobble in her leg when he had stopped for her. And she told him of how she had fallen off her bicycle five years ago and he told her in turn the story of how he had ended up in prison – the first time.

On the afternoon of the murder, Asha Dogra asked him to fetch tea and she drank it with the hood pulled up, as a shield against the sun. He had his, as he cycled at a slower pace than usual. She had insisted that he too have a cup, and he held the clay cup gingerly. Then he had gulped it down so fast it scalded him, all the way to his stomach. She threw her head back and laughed in the manner she had. Strange lady, she looked old, why hadn't she settled down?

The answer he knew was in the man who stood at the gate each time she was late. The old man with the face reddened with worry. Your father will worry, memsahib. He began telling her when her request for detours became more frequent. And she, bolder by the day, would brush away his worries. 'Oh, now he has nothing but to worry about such things. His thinks his daughter will be kidnapped by someone. He behaves as if this is Kashmir. Do you know where Kashmir is?'

Then she had flipped through the magazines and showed him the place. Kashmir. A place where there were mountains, white and snow covered, trees with pointed, triangular leaves, women fair with red cheeks, and houses with slanting roofs.

And he saw the rickshaws too. 'If I went there, I could pull a rickshaw.'

She had laughed, 'You are really funny, Daya.'

The laughter, all that talking would stop once he took the turn away the main road, from where whichever lane you plunged into, her house was only a few minutes away. And that man would be waiting. 'Suppose your father complains about me to Taj sahib?' he asked fearfully once.

He would not. She was very sure of that. Shaking her head firmly while she tossed the clay cup of tea away. 'He hates Muslims, cannot bear to be with them. He would even avoid Taj sahib's shadow if he could.'

This time it was he who had laughed. A loud, happy laughter that drew attention and he piped down, pretending to cough, and she was at once most solicitous. That was also the day she left that handkerchief on the seat.

They found that handkerchief on him when they came to arrest him. They asked him about the knife too. A sharp, pointed weapon, as the forensics inspector pointed out, that must have been the murder weapon. The knife that was missing, only a pool of blood remained to speak of what it had wrought.

The rickshaw puller could not tell anything about the knife, but then he had learnt to forget things so very well too. In circumstances that were eerily similar, he was woken up from sleep by that rough knocking on the door. He remembered the night not long after his father's death when he had fallen asleep right where he sat, dazed and spent, only to be woken by a knocking similar as this, and then taken to jail.

Between the lashings and the drenching with hot and cold water, they screamed at him from every side. He could not see them in his blindfolded state, but only kept repeating the routine he had followed the previous day. From ten in the morning, for the next twelve hours, he had pedalled away, and there had been many passengers, too many of them. How could he possibly remember them all?

They said he was being too clever, threw more water at him. He could hear his bones rattle inside as he desperately tried to remember. And then they held that handkerchief to his nose and he gagged and threw up. The smell cloyed and rushed at him, drenching him with a new disgust. He realized he had never liked that teacher, she was too strange for his understanding.

'Now will you talk? Did you kill him?'

'Kill who, sahib? I am telling the truth. I just did my day's work, taking the usual passengers to the bus stand, to the market and in the evening I was at the school.'

Suddenly there was laughter, he could feel the tension lighten around him. 'So now you are on the right path, at the school indeed. And what happened there?'

He told them once again what he had already said, 'Nothing sahib. I took the teacher back home and went to wait at the station for more passengers.'

They whipped him all over again but he did not seem to

know what they wanted. 'You liar, you know what you did. And you killed him. Where is the knife? You will tell the truth even if we have to flay your hide to know it.'

And they whispered into his ears all night long, as he lay on that hard, cold floor, blindfolded, always feeling the heat of the light full on him so that he shivered and sweated in turns. Flinching when he felt something furry run over him, sometimes lashing him on the face. And there were the moths that kept flying at his face, forcing him to move this way and that, afraid to open his mouth in case the rats jumped in.

Gautam Singh Dogra was found dead in his house that late afternoon by his daughter, an hour or so after she returned from school. Stabbed in the back, as he sat in his study on the first floor, his back towards the window that overlooked the river. It was she who raised the alarm. She did say she had heard the heavy thud of something or someone falling but she had taken her time to come up. They had had a showdown an hour or so ago and she had been sulking.

'Father never liked that rickshaw puller, for some reason...' she sniffed later that night. There she was surrounded by attention, by all of us on every side and it made her very garrulous.

The commissioner gave us all in turn a knowing look.

'He told him off, using words I never thought he knew.' She went red, and couldn't speak for long moments. I had heard the words too, but I didn't go red. Gautam Singh Dogra's vast repertoire of abuse words was something I was privy to and had been the subject of, at least a couple of times.

'He went up and he was still muttering to himself. And then...'

She stopped and reddened even more. He called me names too, can you believe it. 'Get out, you...'

She buried her face in her hands and wept. I held my breath and walked up and away to the long windows, staring out, suddenly aware that from now on there would be no other light to share mine when everything else had gone totally dark. But no one was looking at me. Every eye was trained on her.

'I didn't go up then, those were perhaps his last words, left unfinished and I didn't go up. Because...'

It's all right, said the commissioner. The murderer is in jail, your father's spirit is assuaged for some time.

And his wife got up to get her a glass of water. She had never been in my kitchen so she was a bit lost, disrupting my orderly arrangements. Perhaps that was why I couldn't find the knife when I wanted it later; this was soon after knives became most wanted weapons of suspicion, in the commissioner's own words.

He laughed, and I suppose he was helping her out of a difficult situation. 'It's a good thing too a man can account for the murder. Otherwise, his spirit would have been all over the place, abusing all of us. Kerketta might say this...'

Asha nodded, sipped the water and went on but I didn't wait to hear the rest of it. The bits of how moments later, she had rushed out to the balcony on the first floor of that big empty house, cupping her mouth with her hands to make that announcement. You could hear her right across the riverbank but people did not even look up at her. For one thing, you do not announce a death in that fashion. Asha Dogra tried again and again but her efforts were ineffectual. Nothing stopped outside on the main road, and the paan-bidi shop owner just opposite refused to look up because he did not have his boy to spare and could not send anyone across with the sahib's paan, Velayati who ran the three STD booths next to him did not look up either because just the other day he had a furious altercation with a man he had then wished dead. Besides, as he told the police, he had to monitor the telephones and to manage the queues. Asha gave up, and then walked slowly down the dark tiled steps towards the gate, pausing every now and then to catch her breath, not bothering to stop her tears that were now flowing freely.

She hailed the first empty rickshaw she saw, before she finally arrived at our house in her dishevelled state. There seemed to be no empty rickshaws that day, strange, she said sipping the cold water Kerketta got her. She looked so mad as if she had seen a murder, was what Kerketta told me at the door when I came. He didn't even know the story, so I did wonder just what and how much she had seen. I had been away at the new clinic Prem Aggarwal had just opened, where I was made to wait for half an hour before the doctor turned up. A dog had nipped me on the ankle as I had walked alone by the riverside that afternoon and while the bites weren't sharp, I didn't want the injury to be aggravated. My limp drew too much attention anyway. Prem Aggarwal was apologetic and insisted the delay wasn't really as much as half an hour. He had been my student once and still did not understand that being a punctilious doctor did not necessarily make him a punctual one. And I should know things like these.

When I saw Asha, however, I would agree that she seemed calm, as Commissioner Parida pointed out. But then he didn't know the Dogras, father and daughter, for as long as I did.

The afternoon of the murder, I was seeing Asha after a long time. For a few months, soon after my accident with the bicycle, Asha had been a regular visitor to our house. In fact, she had once brought the oven with her and taught me how to make a fruit cake. That was the only thing I had learnt to make fairly well, for cooking was a wasted effort. There was always just Maddy and me in the house and a cake would take the whole week to plough through. Maddy had always been a poor eater and towards the end of the week, the cake would begin to taste a bit like the refrigerator itself, cold, smelling of all kinds of stuff, especially strong cheese and overripe papaya.

But soon she had stopped coming. When I met her at Mrs Parida's once, she said schoolwork now took up too much time. There were too many copies to correct, question papers to set, more and more children to tutor.

But I knew the reason why, and wondered at Gautam Singh Dogra and the way he had never stopped running his daughter's life. From the beginning, and she was already a young lady the time I first saw her, Asha had been in awe of her father. A disciplinarian who did not suffer fools gladly, he had once fought in the army of the maharaja of Kashmir, and never forgave him for the cowardly manner he had signed the Instrument of Accession, giving Kashmir over. There was far greater honour in fighting and losing for your land, rather than not fighting at all, he had told me once.

Long after his anger against the maharaja had ebbed, the soldier in him had still lived on. In Brooks Town, he had dreamt of a school that would train boys to become disciplined, loyal, ever obedient soldiers, but it was his daughter who rebelled first. She took a job twenty years ago in that missionary school when he wanted her to teach in the military school he was planning to set up. But he never got the land or the resources for it. One by one, over the years, he met all the people that mattered, the defence minister, even the deputy prime minister, all the military schools elsewhere, but his file never moved. I had helped Asha apply for the teacher's position once I got to know her fairly well in my drama classes. Dogra was furious with me when he found out. But those days I still had a way of getting around his anger.

When the school accepted Asha's application, and she began teaching history first to the junior classes and then other classes too, Gautam Singh Dogra remained one very angry man. How could you join that Christian school when your country needs you? He looked at the books prescribed and hated what she had done even more. For nearly a year, there was a cold war in that house. One light on in the ground floor and the other at the far corner on the first floor.

It was this that first brought him to our house, the first of only two occasions he had actually visited. Distant but still very insulting as only Gautam Singh Dogra could be. He knew by then I had influenced her into taking up this job, with all the contacts that Robert had, and because I taught there myself. What kind of history is this? he had said throwing the book in my face. It's all distorted. His face was contorted with anger, and he looked fit to explode. For all that, he was still very handsome and I drew in my breath.

Gautam, do sit down. I smiled, he filled the house up. It seemed to fit into him and it was a thought that made me happy.

Stop your memsahib ways, he sneered. He never really understood, never till the very end. 'I know what you've done to my daughter. And look, have you ever bothered to read this book, instead of the trash you read and write about?'

'As if the Hindu rulers were all peace-loving kings, building temples, converting to Buddhism and it was those Muslim rulers who led their armies into such heroic conquests. That Sher Shah they make him out to be such a hero. Make so much of his battles with Humayun, his fighting with a tiger. Even Humayun, such a wimp that man was, is seen as some kind of a tragic hero.'

I offered him tea, even a glass of water but he refused. He had heroic airs, that man, for all that he had lost, had given up and would never have again. I don't think there was anyone in this town who really liked him. But I for one, could never like him or hate him either. I who had once seen him without that anger around him, could never think of anything else.

Joining that school though was the only act of rebellion Asha permitted herself. After that, she would not allow herself even to fall in love.

Asha arranged a commemoration service for her father that was one of the most well attended in Brooks Town. Even Robert's commemoration had not drawn half as many but then for Robert, there had never been a body and the manager of the club, old Mr Mukherjee, had not really arranged matters well.

All of Asha Dogra's students were there as were the teachers, and the neighbours too. There were many police guards too. At least in death, Gautam Singh Dogra relived a bit of the honour he had lost.

And I spotted Soumen too, still looking like the man I had seen on the boulder only five years ago. He had slipped in at the back, hoping no one would notice. No one would have bothered, the dead mattered more in times like these. I pressed my hanky hard to my face, closing my eyes for a long time. My hands stopped their trembling, I had known Gautam Dogra far longer than most other people in the room. By the time I looked up, I couldn't see him. I couldn't look around the entire gathering and draw attention either. And I didn't know whether to be relieved or puzzled. Soumen had a way of knowing things without really knowing about them. But I was certain, he hadn't been there the day of the murder.

Dogra's face still wore its usual belligerent look. Any time it seemed, he would shake himself awake, tie his pyjama strings more firmly and stride off. I willed it to happen but of course a deed once done becomes engraved into your very life. The white sheet covering his face flapped over his nose, and he could not as much as lift a finger to settle it. It was Asha Dogra who did so, her face stony and composed as she arranged it once more neatly over his face and brushed the flies away. Everyone looked on, saw her too composed and automatically thought of other things, of suspicions that the commissioner had first put together and found that they all pointed to a certain rickshaw puller by the name of Daya Sharan.

Why had Asha Dogra not shed even a single tear for her father? Was it true, and the whispers were beginning to get louder, that she indeed had a hand in getting her father killed? That her father had been upset when he came to know of the affair? Had they – the two, Asha and that rickshaw puller – planned it together? A diabolical plan they had hatched together as Asha Dogra had once again taken a long route back home.

All this was said behind her back of course. Once the rickshaw puller was apprehended, and the idiot had been sleeping the sleep of the dead when he was rounded up, Asha became an object of sympathy instead. Poor lady, she had no one in the world now.

She had me, though. She stayed for a week like she had once before and then chose to stay on. And I let her. Even for me, it was nice to have someone else in the house. From now, it would always feel strange, to not see the light on in Dogra's study, every time I looked out of the window. For a while I had stopped my late evening walks on the dry riverbed. My ankles hurt and I was wary of the pariah dogs there. The newness of all this meant that the dot of light that appeared at times on the riverbank, and which rightly should have evoked some alarm became instead an easily dismissable menace. Asha helpfully attributed it to the cigarette of a tramp woman who strolled there on her own, and who she had seen often. And I, suiting my mood to her casual one, thought it was Reddy, the commissioner's overly smart, too intrusive servant boy who I promised to deal with later. For our immediate need was to adjust to each other in the post-murder scenario.

For weeks and months after, till the trouble with Maddy and his son came into the open, Commissioner Parida was full of how he had solved the perfect murder. Parida aired his views more often when we met at his home, and Maddy's friendship with his son, Ashok, became something altogether different. Asha wasn't usually there because she didn't think it would be proper, so soon after her father's death too. And so Parida indulged in his theory of how it all was a crime of passion, and no one said a word, and no one looked my way, when I was the only one to make a faint protest. I said, 'She looked very calm and quiet, she didn't look as if she had killed him.'

'Ah how could anyone tell, Mrs Hyde? Have you seen a killer before?'

We were looking up at Kerketta shinning up the coconut tree, his muscles rippling against the hard cemented trunk, till he disappeared into the thick green upended thatch of coconuts. We heard him only from the rustling of the leaves. The boy Reddy waited below, and soon enough a green mountain of plucked coconuts bouldered down, making us jump back. I half expected Kerketta to emerge from that heap of quietly sitting coconuts, but the dust floated away with Parida's still excited voice talking about the murder.

'A killer does not have to look like one. And this crime has all the hallmarks of a crime of passion.'

The sun through the gap in the coconut fronds played on his hair and those sideburns that looked like irremovable stab wounds on his cheeks.

'Do you have a knife or something?'

That was Mrs Parida, coming towards us, looking agitated like she was on most occasions.

Her husband didn't listen, he never did. And her tired, always sad eyes turned towards me.

'Do you have one? It would be nice to have some coconut water, don't you think?'

She knew I had one, there were so many times she had borrowed it.

'I will have to check.'

'Yes, be sure you can account for your knife, Mrs Hyde,' said Mr Parida. 'Knives are now weapons of suspicion.'

I laughed as he went on, and there was Mrs Parida putting her plaintive question to him.

'You should not be saying such things aloud. About Asha…'

But her husband had interrupted her again.

'There was nothing wrong with Gautam Dogra,' he said. 'The doctor's report is just complicating things more.'

He scratched his head and appeared to quote, '*Death accelerated by complications caused by heart trouble.* Doctors and their fancy Engish. And how do you explain the knife wound? He just fell against it I suppose, on his back? And what happened to the knife after that?'

The sound of his voice, short and clipped, rhymed with the slapping of clothes against the rocks as the washerwomen washed their clothes on the riverbank.

'He was taking some medicine or the other. So perhaps he did have some ailment.' For no reason, I remembered that ride home on Kerketta's bicycle five years ago and what he had told me then. That he had to get Dogra his medicines. Dogra too had got Kerketta to make a special herbal concoction for him, all of us did, sooner or later.

'There is many a slip,' he went on, 'between the cup and lip. Mind you I am not blaming the lady, not one bit. It's that bastard rickshaw puller. They get ideas way behind their standing, beyond what their head can hold in…'

For the rest of the year, Parida worried over a missing knife, his wife turned more inward-looking than before, and I fiercely set my heart on a new story involving the love between a rickshaw puller and a schoolteacher, and so no one knew when it was that the unlikely friendship that had developed between Maddy and Ashok Parida, the son who had returned after finishing college, turned into something else altogether. All of us, in our different ways, were trying to get away from something. But I might have known, and paid the price for chasing my own love story.

That day as I walked into the kitchen hoping to wash my hands quickly before getting the knife Mrs Parida wanted, I found Maddy kissing Ashok. They huddled together in the alcove under the staircase and I knew what I saw before I walked past hurriedly. His fingers on her chin, her face raised to his. I knew she was in love before Maddy was ready to admit it herself. Shameless girl, you don't know what you are in for. I thought all this and yet did nothing. I had learnt too late that you can't do anything about love. Fight it and it leaves you emptier than ever. Better to love, have the loved one somewhere near, and happy, so you can see him every day; at least have him somewhere near at hand, even a lone light bulb alone in a quiet city can be so reassuring. And now I would never see it again.

When the three of us returned, our faces were flushed, no one looking at each other. Mr Parida stopped midflow, and then turned to his wife, his face a question mark.

'It's nothing,' I said, reaching for Maddy's hand but she laughed a bit nervously and pulled away. While Ashok, already a young cad, was now fingering his father's cigarette case, before a firm tap from his father stopped him.

'Not now, young man, or when your girlfriend lets you.'

Maddy must have felt me stiffen, for she rushed forward to help Mrs Parida with the coconuts. Poor lady, she was fond of Maddy and events were to take her by surprise too. Unlike her husband and me though, she couldn't handle it.

'You need a knife, don't you? I thought we had one,' said Maddy.

I didn't stop her. Of course she wouldn't find it. I had run inside the kitchen and seen for myself that it wasn't at its usual place. I had rubbed my eyes, peered close and even run my hands over the shelf but I knew it wasn't there, it had simply vanished, and then Maddy had come in, now looking suitably composed, her hair in place. It was nothing, we were...

And she stopped when I turned to look at her. Something about my face told her she couldn't get away with subterfuge, not this time.

'Please don't be angry,' she whispered in my ear as we returned to the Paridas'. She had that appealing look but only for a second. Maybe she saw something in my eyes for her voice when she returned was belligerant, deliberately offhand, 'The knife. I couldn't find it. Have you done things with it?'

There were times when Maddy knew more than I suspected, and I stood there, not able to do a thing, hearing her run away lightly to help Mrs Parida with the coconuts and into all this came Mr Parida's loud laughter. 'You look as if you have seen a murder, Mrs Hyde. Do sit down. I was talking to the missus about motives. That's what all detectives tell you – look for a motive. Once there is a motive, things fall into place. And here, in this instance, we have one, even if... even if.'

He drummed on the chair in mock frustration, 'We don't have a murder weapon.'

I wish he hadn't looked at me when he said that; it made me wish I had tossed my now missing knife into the river, simply to evade suspicion or that oily all-knowing policeman's look I longed to slice up into shape.

I never raised the question of the kiss, and later wondered if I should have. Did hiding away a thing mean it's forgotten? A kiss wasn't like a knife; a romantic misadventure wasn't a murder. A quick word, unlike a quick stabbing might have ended a silly experimental flirtation at once. But I kept all my ghosts to myself then.

'As a policeman,' said Mr Parida, arranging his belt, clearing his throat, 'I have witnessed several crimes and understood well how men and women can be driven crazy by want of sex. And remember the first floor window in Dogra's house? Who drew the curtains and why? When Asha said they were always pulled apart because he liked to see the river? So it was obvious that someone had closed the window shut for fear of being seen across the river, and then walked out through the door, that led down to the river again. Someone who entered the house from the back…'

'Maybe he had drawn them himself, which is likely,' said the wife. 'So then that leaves the knife. Where could it have gone?'

But apart from Parida, no one else wanted to have anything to do with the murder any more. One man was dead and gone, another one was in jail serving a sentence for it.

'But a rickshaw puller of all people?' There was only Mrs Parida left to indulge her husband's unfortunate and magnificent obsession.

'Anything is possible, isn't it?' he said, raising his eyebrows. 'Class issues, individual urges, a madness that can drive one to recklessness. What would you know about such things?'

Only Kerketta perhaps with his intuitive powers and black magic could find something that would nail the rickshaw puller to the murder once and for all.

Lawrence Kerketta ko bulao. Call for Lawrence Kerketta. When that message went out, there was a frisson of excitement in the police station. When Kerketta was summoned, it meant something serious was imminent. For Kerketta was needed usually on these occasions, when investigations needed to be sealed up, given that final nod of confirmation. For only Lawrence Kerketta had a certain away of extracting a confession; he could see the truth that compelled the guilty to make a clean breast of things.

Lawrence Kerketta ko bulao. And so as the call went out, constables fanned out in every direction to look for him. It was late evening, Kerketta's official duties were over, the gardens where he worked were now shrouded in darkness and no one was sure where he lived. Batches of policemen kept watch at the four different gardens where he worked, and they stayed up into the night, to be sure of catching him when he turned up the next day. I could hear two of them at the Deer Park gate, their voices unnecessarily loud in the darkness. They were scared of the Christian ghosts from the adjacent cemetery and it took all my persuasion to invite them in for tea, to keep the cold and the fear away. Asha Dogra was horrified when I told her about it the next morning.

'Deliberate murder,' she said. 'Is that what the police think?'

It took her a moment, and then she was all things at one time. Alarmed, nervous with laughter, flushed with indignation, but there was not that evasive nervousness, I thought, those few seconds of silence that indicate some kind of guilty acquiescence.

'I still can't believe why it happened. Father had no enemies, though,' and here she laughed abruptly, running her hands across the table. 'For him I was his enemy number one. He was really getting strange towards the end.'

It brought me up short. 'He should have said something then, instead of telling people off. If you are lonely you need people around you. But he did his best to. You were his daughter, and he never told you if he was indeed terribly sick or something.'

'Don't speak like that about my father,' she sounded angry.

I did not tell Asha that I had been in touch with him till the very end. Ever since Kerketta had let slip about the medicines, I had written to him even more. I had asked him repeatedly how he was, offered to help write his letters, edit his articles, but he had never replied. I had even sent across samples when he drew up pamphlets asking for volunteers to march to the temple that everyone talked of those days. The subject of this temple agitated Mrs Parida considerably, converting her from a pathologically uncertain woman to a passionate one, seething with emotions, eager to set history right.

'An old temple,' she said, 'that Babar's man had demolished, turned into a mosque. Of course, it must be restored. It is a holy place after all. The youth of today need to be aware of such things instead of dancing to pop music all the time.'

I could write poems about the temple that would help Gautam Dogra, if only he would listen. As I walked along the dry riverbank, I thought of jingles that would be catchy as television advertisements, as alluring as billboards. But the sillier I got, and older, Dogra remained ever immune to my overtures. He would always be the only true Kashmiri, as he called himself, unlike those other opportunists who had made those compromises with the Nehrus. The man who had once fulminated against all these leaders in articles that Manik Ghosh published in his *Brooks Town Ramblings*. The weekly was long defunct but Dogra had never given up his old anger. He simply did not know how to deal with the strange, the new, and the very different world he had come to inhabit.

By the time he was gone, eight years had elapsed since his last piece had appeared. In the early 1980s, Manik Ghosh and Gautam Dogra had had a fallout. Ghosh babu was already finding it hard to bring out his weekly on schedule, fighting as he was, a losing battle against the magazines that came from Calcutta. *Sunday, Illustrated Weekly* and now there was *Debonair* too. His magazine lost readers every time one of these new magazines made their appearance, and soon he had no money to pay the pittance he paid to his columnists and after a while no money to bring out his magazine too.

Dogra had pleaded. He wrung his hands, almost grovelled, 'You cannot close down a magazine, it is a veritable fountainhead of knowledge.' For a few moments, a proud man stood pathetically diminished. But Manik Ghosh was adamant, unheeding as well to the many letters I wrote, all in different names, all addressed to him, as editor of *Brooks Town Ramblings*, making common cause with Dogra, though he would never let me tell him that.

There must have been a time in his life in the last few months before he died, when old Dogra must have been terribly and bewilderingly lonely. He had alienated his daughter and he had no friends left in town. He had even come to blows with Mohammad Velayati, the nice, uhealthily curious Iranian who ran the STD booths opposite his house. Velayati unashamedly eavesdropped into phone conversations, the prime ritual of any long distance relationship, that unfolded on a daily basis in his phone booths.

'He had nothing much to do.' It was Velayati who said that to others at the commemoration for Dogra, 'So he tried to remote control his daughter's life. Standing at the gate, going back to check the clock in the drawing room, sometimes shouting across to ask me the time, and then returning once again. And he would then have big fights with the rickshaw puller.'

So it was all coming back to Daya Sharan, the rickshaw puller. That he thought a bit too much of himself. That he was becoming too friendly with Dogra's daughter who was just being kind to him, giving him tips when he performed those errands for her.

And then of course, as Velayati revealed, there were those calls that began coming for Asha late in the evening, or even early morning. The phone stood by the staircase, between the floors where father and daughter lived their separate lives. Calls that could only come from a place afar, when the phone rang out in a clear, long drawn, wailing tone that Asha would run to answer. When her father lumbered down one flight of stairs to answer it, the call was shorter. Whoever it was hung up on hearing his rough, stone-abrasive voice.

They asked Daya these questions too at the station as they waited for Lawrence Kerketta to arrive. It was morning and there was every chance that Kerketta was in the river, foraging for his herbs and animal leavings, which he used for his much sought-after medicinal concoctions. It wasn't just Dogra but even Mrs Parida who had succumbed to their potency.

Was it true that the sahib had shouted at you many times?

Was it true that you came around to their house without your rickshaw?

And then rephrasing this question differently: *Isn't it true that you were seen there in off-duty hours?*

Was it true you made those late night phone calls to her?

He did not even know how to use a phone. He blinked, but even a 'no' became hard to utter. How was Daya to know that the phone calls in particular were long distance ones, made from Calcutta and not really meant for Asha? But the police in their chosen line of questioning, preferred to leave some things out. As Commissioner Parida instructed, 'Bombard them with a hundred, no, a thousand lies, and at last, you will see. The truth will emerge, like a lotus from a mud pond. It has to.'

Say yes, damn it, say yes. The policemen pounded on the table, hammered on the walls, hammered and pounded him too. But the prisoner said not a word, the stubborn, cussed man that he was. Too idiotic too. Kept asking questions in his turn. Which sahib, and who were they talking about? And he really had no idea.

They reported to him a list of his movements the day of the murder.

12.00 took the rickshaw out from Taj sahib's garage

12.10 to the zilla school

12.30 to 1.30 took the children back to their homes in Marwari Pada.

After that Daya did not remember what he had done for the

next few hours. Towards four, he was by the railway station. The magazine vendor confirmed it, to Asha Dogra's mortification. Those magazines Daya bought with the money she had given him, and took with him to school when it was time to pick up the teacher. There had been the usual altercation once again between the father and daughter on their return, for she was as usual late and it was only an hour later that Dogra sahib was found dead.

He was found, a stab wound on his back, his face turned to one side, redder than usual, his mouth open, shocked. *Almost as if he knew who his murderer was.*

Kerketta was late, he was profusely apologetic when he came. More work today, he explained, to the constable, then again to the inspector. Truth was, he had never liked the prison much. More than a hundred years old, some rebels of 1857 had been hanged from the trees that surrounded the building; hanged by the same hemp ropes made by the Brooks Town Hemp Plantation company first set up by Robert's forebears.

The company was in dire straits by the time Robert returned from London; industrial hemp was once used for making sacks, but Calcutta-made jute was now the more preferred option. While Robert steadily lost heart in every way, the spot of the hanging was commemorated soon after Independence with a stone plaque. This displeased Kerketta no end, and not just because his family had been loyal retainers of the Hydes from the very beginning. 'Why give ghosts a chance? They will come back to admire it, and bask in their own importance, you mark my words.'

In my first days at Brooks Town, I had heard him grumbling about it too, 'If I could, I would have written a letter in the papers.' For all his wisdom, Kerketta had this yearning to see his name in print. The plantation may have fallen into neglect once Robert no longer bothered but I believe Kerketta had his own secret plot of land, quietly and illegally cultivating the kind of hemp that made him valued for quite different reasons.

Besides long gone rebels, the prison with its walls of heavy stone blackened with age, also housed counterfeiters, smugglers, a thief or two. There were even an empty cell here and there, and no one remembered what had happened to their original occupants. The prison's records provided delightful fodder to the rats and roaches and termites who shared the premises with prisoners and policemen.

When the commissioner explained the situation to him, Kerketta demurred in his usual way.

'It doesn't look good to me at all,' he said and again, 'not good at all. There is an evil spirit over this town, two unfortunate events cannot happen in the same month.'

'Don't speculate,' said the commissioner. 'We are in this sorry mess because there is no post-mortem facility but we need to know how to fill in the missing gaps. Something crucial happened in the afternoon when this man's hours were unaccounted for,' he said pointing to the rickshaw puller. 'And now, that is for you to find out.'

Kerketta looked at the prisoner when he was taken into the cell. The remaining policemen stood outside, hypnotized by Kerketta's ways no matter how many times they had seen him do it. Kerketta took the man's right hand in his, chafed and rubbed it and then he bent down and sniffed his feet, fingered and pressed them in places. The rickshaw puller giggled. Perhaps he was ticklish.

'It is true, there can be no doubt about his occupation,' said Kerketta. 'It is obvious from the peculiar roughness, the indentation in his palms and the smell of the plastic, and the ribbed marks on his feet. But there is something else.'

He looked confused, he groped in his pocket as if looking for something, and having heard the jangle of his keys he looked relieved. 'Yes?' asked the commissioner leaning forward. Kerketta was taking much longer than envisaged.

'Nothing, nothing.' The commissioner made him nervous. There was something Kerketta knew he had lost but he couldn't possibly report the theft of a small key when a murder had to be solved. And that key, he knew he had lost it a long time so why did it rankle him now? And then his face lightened as he remembered. Yes, it was the key to the Dogra house he had lost, and he was here to help the police solve a murder in that very house. Matters in life worked by way of stranger connections.

He felt the commissioner rolling his eyes as he stood behind him. And panicking, because he was a small man with a small reputation to protect, Kerketta pressed the accused man's soles again, then he turned his hand over in his, sniffed it before turning it over and again, and with a borrowed pair of spectacles, proceeded to read his palm.

'This man has definitely known violence, even murder I would say, and very recent too.' Kerketta shrugged in distaste. The smell of murder seemed close, it appeared to be emanating from his own pocket too, but Kerketta held himself. He was letting his fancies go too far. 'I just cannot express, my eyes will not bring it up,' he shuddered, 'but there has been violence, much blood spilled. I see it in this man's hands, I see it all over the place.'

Daya understood. Understood that it was his past catching up with him. For five years, the rickshaw puller had awaited trial. His had become a forgotten case, like many other under trial prisoners in India's vast overpopulated prisons, who languish in jail, just forgotten. And then one day, just as unexpectedly released with no reason given, just as Daya had been.

The Dogra case remained in the headlines, much discussed and then one day slipped from public memory. Soon other events would come to overshadow it. But the whispers remained. That the matter had been hushed up, because in some way the murdered man's daughter had been involved. The commissioner received great acclaim for solving a murder case so quickly, and in so foolproof a manner. He wrote a paper on 'Method, not Motive, as a tool of Crime' and presented it at the International Criminology Conference in Lagos. The only time he would ever be abroad, the only time that that country would host a conference like that, for in a matter of years, crime would take on such dimensions in Nigeria that criminologists and their conferences would find themselves simply unable to keep pace.

As for Daya, he waited, and waited and waited for so long that he found after a while that his voice had turned to a hoarse whisper, it cracked if he as much as raised it. In his quieter moments, he would retreat to his corner of the cell, and try and remember but could not.

It remained to be asked why the police had not followed his statement or the case up, I put down my pen. It did not matter as long as someone could be blamed for the crime. Finished.

The end of my story. *The Rickshaw Puller's Love Story*, I called it and I was satisfied with it.

I checked the calendar – the last date for submission was still two weeks away. I could send the neatly typed out article by registered post and it would reach with a day to spare – if nothing went wrong.

It was at the post office, where I had sent Maddy with my neat double-spaced typed sheets in an envelope, that she met Asha Dogra. She was all puffy-eyed, she told me later. And her hair had streaks of white that she did not bother to hide. But she still frowned and pursed her lips in the way she had. No one spoke to her, there was an eerie silence in the post office, broken by the slow creak of the two ancient fans whose breeze reached no one and the regular thump of the purple inked stamp pads hitting paper. The smell of old musty paper was overpowering.

And that was what made me go see her. She had gone back to her old house, and was sitting emptily in his study when I found her. His papers still looked as they had the last day, but the blood stain had been washed, and the carpet rolled away. Her eyes had a terrifying blankness but lit up on seeing me. Perhaps she was relieved at seeing a familiar face. It had been years since I had had that effect on anyone. Years. No one smiled on seeing me anymore.

'My dear, you look worn out,' I heard myself say and received a wan smile in return and a shrug like an afterthought.

'It must have been a tough time.'

She looked about to cry, and allowed herself to shed a tear or two.

'It was so sudden,' she said.

'My dear you are not to think more about it.' My hands trembled and I found it difficult to comfort her. Here, and I remembered my flowered, pressed and scented handkerchief. 'No, I have mine,' she said, and a tear like a shiny nose pin lingered at the end of her nose.

'Why not stay with me again for a while?' The offer I made had been impulsive. But perhaps it would work out all right. And Asha Dogra moved into the bungalow.

Midway between these two developments, I received a letter. I despaired even before I had opened it, for I had received such thin, square-shaped envelopes before. *Thank you for your story. We have gone through it and we regret that we are unable to accept it for publication.*

The editor had also helpfully added a post-script. *The authenticated voice of the rickshaw puller somehow does not convince. The narrator, on the other hand, appears too omniscient.*

'I was asking you to assess a story not read a crime report, silly,' I retorted out loud, before bundling it into the wastepaper bin.

I remembered Asha Dogra weeping profusely much later. The tears coursing down freely at last for a man who had towered over her life in every way. 'Towards the end,' she said, 'he was so interested in what I did, he kept wanting to read all my history books and the subject never stopped fascinating him.'

The stories we tell ourselves, I told myself. That was when his death hit her really hard. That, and the incarceration of an innocent man, the only man who she thought had really loved her. She wept for her father, she could have taught him the history her students were just not interested in. And she cried for a love affair that was doomed even as it was born. This was what committed her more to another doomed love affair, one that came alive in the letters that were exchanged and shrivelled in the days one of these letters became strangely public. I envied Asha her tears when I had only my riverside walks that led me past every house, even Dogra's where the light would never be on any more. Every shared feeling stamps itself on an established connection between two people. Maddy and I had laughed together on the phone one night, and the connection had been surprisingly good.

June 1989
The Doomed Love Story

IF ANYONE HAD CREPT IN through that open window and accosted Dogra in his study that fateful afternoon, only Maya could tell for sure. Since the last year, she had been engaged in a great act of propitiation, running up, down, then up again, all 108 stone steps of the Budhiraja temple. It was a performance that began from late morning after her chores for the day were done till early evening, when she had to return home to cook dinner for her father, Old Mr Mukherjee who had once been assistant to Robert at the club. There were only the two of them left now in that house on Brooks Hill. Earlier that year, her brother, Subrat Mukherjee, Physics teacher, had left for Indonesia, barely a month after Agamoni's marriage.

Maybe she had begun it all for her brother; his love for Agamoni had been doomed anyway and he had had no choice but to leave. Or it could be her doddering father Maya worried about, who was cramming the house up with old furniture from the club that was always in imminent threat of demolition.

It was a strange family living in a house I remember visiting many years ago, the time I still taught. A house with its dark silences and that oppressive binding love.

The house lay on the road to Brooks Hill, a ten-minute cycle ride away from school as I found out one hot afternoon, when I rode the streets in search of Maddy.

That afternoon was so hot that even the red gravel on Brooks' hill road burnt in the heat. Maddy was late and as the city slept behind shuttered windows, I rode as best as I could, gritting my teeth to the pain in my ankle, a frown of fierce concentration on my face. I knew I had to make my way to Mukherjee's house, where Maddy had once gone before with a friend. There was no other place at that time for young people to hang out.

The house was in the old Bengali part of the city, with its old shops, soot-covered old cottages, and old forgotten trees. A few bungalows interspersed the smaller one-room cottages, with a scooter and a bicycle in front, and the washing flapped in terraces upstairs. Most of the old houses had porches fenced in with iron grills. Somewhere a straggly frangipani tree sidled against a wall, but otherwise it was an area locked into itself, holding on to secrets no one asked about.

The bigger bungalows had most of their upper floors shut and barred. No one lived there anymore. The children had gone away to Calcutta or farther away, to America. The restaurant that had once been popular was now shared between a television repair shop and a tea stall. There were a few men sipping tea, sitting under a thin cloud of cigarette-grey smoke. They looked at me as I passed and then away, and I found myself willing for them to look at me a fraction more. They did not. It was a world that wasn't mine any more.

I found the Mukherjee house easily enough. There it was, the name on a black and white board fixed askew onto the grilled verandah. There were potted plants along the ledge, and someone's slippers, broad and black-strapped lay outside the door. I had the feeling that their owner was somewhere very near, invisible over those black-strapped slippers.

Subrat Mukherjee, I read. And below in one line, so that the words cut into each other in a maddeningly confusing manner – it said, teacher, convent school, also tuition for bank exams.

I thought I detected a flutter in the curtains, a movement in a balcony upstairs but it was too late to turn back now.

My desire to leave grew as I hunted for the doorbell. A physics teacher, and he can't fix his doorbell and I jangled on the grills. A gentle shake and then a longer one. It made a tiny item of men's clothing fall gently from the moss-stained terrace to the ground. A dotted underwear. Did he wear that under his flare pants? I was looking at it with great interest when he appeared.

I heard an Oh followed by a What brings you here? We were outside the school setting and Subrat Mukherjee and I had no idea how to deal with each other. But it was his voice and it was his face I saw, broken up into small squares by the grill through which we saw each other. He stood at the edge of a dark circle, his face in half light, and cut up, and then he smiled. I knew what Agamoni had seen in him then.

The next moment he stepped into the light. A towel was thrown over his shoulders, the end of his sacred thread peeped out from under it, and a set of keys jangled in his hand.

He was smiling, so that his moustache split and spread across his face.

I came looking for…

Maddy, he finished.

We laughed nervously, but his face had darkened and then he was shouting to someone inside, quick, abrupt words spoken in Bengali. Maya, where is Baba? He is not here.

From somewhere in the darkness, behind the floating green curtain, a voice floated in, He was, I saw him. See his slippers.

The voice advanced from behind the curtains, and a human form took shape behind, What is the use? Muffled at first, the voice took on strength as the human form it belonged to, emerged from behind the curtain. You tell him and then…

The woman who emerged could only be Subrat Mukherjee's sister. Only she did not have a moustache. She had the same curly hair, which she wore longer, and she was fair and stocky, a round face with features arranged neatly on it, topped by a pair of pencil-thin, parlour-straightened eyebrows. She stopped when she saw us and withdrew a step, holding onto the curtain.

I will go and look. He must have gone to the restaurant…

Brother and sister looked at each other in annoyance. Till he remembered me again.

You please step in, step in, do. He was speaking the strange English that always made the girls giggle. Perhaps that was why his love letters confused Agamoni. He sounded brusque too, perhaps he was worried about his father. She is my fellow teacher, and so he introduced me to his sister. And in that abruptness, those words spoken were oddly touching.

His sister looked uncertain, stepping back even more as we stepped in.

Shoes…

She said pointing to my black-strapped, buckled up outdoorsy shoes. The one doomed to be irrevocably spoiled when Jaspal Singh would push me, one afternoon as hot as this one.

Shoes? I asked.

She pointed to my shoes and then the door. It was Mukherjee's voice that sounded from behind, it had taken on its old tenor and form. Shoes to be deposited at the door before entry. But in your case, we make an exception.

I rose, relieved at not having to take my shoes off. The floor was unevenly patterned, and I caught sight of Maddy's black pointed school shoes and felt an odd relief. So I had found her after all.

What class you teach in? she asked, shouting the question, and so I couldn't even correct her. It wasn't rudeness, just the way she spoke her English.

Needlework.

And it was Mukherjee who explained, she is the needlework teacher, no classes to teach.

Oh.

That one word said volumes, it was said softly but carried a wealth of meaning behind it.

'I used to be the drama teacher once,' I said, louder than was necessary.

'I see you sometimes on your bicycle,' she said, not hearing me at all.

I realized then that there was really little that escaped her notice. She nodded and abruptly walked back in, Subrat too vanished behind the green curtain and after a while, I walked in too.

Behind the green curtain, past a rack full of old newspapers and more shoes, I advanced into a small room made narrower still by the bamboo wicker chairs placed randomly. These were chairs I recognized at once. The Brooks Hill club that Robert had once run was now falling into a state of dishabille before my very eyes. Every day someone would carry away a sofa, the garden chairs and once an entire four-poster bed was carried away by two men, with three joyful children on top. And then Mr Parida as commissioner had put a stop to it, ruling that Mr Mukherjee, as the former acting manager would be official caretaker till a decision as to what to do with the club was made. And now it was he who was siphoning off the furniture.

Still I found the very familiarity of the chairs comforting. It was strange how I only felt pleasure as I saw the round table squatting in the middle of the wicker chairs, its glass surface hidden by a mound of papers, including old Bengali magazines. On the walls, hung an assortment of things. A mask of Durga, photos of Kashmir, the usual cross-stitched design work of an English country cottage and towards a corner over a table that had to be Subrat Mukherjee's for his cloth bag lay careless on it, a black and white framed photo of a young bride. It was not the usual downcast photo of a young bride, instead her veil had slipped off her head and she stared at us sideways, a bit cockily too, with her elbows on the table.

I found Maddy there too, with a classmate. Because she did not get up to greet me, neither did the other one, though I had been her teacher not so long ago. But I was used to this now.

Mukherjee Sir's mother, Maddy told me matter-of-factly seeing me look at the photo. I could tell of course. There was something about the way she looked that Subrat had inherited.

Only his eyes had a more narrowed look, as if he would never find what he was looking for.

The three of us were alone in the room. We sat on the chairs, knees knocking against each other's. I shifted and asked her, What are you two doing here?

But I didn't hear Maddy's reply for just then we heard voices. The son berating his father. You should not go out like that. People will think you are mad. And no slippers too.

Then the curtain was tossed aside and the two men walked in. And I saw a face I had last seen long years ago. Someone who could only be Subrat Mukherjee's father, the man who I had once known as Robert's assistant at the club. But his thin quavering voice had taken on an old man's querulousness, the spectacles in his hand shook as he shuffled in, hesitant, into the growing darkness.

Good afternoon, said the older man, and the younger girls, more innocent, smiled at his cheerfulness, at the way he had greeted us.

'You girls,' he said and smiled. 'And what brings you here?' I had liked him once, his old world courtesy reminding me of those old time British gentlemen who were Robert's friends and paid me attention.

We were thirsty, Maddy lisped in the way she had when she wanted attention.

The older man shuffled to a corner and switched on the light. A naked bulb blinked alive in surprise, hanging on to a wire that disappeared into the low roof. And time froze as he turned around and looked at me.

We looked at each other and the silence waited to be broken. There were more creases on his cheek, his eyes were narrowed as they tried to take me in and take in the past too, and then, amazingly, he shrugged it all aside, and lurched to the nearest chair.

Sit, sit, said the older man, as Maddy made to get up and he made himself more comfortable in the wicker chair that had once belonged to the club.

Your father, what does he do?

He has business, said Harpreet, Maddy's friend, biting her lips.

He turned his polite curious eyes towards Maddy.

And knowing somehow just then that Maddy was about to make up yet another story about a father she had never had, I stiffened, knowing I had to intervene.

Yes… and he was British, I heard her say.

Well, well, he smiled then toothsomely, You are quite a lady then, and you?

I am Mrs Hyde, and perhaps the devil resided in me too and I blurted out, I used to be Chatterjee before.

He smiled, slapped himself on the thighs, Ah a Bengali, and just then his son came in balancing a tray with several coloured glasses, some orange, others yellow. He couldn't have heard me.

Drink up, girls, he said.

They watched our faces as we took our first sip. It was water in the coloured glasses and Subrat said with apology in his voice, 'The cold drink has just got over.'

But no one heard him. His father was looking at me with great interest and I willed him not to remember, to ignore any hazy stirrings his memory could have evoked, on seeing me there.

'It has been a while since we had guests,' he said finally, looking at no one in particular, in a sad, forlorn voice.

Subrat Mukherjee looked uncomfortable, he looked at each one of us in turn, did not find anything to say and we waited for his father's rambling reminiscences. It was a possibility he would soon get tired or forget.

Last time we had anyone, and it already is some time now. Why, it was that man from Kashmir, Dogra sahib, who wanted to train all those youngsters in the park. Before that, there used to be people from the club, but that was so long back…

'My father,' the son broke in, 'he speaks of a time in history.'

But his father would brook no interruption. 'It used to be the most popular club those days. It was not so sleepy as today. And people would come, complain but learn to feel at home. I was the manager of the club…' He laughed, leaving the sentence unfinished, hoping to convey a bit of his lost importance.

'There was this English officer when I had just come. He was so out of place. Not for him the hunt in the jungles. He would look so lost when he came to the club, there was not that usual swagger, the aggression, you follow what I am saying?'

He didn't wait for us to confirm but continued with his story, 'And at night, soon after he had left after a few drinks, he would ride the entire stretch of the Brooks hill road, up, down and over and over again. He would not sleep, not let his poor horse sleep and not even the rest of us. It seemed he did not want to go home either. One day, I asked him why. And do you know, he said he could not remember why.'

Harpreet shrieked, and the older man smiled, glad of the effect he had created. I sat, stiff and straight, knowing it was time to go. But Maddy listened to him, fascinated.

Maybe he was sleepwalking, I suggested, icily, hoping he would take the hint.

It was then that Maya, Subrat's sister came in. She had had her fill roaming by herself in that small house and had come in having run out of all options. Now she sat next to her brother, tossing baleful looks once in a while at her father.

'He was the last of those Englishmen. I never called him by his first name. I never remember his last name too. He seemed too young and brash. And then he left suddenly, upped and went just like that. A long time ago, it was. They did find a dead body but it was never...'

'Don't scare them,' interrupted Subrat Mukherjee abruptly but he was smiling kindly at the girls. And no one, no one could have heard my heart beating fast, even his sister who continued to look balefully at me, at her father and then everyone in turn.

'Father would scare me too, with the same stories... it didn't work,' she said with a relish of her own. 'I can't be fooled any more.'

There was a pitiful defiance in the manner she said it. She was a woman one had to be wary of, I knew then. The plainness of her face gave nothing away. Her petulance too was momentary, as if she was afraid to express any more of herself. I felt sorry too. She was one of those whose best years had left them far behind, or perhaps she had never had them either. Her straight, pencil-thin eyebrows, the quickly applied powder now lying in white patches on her face, the wristwatch tight on her arm, and the clip in her hair, holding it punishingly in place. She did everything right but already time was too far ahead. Perhaps that explained in part the running she would do later up and down the steps of the Budhiraja temple. It was also a hope to catch up – on life, on time.

'No one respects me any more,' said her father. She blushed and her face looked more splotchy than before. 'It's the trouble with the times. No one respects the past, or the old... that old club is falling to pieces. The owners don't seem interested in it, how long can I keep talking of it?' he asked querulously.

The son leaned back in his chair. He had the non-committal expression he wore in class when a particularly stupid student fumbled his way through an answer. We knew then it was time to leave. I was relieved to get out into the sunshine, away from the darkness, that house crowded with furniture where love had no chance to creep in.

Agamoni Gupta was the woman Subrat loved secretly. Even otherwise, she had a mesmerizing effect on all those who watched her. There was the almost unconscious way she had of pushing back flyaway strands of hair behind her ears. The rest of her hair was tied up in a thick plait that swung low to her hips and moved when she walked. Mukherjee must have fallen for her the year they both joined, the early part of 1983.

Perhaps Agamoni returned his love but they were both always careful, first smiling at each other across the crowded staff room and playgrounds. Not a word out of context was ever exchanged, no one overheard them saying anything scandalous and it was doubtful if they had ever met outside the school. But we knew still, even those of us who had known love fleetingly, and others who had never known it at all. It was obvious in the way they smiled at each other, lightly and almost playfully and the world stopped, as it must for lovers. We looked up, work forgotten and looked at them. For a second or two, the wind hung in the curtains, it swelled up balloon-like before it swung back wallwards, and only after that did the children's screams, momentarily muted, become apparent to everyone.

It was a delicious secret that belonged to everyone, and never aired. We followed with eager eyes the two of them every time they walked towards their respective classrooms, her languidness a contrast to his determined strides. It was a romance we carried in our hearts, everyone referred to it off-handedly, nothing was certain and this is how we wanted it. Real love was for the films and never survived. People who married, had babies, ran homes did it for the simple convenience of living. And love was reserved for those shameless and disobedient. Because this was a secret love, we never really knew what it was, and let it be.

Yet, it was Agamoni Gupta who got married six years later to a businessman. The same year that Dogra died, and Subrat left soon after, and Maddy was still around, she hadn't left yet. Agamoni's husband, Binduteshwara Thakur was a well-off businessman. His family owned resorts and hotels around Digha, Gopalpur and Puri. He had a name like a Hindu God but marrying him was the most practical thing Agamoni could have done. He would provide well for her and she need not work if she did not want to. She would be another Mrs Commissioner Parida, I thought. She would become too fat, too rich, too frivolous, too fond of jewellery, too friendly with all her husband's friends and always too unhappy.

Subrat did not show his heartbreak. I noted Asha's silence and put it down to her distress over her father's death. But from Maddy I gathered, how Subrat had begun taking his work more seriously, volunteering for those extra duties that were part of a teacher's life. He was in charge when the boys played their Saturday cricket matches in the empty grounds next to the cemetery, the very place Dogra had eyed for imparting his brand of military training. The place everyone was secretly afraid of.

Only a vagabond woman of recent vintage lived in a shack near the cemetery. No one knew where she came from or how she came to occupy that shack, left behind by a long ago labourer. She appeared and vanished at will. She was scrawny, hobbled because of a misshapen ankle and had a mass of shaggy matted hair that was of uncertain colour, except it turned to silver when the sun caught it. She always dressed ridiculously, with stuff that someone had thrown at her or she had picked up from some place or another. Often during the course of a cricket match, she would emerge from her shack or walk slowly up from the riverbank, only to hurl a volley of abuse at the fielders on the boundary and at the few spectators who happened to be around. Everyone put up with her best as they could.

But there was a day when someone responded and it was Subrat who did so, nearly a fortnight or so after Agamoni's marriage. The school cricket final was on and the tramp lady had appeared and was peering over the railing when he rose from his chair.

'You there, make no noise,' he said, his anger making his hair fall over his face and his moustache bristled as well.

The woman directed a torrent of abuse at him.

'All your vituperation is for nothing,' he responded in cold clear tones as if he were reciting the words aloud. 'It does not make sense. It would be better if you went in.'

She began again, and Subrat picked up a twig and walked towards her, shaking it, 'Be off, or I call the police.'

Maddy asked if I had heard – the cheering and clapping that were loud enough to reach my study. I nodded absently, 'It would have been fun to watch. Did she come back?'

But Maddy was now talking of Agamoni Gupta who only smiled her new vague smile, as she sat in a plastic folding chair with the other teachers under the leafy pipal tree. Everyone clapped but not Agamoni who suddenly developed an interest in how her sari was arranged. She bent down to rearrange the pleats, and I knew the tramp lady must have hobbled back to her shack. Soon she would move herself to the river, and in time, she would use some of my old things, like a pair of shoes with a torn buckle I would never need any more. 'That's quite an act, isn't it?' I said but Maddy never heard.

And Subrat's new found heroism only lasted as long as the day Mahesh, Maddy's old friend and classmate, produced that letter that he said had fallen out of Subrat's pocket.

Mahesh wanted terribly to impress Maddy and it wasn't difficult. She had never had much male attention, having grown up without a father. So he produced that letter that was to have great repercussions. What was a secret was now openly known. It speeded up Subrat's departure by some months, to a place as far away as Indonesia. It flushed out in the open Asha's role in the entire matter, as a go-between in the secret romance of six long years that Agamoni and Subrat had indulged in. A romance lived through letters though both lived in the same city, helped by fairy godmothers like Asha who picked up letters he wrote to her every time she made a detour to the post office as she did the railway station. Who answered his calls even later from Calcutta and for a month or two even from far away Indonesia especially when he had something urgent to tell Agamoni. The question was: Had Dogra known about this too? Did he disapprove? Or had he misunderstood the whole thing?

Maya, Subrat's sister would know for sure. I could picture her, with her everyday scowl in place, cursing Agamoni under her breath, blaming her for her brother's unhappiness, and yet happy that she had married someone else. She was a woman who wouldn't want to share anything – especially the men she was used to all her life.

Mahesh had pulled out the letter from his pocket and we recognized it for what it was. A piece of paper torn away from a writing pad, folded up in a manner to fit into a one-rupee postal envelope, and there was her writing. A teacher's writing, displayed on blackboards, on the margins of answer sheets, and in attendance registers, is easily recognized and placed.

'This fell out from his pocket,' he said. 'He did not see.'

Maddy made a lunge for it. But Mahesh held on to it, before putting it back in his pocket, a smug smile returning to his face, 'Sorry, can't give it to you. Need to study it myself.'

And his fingers tight over the letter now secure in his pocket, Mahesh Aggarwal walked off.

Only a few hours ago Subrat Mukherjee had returned to Agamoni all the letters she had written to him, except for one he didn't want to let go, the very one that had now gone missing, the one Mahesh found.

It happened as they met in a group with the other teachers at the new café on Brooks Hill. The Brooks Hill café was a new addition to the landscape dominated by the old, scarred hill. It was close to the Deer Park and was owned by a former student of mine, Raja Mohanty whose family was one of the richest in town. I had once known his father, Rabi and the Mohantys had made their fortune through a clever manipulation of other people's land. Raja's new café looked pretty, and with its red and white checkered tablecloths, its English teatime snacks, screening of old black and white English films, it was a poor imitation of the older club. I longed to visit it, but till Asha moved in, sorely lacked for company.

It was in this new café that Subrat asked for and returned in turn all the love letters except one they had exchanged. It would be the last time they would ever sit next to each other. His hurt meant he had to come back one last time, and Agamoni, for her part, was too newly married to ask herself how she really felt. For the past week since she had returned to school, she had been much admired and envied, for the saris she wore with jewellery that matched. She had a glow on her face and blushed often. The glow came from Farah Velayati's special face pack made from a mix of soya flour and sandal paste especially got from Iran, the blush came from things Agamoni remembered about the wedding that she had not known before.

Now she remembered as she felt Subrat next to her, blushing at what her husband had whispered in her ears, how he had smelled her face and said, 'You can call me Bindu, Aggy,' and had then proceeded to put her on his lap. They all called him that, he elaborated. His three spoilt rich sisters and his mother who had not come for the wedding but who waited for him to return to their three-storeyed mansion in Puri.

Subrat had something of his sister's scowl as he handed the letters over. He remembered how his sister had looked when he had lingered by the door waiting for Asha to bring him Agamoni's letters during the holidays. Asha was older, and no one would ever suspect anything if she came to their house. It's no use. She doesn't care, his sister had sniffed. You write to her everyday and she writes to you, maybe once a week. Anyone can tell, she doesn't care.

She must have a black tongue, and it was perhaps that he was thinking this that he looked as grim as Agamoni looked vague. And that was why he had chosen not to intervene when his sister took upon herself that act of penance, running up and down the 108 steps of the Budhiraja temple afternoon to sunset; not telling Maya either of his friend Dipankar's efforts to win the contract for a motorable road all the way up to the temple.

Subrat returned instead to the task at hand, of returning all the letters she had written to him. Letters written during the holidays, or whenever she wanted to write. All the letters that Asha had carried between them, except one. The last one Agamoni had written to him during her honeymoon. The one that Mahesh would soon put up on the notice board, simply as an act of bravado to impress Maddy. Where Agamoni wrote to Subrat that she would never love anyone but him and would carry his memory with her in her every breath, till her death.

'You are smiling,' and he spoke to her in a low voice.

They used that undertone when speaking to each other in company, and though the words were eaten up by his moustache she understood, and then his hand slowly pushed the envelope across. All your letters, he said, and she smiled, going along with the subterfuge. She played with the strand of hair that always strayed across to her cheeks.

They stared at each other briefly, and as his hand reached for the salt cellar and hers for the ketchup, they touched for the first time and wondered why it was always so difficult to say anything.

The letter was put up on the school notice board in the beginning of the week that Subrat announced that he was leaving for ever. Mahesh had made a photocopy of it, smudged out her name, before he put it up. Till late in the afternoon, crowds of students surged around it, laughing and reading it aloud to themselves.

Maddy accosted Mahesh about it, the very next morning. He was playing table tennis and grinned unctuously.

'But you should not have done this. Did you think at all about the consequences?'

'I cut off her name,' Mahesh said, 'so what's the problem? No one knows.'

No one knows? Come on no one is a fool. Everyone knows her handwriting. If her marriage is spoiled, you will be the one to blame.

I will take it down soon, I promise… he said looking confused, not able to follow.

But he didn't have to do that in the end. It was Subrat who walked up to the notice board, his bellbottomed pants flaring out with his every determined stride. He ripped the letter off the board, folded it with minute care into his pocket, and rode off on his cycle, returning only the next day to tell the school of his decision. It was his sister's reputation he had to protect, he announced. His sister Maya who for these many years had been involved with Dipankar, Manik Ghosh's good-for-nothing layabout son who had only recently turned contractor. Now Subrat hoped to earn enough for her marriage, before it was too late. A job in Indonesia would allow him to do just that.

That was what he told Binduteshwara's goons when they surrounded him the next day as he returned home from somewhere. It was his sister Maya's letter to Dipankar that he had spirited away from the school board, it had nothing to do with Agamoni, he explained, his arms crossed around himself. His old father shuffled in the background, a look of uncertain delight on his face. He might have thought they were having guests again.

But Subrat Mukherjee's explanation left everyone confused. How could anyone not have known about this other romance?

Manik Ghosh had immersed himself in bringing out the *Brooks Town Ramblings*, which had only some years ago closed down. Gautam Singh Dogra had written for it, and Robert had been an avid reader. At one time it had been very interesting. It was about the town, the history, the people in it and it also had debates about things happening in the city, in the country and the wider world too. But of course as the papers from Calcutta began reaching on time, Manik Ghosh's paper began to be read less and less till he was forced to close it down.

One of Manik Ghosh's pet grievances had been the younger generation, he called them the 'don't care, do nothing' generation. And his son Dipankar was an apt personification of it all. He was now a contractor, that is, he fixed things for people, especially the government, arranging for labour and supplies each time a project came up such as a road, a canal or a food godown. He had as his office the ground floor room that had once been his father's, and with his feet up on an empty table, he was always on the phone. And when Dipankar was not on the phone, he drove around town in his smoke-spewing open jeep with two or three other men, and it all made for a very menacing picture. When he was not chasing up a contract somewhere, he would park his jeep near the women's college, at the sugarcane juice stall by the gate and simply look. And that was how, Subrat insisted, Dipankar had seen his sister six years ago and how the love affair had begun.

No one knew either if the friendship that Dipankar and Subrat Mukherjee shared was related to the love that blossomed between Dipankar and his sister. But every night for a month before Subrat left, everyone heard Dipankar Ghosh's ramshackle jeep as it jolted and grumbled its way up Brooks Hill. It was always past eleven, when the television programmes were over for the night, and people looked up, and at each other knowingly as they heard the jeep make its way up.

In the Mukherjee household, with its furniture spilling outside the house, they heard him come. And Subrat emerged in the open and berated his father in full hearing as everyone listened behind drawn curtains and switched-off lights.

Look at you, so much furniture in the house and no space for guests.

The old man only looked at the furniture lying outside and smiled thinly.

The two of them, Dipankar and Subrat, would sit together in the jeep to talk. There was no way he could be called into the house. It was late and there was too much furniture around.

No one knows for sure what was discussed, as they sat in that darkness, swatting away the mosquitoes, unseen and unnoted except for that red dot of light that was Dipankar's cigarette. Maya watched from her darkened room, her eyes lit up with feverish hope.

'Are you asking him for a job?' the father sneered later. He never had a good word to say about the Ghosh boy.

'Going tramping down the roads and highways managing his contracted labour? He siphoned off the entire money instead of paying either the suppliers or the labourers… you be careful of that young man. He seems just like Soumendra Mohanty.'

Soumendra, that man on the boulder Maddy had chased away, had a disrepute that preceded my opinion of him. He was rarely in town and yet people, whoever you asked, had a definitive one line opinion about him. And he had never really cared. He didn't after all have to belong here.

Between father and son now, were tables of various sizes. The circular dining table, the smaller serving tables, the ornate writing table with its secret drawer, and the stools too small and fragile to hold anything. Maya would have put vases with flowers on them but for the fact that she would have to walk around the tables and the stools, and there was every chance she would topple them over.

The thought that her brother was meeting Dipankar excited her for some reason. She had seen him often outside her college, the girls would talk about him because he was so different. So daring. So confident. So smart. Just so different. There was also the way he spoke to girls, he did not feign a shyness like the other guys. Instead he laughed at their jokes and sometimes made a few of his own.

Of course, she knew men who were like that never settled down, never made good husbands. Soumendra Mohanty, the name her father had mentioned. Cousin of the rich lawyer Rabi Mohanty and his son Raja, and what a useless rake everyone, and not just her father, said he was. Living in Bombay, travelling to the oddest places, and turning up once in a while in Brooks Town, where his own family wanted to have nothing to do with him.

But Maya never having known love, and the addictive poison it could be, believed in its magical restorative powers. If Dipankar made the right moves, she would make sure that he never regretted this decision. The intensity with which she thought this was matched only by the desperation with which she wanted to leave the house. All the more desperate because of the suddenness with which the thought came to her. That she in effect hated the house that was now trampling all over her, where the only space she could claim as hers was that before the window from where she looked on hungrily at the red dot of a cigarette, trying in vain to catch the conversation between her brother and Dipankar. The many ways Dipankar held his cigarette, the ways it flitted and moved as if it had a life of its own in the darkness everywhere made Maya believe that she could tell Dipankar's every mood. She could, thinking of that moving light, make her next plans, however laughable they seemed, then steel herself to any mockery and speculation that would automatically follow. Once upon a time, before days and evenings were taken away by television serials, small towns had their own ways of reading and defining love.

Looking across the river, it was welcoming to see the twin headlights of the slowly climbing jeep. The darkness was upsetting, I missed the light that had been forever on in Dogra's study. Now the sound of the jeep rolling up the hill filled up the vacuum I felt inside, told me I had company once again in the hours when everyone slept.

In the darkness it was so easy to lose count of time, and forget the sequence of events. Had Maya begun her penance soon after to win over Dipankar or much before that, when news of Agamoni's wedding had just broken and her brother's heart broke too?

In the morning, I would hear her all over again and know in my own fast beating heart, that perhaps she would stop all that running, once the identity of who had really murdered Dogra came to light. But it was beginning to be believed, even secretly, that just as Asha, an unhappy woman with no prospect of marriage could play a part in murder, other unhappy women with no prospect of marriage needed patience and penitence in ample measure. No one really believed that anyone, especially a wastrel like Dipankar could fall for Maya. But love could bloom in the unlikeliest of situations, even in a town such as ours, and apart from me, no one was really bothered to know Maya's reasons. She ran, with her eyes closed all the time. She knew now how every step felt under her feet. She did not need to see a thing, she would never see a thing. For even the sight of a loved one, driving around town in his terribly noisy jeep, leaving pockmarks of dust clouds in every place he went with it, could be distracting. Later, of course, if all worked out well, she would tell him what everyone knew: that cigarette smoking is indeed injurious to health.

October, 1989
In the Hospital

No one was more disapproving than Kerketta when Asha moved in. First, he was convoluted and confusing in his warnings. 'Her father's death,' he shook his head, 'it's not a settled matter.' And then he was more direct, 'The heart in her is bad. She gave her father much trouble.'

He looked darkly at Maddy and me and I wondered what he really saw. But maybe he used his powers of perception only in police stations. 'It's all right, Kerketta. You can't really tell one heart from another. And these days, they are having transplants.'

Maddy giggled; those days I could still make her laugh.

And so Asha moved in, it had been years since I had been with anyone my age. In the last few months, Maddy had taken to spending more and more time in her own room. Asha came with her boxes packed with stuff gathered, treasured over the years. Her black and white albums from a time when we had both been young. Every time she withdrew into her silences, she would retreat into her room on the ground floor, shuffle through the photos, sniff with all the effort it took her to remember and emerge only when an idea for a new recipe struck her. But with that death between us, we managed to soon resolve the smaller differences we had.

My hair was now a light gold in colour, it had always been very light. I liked it that way, sometimes going to Farah's for a trim to keep it a decent length. Maddy was a teenager and she would become a lovely woman one day soon, I knew. Her green eyes and hair of burnished gold was so like someone I had once known that I lived in constant fear that someone, especially the sad, all-seeing Mrs Parida, would comment sooner or later. And in all this, there was Asha Dogra who still carried on her Sunday morning ritual with the same vigour. She would set the henna paste the previous evening, mixing the mehndi leaves with the amla and the egg. That first day, it made me wrinkle my nose. It stinks, I said, the egg seems to be everywhere, even in the milk.

Asha had retorted, It's an old traditional treatment for the hair. And it is not just for looking young. I have been teaching in the school for nearly twenty years now, everyone knows my age. The amla keeps your hair silky, the mehndi gives it a thickness...

You haven't still explained the egg, my dear? I asked.

It's for the glow, the bounce.

It struck me then how this same smell had pervaded the Dogra house over many Sundays and so it was I who offered to smear that paste over her hair every Sunday, parting her hair to apply it to the roots, then on every strand of hair.

Asha was soon her old, girlish, flighty self. Don't leave anything out, she pleaded, but the smell stayed on my hands for all my frantic repeated washing. I had been splashed with all the colours of the world and I couldn't, it seemed, ever wash them away.

When they, father and daughter, first arrived in Brooks Town, Asha had finished high school, and I was Robert's young wife, the adored Mrs Hyde. She looks older than that, I told Robert and later it was Dogra who told me of the years she had missed in school because of her itinerant living. He did not tell me of the mother she mourned for in a way that even she couldn't explain. All this was from a time when the illusions had not broken yet. I had not yet been deserted. Robert, my husband with his roving eye, was the first and the last British manager of the Club and Brooks Plantation. The company made hemp ropes that were trucked to Calcutta, then on to Rangoon in the east and Vizag in the west. When the company went into a sudden decline during the 1950s, Robert went downhill too. When not flirting with anyone in a sari or a skirt, or riding up and down Brooks Hill, he would while away his time, drinking and playing the piano at the Brooks Hill Club. He had a divine voice that charmed all the women, even Asha, every time she came home for the holidays. But the club was on its last days too, the last British officers left and the Marwari businessmen and native lawyers wanted a new club of their own. And of course, there was Robert's drinking problem. We fought constantly, he was always jealous and suspicious, and this was how it had all ended. One tempestuous night, Robert had driven off in his car and never returned. Not on a horse, as old Mr Mukherjee had it.

The year of Dogra's death, as summer stretched into autumn, for a brief while, there were three people in our house. The room in one corner of the ground floor was redone for Asha. The roof sloped at one corner and the smell of the neem leaves filled the room in summer. There was the noise of the typing as I composed, erased, recomposed. Stuff I knew that Asha or someone else would read on the sly the very next day. Someone who would take care to leave the pages just as I had left them, in the file, the crease in every fold just the same.

There were other new sounds too. Sounds that came as Asha worked in the kitchen. She cooked, baked and grilled, and more when she wanted to forget. Instead she forgot things she never had before: sometimes she would mix up ingredients or add them in the wrong quantities, or miss the steps a certain recipe required and so all of us were roped into a rescue effort to preserve the perfect reputation Asha's cooking enjoyed and also her equanimity, as Prem Aggarwal, the doctor, advised. Food she made that I would get to taste first, for she wanted me to check various things – the salt, sugar, the oiliness, food I knew she was making, for when she would forget some ingredient she would send Kerketta rushing off to Govardhan's. Once there were as many as five trips in one day as she made sambhar, a simple dish with multiple ingredients. Poor Kerketta made trips for curry leaves, a coconut, tamarind paste and last, for lemons. It could have put me off her food but it didn't. The image of what she cooked, the aroma, as the kitchen was just a floor below mine, was too strong to allow that. That accounted for my night raids into the kitchen. As did Maddy's and perhaps all the other footsteps. In my always fevered imagination, in the days following Dogra's death,

Asha's cooking brought into the house, too many people, even the non-living.

When I first heard the footsteps, I thought it was Asha. They were new, and hesitant and uncertain, as if the feet were testing how the floor sounded. Perhaps she had a habit of getting up for a glass of water, or she was just sleepless. But there was a different sound too that followed, and it came to me just as I was about to fall asleep.

The sound of someone moving across the roof, across the garage, someone who had scaled the wall to come in; I heard the creak of a twig under the feet, the swiftness with which the leaves scattered.

Next morning it was the cake Asha had baked so very painstakingly the last week that looked diminished, a slice cut away, cleverly, and very neatly. Evidently with a sleek, sharp object. My old Tibetan knife that I had been unable to find for Mrs Parida's coconuts, would have sliced up pieces as neatly. Someone else had had access to it and used it. But why?

There were sudden other nights like that. When the darkness stretched all around and no lights came on, as they never would any more, at any window, I heard the footsteps again. Sometimes looking out of my window, I longed to see the dot of red light I had seen so many times before but Soumen had not returned. I wondered if I had really seen him the day of Dogra's funeral; had it really been him or had I imagined him watching me as I sat by the riverside that terrible afternoon of his death, unaware and uncaring of a life ebbing away not too far away.

I thought all these thoughts as I heard every other sound expand and grow those long nights. The clock in the outside verandah, the even, faraway snores of the orderly on night duty at the Paridas', a car sweeping past, a sudden angry cawing somewhere, and then a long while later, to break the silence almost, the sound of the fridge door opening, and what I did not see but knew: the bluish green light from inside the refrigerator, scattering itself like a bleeding knife across the hallway, up the staircase, moving up the walls close to me.

As the refrigerator humming picked up in the silence, I realized it wasn't Asha, it could never have been Asha. I sat down on the steps, unable to go down. My legs were trembling and wouldn't hold me up. Was it the same person who had taken the other things too – the Tibetan knife, for instance?

Over the next few nights, I would hear the same footsteps and others too, and never be sure, till the time I did hear Maddy, and learnt too late her terrible secret – on that one occasion when I heard her steps move away from the open refrigerator door, the sounds I heard later from the bathroom where she had shut herself in.

In the half-darkness, with only an overhead skylight, and a door half-ajar Maddy thought no one saw her as all the stolen food she had eaten burst out, noiselessly and in a smooth, yellowy brown flow. Afterwards her fingers would ache, her fingertips would appear sore and reddened to my newly alert eyes and I would remember always that dewy, pale look on her face, I caught in the faint light.

Maddy, I whispered but I knew how horrified she would be if she realized I was spying on her. What if the name came to me more matter-of-factly. Maddy? But once she knew I knew, she would brush away all my efforts to reach her. Maddy, more gently, more pleading. Maddy, calling her as if my heart would break. But I had left it too late. My lonely daughter was lost in her private hell, lost in the food she gulped down and threw out, in an equally frenzied way and all I could wish for was that somehow she could get out of it, if possible get out of Brooks Town. Like the food she no longer wanted to hold inside, she was now gagging on the town that had been her home since she came here as a little baby, of three months. I remember that day still, a smile on her small face as she slept in my arms. Not even waking up once as the train lurched and heaved, and I jumped down the last steps, happy to be back in Brooks Town after nearly a year. I never saw her leave and I always hoped she had a smile then too.

I descended over an hour later, when I knew for sure I wouldn't hear the footsteps again, I saw that the cake looked substantially diminished but I pecked off a corner too, and a cherry and then reached out again a second time to take off a nut, before I closed the fridge door, licking my fingers, returning as quietly as I could to bed. Only the night watched over me like a protective umbrella and perhaps understood why I had to share Maddy's guilt, the way I did, even if I did not know how to help her.

It would be only some weeks later till the footsteps quieted somewhat. One afternoon as I sat on the boulder by the river, I saw Reddy, the Paridas' young servant boy, clambering over the roof, softly treading over the cracks. He had jumped onto the roof over my study after coming up the stone steps from the river, and then shinnied up the tamarind tree, a branch later had cracked and fallen onto the wall, but he was already gone, over the compound wall. That was how he would escape one day soon never to return. But by then Maddy was already making her own plans as well.

The next morning, Asha talked of the noises she had heard. It must be the rats in your house, she turned to me accusingly. And a few minutes later, she insisted, the house must be haunted. Perhaps it's a ghost, even Robert's.

I listened to her fears, and though I knew of Maddy's night time raids on the fridge, she scared me. That it wasn't Robert's ghost but someone else's just as well. Someone who had come once to the house nine months before Maddy was born.

Don't be silly, Asha, I said, my voice louder than usual. Maddy's face was pale and dewy, her knuckles were red, she was already drifting away from me but I did all I could to end the matter. 'You are listening too much to Kerketta and he's getting old. The stairs are older, they are creaky and wooden anyway. That could account for the noise.'

Maddy did not care to look up, she was toying with her food. Asha's concerns would move onto her disappearing appetite and my indifference to it all. It was an act I became desperate to keep up more than anything else, I never wanted Maddy to know I knew. And all that Asha couldn't explain, all that began to concern her, gave the frown on her face a more entrenched life.

On Saturday afternoons, the intruder returned again, the only time he did during the day. It was the time Maddy went for her extra classes, Asha went to the club to play cards, or to Farah's for a do-up. And I trudged down the river bank, all the way to Dogra's house, letting myself in with the key I had stolen from Kerketta those many years ago.

I looked among his papers, ran my fingers over his spidery handwriting and looked at the photos he had. Pictures of long ago happy days. His wife, and a younger looking Asha still with a frown on her face. Looking at those photos, I almost understood why he came to distrust happiness so much.

In the same manner, I made the long walk to the police station too, with the jail a stone's throw away. *Parcel for Daya Sharan*, I wheedled, pointing to the label I had stuck. *From the Welfare Society*. I always picked a time when a different man would be on duty, but that never mattered. They never checked the parcel, or asked questions, sometimes they laughed, openly in disbelief. 'A parcel? Oh my, so he's got admirers.' A small town could be small and get even smaller but they would never do a thing like cross-checking things with each other. The jail authorities would never check with the school who ran the welfare society, and who really cared for a rickshaw puller who had been put away for murder?

Those late Saturday afternoons another intruder had another house, entirely to himself. Of course whoever it was could not put on the television or the radio for Mrs Parida next door, who had taken to spending her afternoons locked in absolute darkness in her room, would hear everything. But he had the run of the kitchen, gorging on the appetizing things in the kitchen and in the fridge. Whoever it was had also read my story as he had the cake. The intruder could have told at once that I was obsessed with the death of Gautam Singh Dogra, a fact that would have struck the police, if they still hadn't closed the file on his murder, as very suspicious.

Some Saturdays I returned early just so I could catch the intruder. I am back early, I would say, opening the door. The habit of talking to Maddy, of hearing my own voice in a quiet house remains with me. Are you all right? I asked again but of course no one answered.

The trees brushed against the window, their shadows moved against the walls, a window creaked somewhere, as did a stair, or was it a footfall? The afternoon sun slanted in through the blinds and as my keys fell on the table, I could tell time had stopped. The shadow that fell across the wall, moving across the stairs could have been Robert's.

The phone rang that one time I came back. I let it ring once, twice. No phone calls now came for me, they did for Asha. But Asha's calls were the usual long distance calls, where the operator first called and then she had to wait, fretting and fidgeting. And then she spoke so softly that I couldn't hear much at all.

That one time I answered, no one said a word. I assumed it was one of Maddy's friends, I almost hoped I would hear Jaspal, his voice hoarse, with the occasional lisp, at the other end. So I told him off, feeling fiercely protective and glad that I was getting back at him somehow. I could learn to live yet without a man's attention. I had nothing to do with his mockery.

It was Asha who connected the dots, sort of. She pointed to Maddy's absent appetite and pointed to her friendship with Mahesh. Something I knew nothing about for I no longer taught at the school. After that episode of the letter that sent Mukherjee away, I learnt the two of them were indeed often seen together.

I asked her, as Asha said I must, and Maddy replied, as

I knew she would, that it was just a friendship. She's your daughter, you must ask pro-per-ly, Asha hissed into my ears many a night over dinner. She might get into bad company, do something...

But I no longer had the will. Every day I saw her grow even more beautiful, and it was a beauty that drove her apart from everything and everyone in this town. For it seemed her beauty was not helping her win the attention of the one boy who would never really care: Jaspal. A boy who had everything was growing into a man who would never be denied anything and Maddy was something he had grown out of. Or he knew the one truth, I hoped Maddy would never know, and knowing what I did, I ignored Maddy's obvious need for help and attention. My daughter noticed my efforts not to help and in the many ways our subsconscious comes to rule our lives, a distance developed. The crack once opened grew so wide that soon I was afraid of stepping into one. It didn't matter. Since I no longer taught at the school, and did nothing much, I bore the full force of my daughter's contempt. And I welcomed this, it was better than thinking she knew far more than I wanted her to.

I protested at things that really didn't matter, and asked her why Mahesh had to come around so often.

'He needs help,' Maddy said finally one day, 'with his English.'

Asha still saw things differently. 'Why can't his rich parents hire a tutor? Why do you have to coach him for free and get a bad name in the bargain?'

'Surely you don't have to come home with Mahesh too, people notice, you know?' I asked, emboldened, as Maddy chewed endlessly on a sorry looking carrot. 'And he has such a terribly unique sweat smell,' I went on, petulant, hearing the sound of her cutlery on the plate, mirroring her unresponsive self, 'does he ever wash his shirts? And anyway they are always too tight for him. And his phone calls, always timed when no one is around and he doesn't say anything either.'

I remember how both of them looked up startled, then at each other and still said nothing. Was there already a secret pact between the two of them? Or had I, so immersed in this recent death, already lost the plot?

But I can still hear Asha's whisper, 'You should tell her not to get too mixed up with him.'

But he was important and Maddy's only friend at a time when it mattered.

He came around every Sunday afternoon with his English Reader. I remember the first time he came, the way he stood up awkwardly to say hello, his plump face reddening, his chipped teeth bared in an embarrassed smile.

'I need some help,' Mahesh said when I walked in, his hand moving in a wide circle to indicate Maddy.

'Yes,' I nodded, graciously. It had been a long while since a man, even a relatively younger one, had sat on the drawing room sofa. The room looked different, even happy in a way. And I felt different too.

He blushed even more and fidgeted. 'I am happy Maddy is here to help you,' I said gesturing ineffectually.

I watched from the window as Maddy sat on the low platform outside the grounds overlooking the river, and gave Mahesh his basic lessons in English. She would ask him to describe what he saw, and then would correct Mahesh's rendition of it. 'You can't say the trees are green, it is the leaves that are.' But he was stubborn. 'I am looking at the... at the... *pura* picture.'

'There you go again, see. You don't even know the word – whole,' and I caught that affectionate reprimand in her voice. Her voice that was otherwise so expressionless, also fighting the loneliness she must feel. And Mahesh would laugh his rabbit laugh then, biting his lips as if he hated the sound of his own laughter, 'Yeah, but you got the meaning, right?'

But as with Jaspal, this friendship ended too soon, after the other letter was found. Life turned full circle for Mahesh. In a class of fifty who could tell who had riffled through Maddy's desk and produced that other letter, the one she had written, copying it out from my *Love Letters for Every Occasion*. Or it could have slipped out of Mahesh's pockets some time? In no time, the letter was on the principal's desk and it was Asha who was summoned to identify Maddy's handwriting.

After a magnifying glass and a scale were produced, Asha made her fatal pronouncement, without looking at Maddy, or at anyone, looking at the table instead, 'Yes, the handwriting is hers.'

'Did you write this letter?' The principal asked Maddy then, and Asha Dogra's eyes reverted to the floor, and my daughter said, Yes, I was giving him English lessons.

Asha Dogra burst in, 'The boy used to come over every Sunday and they would go down to the river. I did warn Mrs Hyde about it, but... do children or anyone else listen these days?'

The two of us were subjected to Asha's harangue that evening. She blamed Maddy for her lack of morals and me for my poor parenting skills and everything else. She was careful to say 'guardianship skills' however; being exact, and she must have learnt this from her father, always imparts a greater clarity to things. It staves off other things too, like having a good conversation to clear up things. But that evening, all that she said, made me wonder if between the two of us, we had driven Maddy to write that letter.

'It is your fault. Bringing her up with no restraint,' Asha still goes on at times, even after Maddy has been long gone now, and Mahesh has paid with his life for joining those rowdy boys Gautam Dogra had been training to send to faraway Ayodhya. And Kerketta who could tell the future with some certainty was dead too, in those riots that followed the demolition of the temple in Ayodhya.

I listened to Asha. The two of us made Maddy cut off all contact with Mahesh. It was perhaps too drastic. No wonder she went away, without as much as a warning. Only I got the blame. Much later I saw the admission forms that she had filled up, all on her own. And of course Asha helped, they were both in this together. The bitterness still rises like bile inside me.

I have a form that never got sent. And the pang in my heart returns when I see once again the option for parent crossed out and Asha's name filled in, as Maddy's guardian. I remember too Maddy's puzzled look from a time farther back when she had shown me her school identity card and asked what 'ward' meant. It means *you*, and *you*, and *you*, I pointed out, thrice to stop her from asking anything else. And she asked very seriously, 'A ward, how can I be one?' Someone who is under one's guardianship, I replied, looking away. And she said not a thing.

It was the next morning, Maddy played with her food as usual and Asha had a 'taking her in hand' expression on her face. Hoping to make up for the day before, Asha had made for Maddy some of her favourite foods, things she had nodded to and said 'yes' on other occasions: upma, French toast, and a raita. But Asha had not understood the degree of injury she had inflicted on Maddy. It wasn't just cured by well-prepared dishes. If the heart is hurt, the stomach can never be appeased.

And Maddy had mumbled, not looking her in the eye, 'I really do not want breakfast today, thank you.'

Asha pursed her lips and I intervened, as I always do at the wrong moment, in the totally wrong way. I had no idea of the consequences it would evoke then.

'You need not be upset, my dear. It's usual at this age.'

'What's usual?' Maddy frowned and then repeated again, softly, enunciating each word more clearly as if I was Mahesh, 'I am sorry, I did not follow. What's usual at my age?'

The coldness in her tone was unnerving and made me say things sillier than I would otherwise have.

'Come on, my dear. I'm sure you understand.' I reached for her hand but she flinched and withdrew. 'Sometimes when these infatuations take over one, common sense is the first casualty.'

It wasn't me who said these words. I wanted to hold on to Maddy and already she was far away. The contradictions within ourselves that appear so straightforward, sometimes even to ourselves.

Asha coughed and spluttered into her sandwich. And Maddy replied, taking her time, letting the coldness gather in her voice, fed up with the two of us beside her.

'No, I am all right, really. Just feel a bit under the weather.'

'Oh, would you want to spend the day at home then?' I exchanged a quick glance at Asha, hoping she would not say yes. The last few months, now that I had stopped teaching I had got used to having the house to myself in the mornings when the two of them were in school. For those few hours that I was alone, I recovered myself in slow degrees. I would put the radio on full volume, clack away happily on the typewriter, jump off the chair in between, stroll down to the river, be someone else for a while, and then creep back, to my typewriter, and the pattern would be repeated day after day. For a few hours every day, I would return to the mad, flighty young woman I had been, a period in my life that had been too short, that had ended too abruptly. A door that had banged shut, when someone had walked out of my life forever. I mean someone who literally walked away, not drove away in his car, never to appear again.

'No, I am fine,' said Maddy.

'Brave girl.'

Still tight-lipped, Maddy got up and left the table. Asha looked at me angrily.

'Stop insinuating that she's not over the imbroglio yet.'

Imbroglio. It was a moment I too had had enough of. I stretched that word out mockingly, imagining a piper leading all the letters that made up that word, marching down the streets and the letters twirling out of his pipe, shaping themselves in the air.

'Im-brog-lio. And it's not an affair,' and my voice was as icy as I had learnt to make it.

Like the cold hand Bob pressed over my neck when we fought. Even the memory of it is enough to make me cry out, my cries like shrieks in the stillness of the night setting forth a strange rustling in the branches. My fingers rasped at his throat in desperation till he let go, but I would be forced to wear a tell-tale band to cover up the marks of his fingers. The band would stretch tight over my neck, my hands, making me feel in part like a bound-up hemp sack, the kind that was used in the plantations once, when they were still running well. The days when those sacks were being sent all the way to Calcutta and before that, to Rangoon to the rice processing plants. Before the days nylon came in a big way, before he took to drinking and ran away.

Asha and I must have argued a long time, the past must have stayed with me longer, and it was only later we realized that Maddy was taking her time to come down. Asha fretted, the two of them had to leave for school together. But that silence as we waited, our faces turned away from each other, was finally broken when we heard her fall to the floor. That heavy thud could mean no other thing, and by the time we rushed up to Maddy's room, our slippers slapping the steps hard in some rhythm, she was already in that dead faint that made us look at each other in alarm and rush towards her, in a race to see who would reach Maddy first.

The two of us groaned and grunted as we carried her to the bed, where she lay prone, a delicate branch cruelly twisted out of shape, and there was foam around her mouth, as she gasped for breath. She wasn't heavy but we were not used to such hard labour after all. Asha sprinkled water, chanting prayers under her breath while I crossed myself, subconsciously. We darted scared looks at each other and when she slithered away from us, a third time, and her skirt rode up, well above her knees, it was Asha's resolve that first gave way, 'She is not going to die on us, is she?'

I looked at her, crossed myself one more time and whispered, 'No, she is like her father, strong inside.'

I thought Asha gave me a strange look, but I concentrated on looking at Maddy instead.

I saw the tears too on Maddy's cheeks some time later, as we moved her downstairs to the carpet in the living room.

Asha and I looked at each other for everything, refusing to do anything without the other's sanction. There was Maddy sprawled inelegantly on the floor, and I felt the soft scratch of Asha's nails on my wrist as she straightened Maddy's skirt that rose and flew in the breeze from the windows. She bent and peered at Maddy so carefully that I finally snapped, What's wrong with her now, stop staring at her like that?

I was wondering if she is pretending.

I peered too. Saw myself in Maddy's vacant open eyes in a way I had never seen myself before. I saw how my eyes blinked repeatedly in nervousness, the twin lines on either side of my face. I was beginning to look old and tired and very frightened. Maddy was unconscious and one day I knew she would make a wonderful actor. Life's truths come to us in the strangest of situations.

No she did faint, I said and then oddly I felt myself weep. For so many years I had kept it a secret and promised myself never to weep. But then I had never known I would see Maddy this way. I wept for her, and all that I saw was slipping away from me.

In that terribly long day, one of the worst of my lives, that stretched forever, Maddy moved from life to death and came back to me, but not in the same way. Besides the three of us, there was Kerketta and the doctor, Prem Agarwal. He was Mahesh's brother and had just set up a clinic next to the sweet shop the Agarwals owned.

It was Asha who had called him after Maddy had already begun to breathe heavily and with difficulty and her face was a terrible mottled red. Every time she rolled her eyes briefly and blinked, we moved our faces closer, in the hope she would see us, murmur something.

Beta, are you trying to tell us something?

It was me who should have spoken but was silenced by Asha's head repeatedly coming in the way.

And I heard Asha's voice over my own ragged breathing.

Shall I call Prem?

It's the shock she has borne for a long time. The embarrassment and ignominy forced on her.

My voice as I said this sounded distant and faraway, even to me. Was it the letter and the humiliation or was there something else?

Prem Agarwal said he would come at once. Asha after all had been his teacher. Prem of the exquisite skills, who simply had to give women his all-knowing glance to know without being told what was wrong with them. That it wasn't something physical but emotional. Most women's problems, he would say to his other men friends, are to do with their feelings. They feel so much that it begins to tell on their health. And he would never understand why his carefully considered statement was greeted with much raucous laughter.

The operator at the phone exchange who dialled Prem's number once Asha had called must have been curious. For never before had a doctor been called to our house.

A doctor to Gleneagles? It could only mean death and that was why George Singh, the operator, eavesdropped so very shamelessly on the conversation and in an hour the news was all over the town. Prem Agarwal and Lawrence Kerketta arrived at the same time. One through the front door and the other by the back. Kerketta said he heard voices in his head, telling him to come.

It was almost a competition between the two of them then. Kerketta whose presence that day was menacing and brooding, and Prem jaunty and exuberant, determined to put quacks such as Kerketta in their place. And they argued as Maddy's condition worsened.

Later they would tell Maddy I had let it all happen. That I was adamant about having Kerketta see her, when a qualified doctor was already on the scene. But I was really clueless about everything and also afraid. There was a heavy, unmoving cloud in my head and every word I tried to think up, broke up, smashed into a thousand pieces before it was devoured by the cloud.

The arguments and speculation would last for a long time, long after Maddy had run away from Brooks Town. But that day as Maddy's heartbeat vanished to a low murmur and Kerketta finally began shaking his head and crossing himself, Prem's joviality turned to panic. He had been charming when he came in, asking if my ankle had healed, if the dog bites still hurt. And I shrugged, hoping Asha had not noticed the question. Asha for her part was always one to ask unnecessary, pointed questions.

Thankfully Kerketta chose that moment to show off.

'There is too much death here too,' Kerketta said, looking dangerously around, and a film of cold sweat grew on my forehead; it was some seconds before Prem's words made sense.

'We must move her to the hospital,' he said, almost defiantly, as if daring the quack to contradict him even more.

We must. I turned and there was Kerketta, his eyes closed, sniffing the air. Kerketta, if you don't mind, we must leave.

He got up, shaking his head, still in a daze. 'There is something here, I don't understand. Too many deaths.'

I glared at him then, hating him. What did he mean? Was he blaming me for Robert? Or for every other death that had followed?

'There is really nothing to understand, Mr Kerketta.' And Prem was calling for the ambulance, and I knew I would soon have to deal with Kerketta. I washed my hands meticulously, let the welcome cold water soak my face and by the time I returned, I could hear the ambulance not too far away.

The ambulance had been bought second-hand. It had been left half-painted, its doors flapped open, as the paint had yet to set. A crowd had gathered outside the gate and Prem vented his fury on the incomplete address painted on the ambulance.

Prem Agar... what on earth is that supposed to mean?

Job not complete, sir, said the hapless attendant on whose lab coat, blotches of paint gave away signs of his recent activity. Last night no power cut. But the lettering has been traced out, see...

And he showed the outline of the remaining letters, in faint dark lines.

Agar indeed, you people think it is a joke running this hospital.

In the ambulance, Asha tried to speak. Her lips moved against my ear, and I squirmed. Then the jolting, the incessant wail of the siren made her shout.

Will we be arrested? screamed Asha Dogra.

What for?

Abetment.

Abetment of what?

That… we drove her to it, she shuddered and thrust a finger at me.

Maddy looked like a small sea lion to me, sometimes a bolster, shapeless and ever changing. I could see Prem Agarwal in the rear view mirror wiping his forehead, taking off his glasses and then putting them back on again. A critically sick patient, two already hysterical, breathless ladies, and a nervous doctor with shaking hands. We were a disaster in motion.

There is no proof…

Who needs proof… it could be mental, Asha snapped.

I wondered what Maddy had eaten though. All that food she had stuffed herself with and gorged out – it must have destroyed the system entirely. These were all new sicknesses and we knew nothing then. But with my old icy calmness in place, I replied to Asha, 'For a person as old as you, you clearly lack common sense.'

Prem Agarwal looked through the mirror, smiled nervously, Please don't be upset, mis… madams, er… my English was always poor… what is the plural for two ladies…

Why, you could just say ladies…? Asha Dogra laughed. She loved it when her former male students flirted with her. Only I caught her glare, and the softly hissed words, 'I am not old, you hussy.'

Not too long ago we had come to an exchange like that, and this time before it could erupt again inside an ambulance with an incomplete address, Prem's voice joined the rattling and the jolting that made ordinary conversation in any case, difficult.

Ah yes, Ladies… that's the word they put on bathroom doors, he laughed.

Asha laughed too. It could have been a perfect day for a picnic. And I chose the moment to spoil the fun, show off my knowledge, that I had once been to London, had once in fact been in love with an Englishman.

The correct word, if you indeed are looking for a plural for madam is mesdames. But, really, ladies would have been all right, if you could allow yourself to forget the other facetious connotations.

He was laughing now, into his handkerchief. 'You really should have been teaching in the Brooks Town College, Madam. Your English is too good, too good really. I tell Raja Mohanty to open a new college in that vacant plot of land he has been eyeing near the school, the place where the hemp company used to be, instead he's thinking of a shopping complex. And you should be principal… or at least head of the English department.'

'Has he already bought that land?' Asha Dogra asked, her eyes shining. I wondered what her interest in it was. The matter of that land had piqued her father no end too. Poor man, he had written so many letters to the government asking for a permanent piece of land to set up his military training school, instead of using that clearing, so close to the Christian cemetery too. Hemp still grew in wild abundance there, and who could tell if the wild excitement so evident in the boys he wanted to train had its origins in the elusive tangy smell that pervaded that lost place or if there was indeed something in Dogra's speeches?

'Almost,' said Prem when my thoughts returned to the present, 'Raja knows the right people and perhaps he might get it soon. But even before these formalities, there are already people who want to set up their own big shops in that complex. Jaspal Singh wants to set up a big cloth store, selling everything, even imported stuff like jeans, cosmetics… even ladies… er… er… things…'

I butted in, 'What about your father, Asha? Didn't he plan to set up that military training school on that plot of land. All those meetings he had with the government, whatever happened?'

Asha Dogra's lips stretched into a tight smile. It was only after a long time that she replied, 'Dreams have a way of becoming real.'

My laughter rasped against my throat as I responded, 'Don't we know, don't we all know.'

And then I turned my attention to Prem Agarwal, who had begun to relax as we rode to the hospital. 'I hope there will be nurses and other doctors to attend to her.'

Everyone remembered Maddy then, bouncing on the floor with every jerk of the ambulance. 'We will do a thorough check-up, don't worry, Mrs Hyde. I will need to ask the two of you questions please if you don't mind?' He was no longer nervous.

As we neared the clinic, some of his blithe self-assurance was returning.

'Oh, will that be necessary?' said Asha, her eyes blinking nervously, her hands twisting in her lap. 'I do feel sorry for her,' she pointed to Maddy, and then screamed in alarm as we took an unexpected turn to the right and Maddy rolled right over to her.

'I think it was because of something she ate,' I muttered, glaring at Asha. It irritated me, how she managed to garner the attention all the time.

She turned her brown-eyed gaze on me. In other circumstances, the hostility there would have floored me.

'Are you going to keep harping on my cake again? If so, it really doesn't behove you and it is quite off the point.'

I turned to look at Prem, who was already turning away to bark instructions, perhaps about repainting the bus. I looked at his head of neatly coiffed hair, arranged in that new hairstyle he had adopted – floppy at the back – and I remembered how the curls had danced and bounced on his shoulders as we rode over a particularly bad stretch of road.

'Dr Agarwal,' and he smiled at being addressed thus.

'Prem...'

'Oh Doctor sounds much better,' butted in Asha yet again, 'besides, you are a trained doctor from Calcutta, we should show you the respect you deserve. What do you think happened? I mean people will ask us, you know? And you know how nasty they can get?'

He raised his hand god-like. 'Leave it all to me. I would just need to ask you a few things of her family history.'

The light was fainter now and I was glad they did not see my stricken face. Would I be asked to reveal everything. The secret of Maddy's spoilt fair skin, her green eyes, that brownish hair?

But I wasn't letting on quite so easily, 'I could tell you whatever I know, but some things, my dear boy, are best left to themselves... some things even I would not be able to tell you.'

And of course he knew the old story, as did everyone in this town. Of how I had found Maddy the time I went up north, to look up one of Robert's old grandaunts. Maddy had been left to me as an orphan to look after. Her parents had died in a landslide, and she had been the lone survivor in her village. I came along at the right time, to adopt her, give her a good life, one in which happily-ever-after endings were assured. Even Soumen, that other long ago time when he had sat on a boulder by me, the valley at our feet, had agreed it would make a good story. 'The most original one you've ever written,' and I realized only now he meant it seriously.

Prem Agarwal heeded my request, he understood. Besides as a young, newly prosperous doctor, he really didn't have the time for too many details. 'Yes, there are things difficult to explain. Some disorders such as a weak heart could be con... con... gruous (and I corrected him again, congenital but of course he wasn't listening) but who knows why such a thing happened. You tell me she was fine in the morning (we nodded seriously). Then perhaps it was destiny. I am a doctor,' he laughed ruefully, 'but there are some things such as destiny. My mother always says. Not all fingers of the hand can be alike but we were very disappointed at the way Chhotu turned out.'

Chhotu, I realized, was what they called Mahesh at home.

The boy who almost became the fat, paunchy, balding sweet seller that befitted someone with a name like Chhotu. But then Mahesh decided to write himself a different story, and perished as a soldier in the cause of the temple that so excited him, as it did Mrs Parida, Dogra Sahib and indeed a great many others. But all this was still three years away.

Prem laughed, spreading his hands helplessly, but on his face there was a look of utter desolation. 'There are things I don't understand,' he was saying. 'Chotu has everything, too much of everything, maybe that is why he cannot decide. Gets mixed up in all the nonsense the television carries these days.'

We nodded. There is something about someone's troubles that breaks down all barriers. A warmth had crept into the coldness now, a mist had gathered in the windows. We were climbing the steps towards the small clinic that Prem Agarwal had constructed recently, next to the maternity home used by the planters' wives. Our breaths were short, and we felt lighter as we climbed the twenty or more steps. As did the attendants carrying Maddy up. Soon there will be a ramp in place, Prem assured us as he led the way.

Below the ambulance already looked as fragile as a matchbox, on that ribbon of a road. Not too far away we could see the old temple and Maya still running down at what looked like breakneck speed. All those weeks' experience, must have added commendably to her pace.

Amazing isn't it? At such a great height…

It's the forests all around, it keeps things cool, explained Prem. He was looking with interest at the woman who ran with her hands raised over head. Sometimes I try to race her, he said.

'She must be very fast for you,' I said. 'She has had quite some practice.'

'Yes, poor girl. Doesn't see sense,' it was Asha Dogra, 'all this love business. Suddenly, it seems to have gone to our heads. We expect too much from it all.'

Love, yes. Why, that's an interesting statement. I wished I had my notebook to take it down.

We stood there for a while, in the camaraderie that had been forged. The only sound was the wind strangled in the branches and the echoes of the footsteps of the girl now climbing up the stairs, followed a few seconds later, by her harsh panting. Far away, all other sounds were muted. A sudden clank of the rickshaw bells, the temple cymbals, a shout from the football field, even the sounds from the future that only I could hear. The crush of bricks falling in a thud, the crack as a branch shook itself loose, and a breathless hush.

And once inside, we remembered Maddy again amidst that clinical smell of antiseptic and disinfectant. The room was clean and white, and a lost nurse stood in a corner as Prem examined Maddy.

She is too weak, with low blood pressure. She has not been eating.

He did not see what I saw. The red welter marks, the scratch marks and the boils on her fingers that came from putting them too often in her mouth. 'More protein, in large amounts. She needs to build up her strength.'

The Parida's servant boy Reddy was soon going to disappear. It happened in the time Maddy recovered in hospital. And only after he had gone away for good, most people, at least in the Parida household, let slip how for some time he had been distracted and restless and too thoughtful. It made you wonder why they hadn't said so in the first place, before he did the disappearing act. With him gone, there would be no one to care for the hens. Perhaps things happen for the best, even when animals and silly birds are involved.

For Mrs Parida, who had always had a soft spot for Maddy, till she chose to elope with her son, insisted that the protein now medically recommended for Maddy was readily available. Her famed leghorns could supply it and in any case, there had always been too many of them for Reddy to manage effectively. Or maybe he never wanted to. His gaze always sought things farther away than were visible from the high reaches of the tamarind tree, to where the king rooster would occasionally fly up when his squabbling brood got too much. They were killed one by one, their numbers dwindling as the weeks passed. Some died at Kerketta's hands, and he used their detached heads to make some special medicine, a few others died of heartbreak, only a few would survive Reddy's desertion of them. For some weeks, as Maddy made her plans in secret, Asha made chicken dishes for the Paridas and for us too. And Maddy recovered.

By then her mind was made up. She was going away, just like Reddy. 'I am leaving,' she only said one day, when she was all ready to go, and a rickshaw stood outside waiting to take her to the station. For a long time, I told Asha she wanted to get away from us, by which I meant a whole lot of people and I didn't have need to specify. Three years later, Maddy would come back surprising us all; my own words too would return to haunt me.

October, 1989
The Disappearance

To most people, Reddy's disappearance that same year was an afterthought, perhaps facilitated more by topography than any grievances he might have had, working as a servant for the Paridas for five long years.

There were walls that separated one house from another and between the walls and the houses were gardens, in various states of existence. Mine had gone to seed a long time ago but it still had a wild beauty of its own. In some places the walls were higher, nearly insurmountable because of those old trees, some that had been standing even before I arrived here, as a young wife.

Sometime between 1.16 p.m. and 4.02 p.m., in the month of October that year of Dogra's death, Reddy KV disappeared. The timing and manner of his disappearance remains contested, everyone had a different opinion. I was glad to see him go, he was getting too friendly with the tramp woman with her now permanent hobble, forcing her to engage in silly inane conversations for minutes on end. I hoped he had taken away the knife for good, too. My search for it had proved futile. I had looked for it all along the river bank and even in Dogra's room but my lovely, long-handled, curved Tibetan knife remained well and truly lost.

Reddy was one of the retinue of orderlies the commissioner was entitled to. In that big, sprawling house, its walls overhung by branches of trees that had grown too tall in a neglected fashion, there had always been five orderlies, three gardeners and one sweeper, the woman called Dasi. The orderlies were there to be ordered about, but each one had their duties fixed and already decided.

So Reddy KV did all the jobs that were new, came up too suddenly, or those that involved more physical effort. That is, he did all the work the more senior orderlies would never deign to do, which meant that he ended up doing quite a lot.

It was Reddy who managed Mrs Parida's poultry brood, clucking repeatedly to send the hens back into the henhouse after their daily outings in the sun, twice a day.

Reddy KV also fetched the ball when the Parida boy, Ashok, played cricket with his friends. He was sent up to the roof every time the television antenna needed fixing. Whenever he did this, Reddy always took a long time returning. It was the orderlies who first began joking about it. He goes there to pee, they laughed among themselves; for the cache of magazines and comics that only Maddy knew about, would come to light much later.

Sometimes apart from the lone guard at the front gate, Reddy was the only one at the Paridas' home when they went away somewhere, or when Mrs Parida missed her son too much and the two of them went to look him up. Reddy would then be found sprawled in one of the many bamboo chairs that crowded the open verandah, overlooking the river.

On quiet nights as I walked along the river, I would think someone was indeed sitting there, the way it rocked and creaked in the wind, even when no one could possibly be there. The driveway lights would shut down for the night, except for the lone twin lights on the gate that led down to the river and I could only hear that softly creaking chair, the sound of a lone crow flapping in the branches, and the distant howl of the jackals.

Sometimes, I would see a flicker of light on the river, someone moving with a lantern but then it would soon disappear into the trees or I lost track of it just as one cannot follow a shooting star for too long. And nearby, there would be a few snatches of a song that I knew only Reddy KV could be singing in the darkness. It was because of his presence somewhere near, where one could hear but never see him, that Maddy lost her fear too, that she learnt to love the darkness as well.

But unlike Maddy, I disliked Reddy KV because he saw too much with his bulging eyes, and because he was not what he seemed.

Reddy's addiction to film magazines, women's magazines, horror comics grew from the time he ran errands for Mrs Parida. Each time Mrs Parida sent him to Asha Dogra's house, the time she stayed with her father, for they borrowed each other's magazines, he took carefully arranged detours. For Reddy loved riffling through the magazines and comics before he delivered them safe to the two ladies. He would sit at a roadside dhaba or under a tree, or be up on the roof, flipping through the magazines and return a good half-hour later. For a while, he had even lent Maddy some to read.

But Reddy also borrowed comics from the vendors at a daily rental price and others he bought with his salary. He hardly saved anything in the process. No wonder everyone automatically assumed that he ran away because he had stolen something. In his hurry, he left behind those comics that in the beginning only Maddy knew about. Comics full of lurid sex, macabre murder stories, and evil fantasies, that he chose to hide away in the loft above the garage. And they were scattered in other places too. For only he knew all the shortcuts, the hidden ways that led from one house to another, across walls, over terraces and through the trees.

Sometimes he took the long way home. That is he climbed over the walls into my part of the compound, jumped onto the terrace, up and down the windows placed at different levels, before swinging from the mango trees back onto the wall and his own guava tree. He just did it to throw everyone off his scent or simply for his own pleasure. But Asha chose to air her suspicions to Mrs Parida.

Someone steals food from our refrigerator, Mrs Parida.

Oh dear, she said. She was most often sad in the way lonely women are. And she left it at that. Are you sure there's nothing else?

I don't think so. It's the food.

But before anything could be done, Reddy disappeared, that is, he simply upped and left one afternoon. I could have told them as well that not having solved one murder effectively, the police could hardly have done much about a refrigerator's stolen goods.

Maddy would badger Reddy for his comics for she always read them too fast. I had often heard the two of them talking on the roof, and their voices clearly reached me in my study just a floor below.

The new ones haven't come yet, he would say. That was his way of teasing Maddy. He had to go to the wastepaper market, the raddi bazaar, to pick up the second-hand magazines and comics and he hadn't had the time. But I knew these excuses were partly to throw Maddy off track. It took him a long while to show her where he kept his comics.

The overhead loft, where he kept his comics in an old aluminum trunk became his home when he first began going up to the roof as part of his everyday chores, and no longer just secretly. After the television came to the Parida house, the onus of fixing the television antenna, checking it for rat bites and to ensure that it always stayed fixed, pointing towards the television station on Brooks Hill, fell to Reddy. The other orderlies were too old, too fat, too unwilling. Reddy went up to the roof on other occasions. During the rains, he went up to check on the rising river levels, and the roof allowed a clear, unobstructed view of the dam at Hirakud. After every storm, it was Reddy who swept away the leaves that gathered on the roof, making several trips as he did so, carrying on his head a wicker basket laden with dried brown-yellow leaves, rotting fruit and always something unexpected. Beads of a necklace, a scrap of cloth, a ribbon, a precious stone, and on one occasion a piece of paper with a simple message written in bold black letters.

Keep away from me.

Only I knew it was Dogra's handwriting, but how everyone

else, even the orderlies laughed over it especially after it was found pasted on the walls of his loft, days after Reddy had gone.

My cheeks burned as I remembered the story, heard their laughter as the orderlies tore off the paper and held it high.

I had just heard from Soumen, and so had Dogra. He had stolen something that belonged to both of us. A certificate, and there he was blackmailing Dogra with it.

Blackmail? No, I am only being ingratiating, Soumen wrote to me. He always wrote like he was speaking. I could picture the dancing glint in his eyes, the earnestness of his tone and suspected he was not exactly telling the truth. He had also spent a lifetime trying to convince people of his dreams and there was hardly anyone willing to believe him any more. Least of all Gautam Singh Dogra, who he had betrayed terribly.

I am hoping he gives me a chance to talk to him. I know the people in Delhi he can meet, but he refuses to have anything to do with me. All I am asking for is a little money.

Do something, Charu.

It was Soumen but no one made such requests to me any more. I could hear the break in his voice almost, as he wrote.

It must be another mad scheme he had in mind. A film he was hoping to make. I learnt much later when it didn't matter any more, about the land he wanted to buy back, and his plans to begin cultivating hemp again. Hemp that suddenly, decades after its declining value, had taken on greater value – medicinal and commercial. That time, though, finding myself once again in demand, I did intercede on Soumen's behalf. It gave me a chance to write to him but of course Dogra thought I was an accomplice too. Just like he thought the certificate was another bit of drama. An old bit of forged paper, to lay claim. Claim on what? I wanted to ask and cared enough then not to laugh. What is it that make people so self-oblivious, so blind to their own diminished selves?

But Dogra knew nothing and the venom in his voice choked me like nothing else. After that I had no chance either to ever explain things. He turned away from me even more. He altered his schedule so drastically that there was little chance he and I would ever meet face to face. In fact, he put so much distance between us, that I was afraid it would be noticeable to everyone else.

And then a few months after his death, as I hunted in his room one Saturday afternoon, I found the birth certificate in his study, hidden away behind a very old photo of his wife and daughter. He had perhaps put it there because no one would dare disturb the photo. And I who had imagined Dogra's face on every other occasion could not picture how he must have looked when he had held it. Why had he not torn it to shreds? What thoughts had run through his head then, or had he already closed his mind to all other possibilities? Ever since one long ago war-scarred afternoon, when I had seen emotions change at too seething a pace, I distrusted them. But it was after many days, months, that I was able to think of him more gently. It was too late to think about other 'what ifs'.

Reddy made his escape one afternoon. The hens had been out of their roost for an hour or more beyond their usual time and no one had heard Reddy's usual clapping and whistling, the noise he made when he talked to them. He usually let them out around one in the afternoon. That day he was late, an orderly saw him jumping down from the wall that divided the Paridas' bungalow from ours and had pointedly gestured at his watch. 1.16 p.m., it said then. Now the hours had passed, the sun was waning, and the hens were still out. They looked a bit surprised, staring at each other, the black and white speckled rooster with the curvy red crown on his head looked particularly nonplussed as the other hens clucked away at him.

Reddy, Reddy, and the call for him went across the walls, towards the river and the crows lifted off from the tamarind tree once again and the roofs were full with the noise of clattering feet as other crows slid off every roof and burst into the sky.

Reddy, Reddy.

But still he did not appear.

Must have gone to the river, said Mrs Parida. She looked at the wall clock that another orderly winded up every week and noticed it was past four.

And the orderlies, the two of them on duty then, trooped down with the gardeners to the small side gate that led to the river. Where I was, not too far away from the riverbank, I could hear the clink of the keys in Kerketta's pocket. Five years since the one key had gone missing and he had still no idea that he had lost it. But then he had no need to tend Dogra's garden any more. Asha stayed with us and already there was talk that the house was going to return to its original claimants, the Mohantys, the family that had once served as ministers to the maharaja who had originally owned the house. But that story is for a later time, when I have all the pieces that fit in.

Reddy, Reddy.

Kerketta's voice floated across the river, past the shallow pools and gorse hedges, and came back, louder and more forceful after it struck the bald-faced, grey boulders that lined the river at the far end. The forests that were sometimes lit up red at night looked now bone-dry and stick-thin like some of the old village women who ventured into it every day for timber and grass. The echo sounded from everywhere, magnified several times over as those on the banks shouted back with gusto.

Reddy, Reddy.

But he did not emerge from behind the rocks nor did he step out through the curtain of trees. Nothing stirred. The ever-foraging tramp lady, a white plastic sack almost bearing her down, on her back, looked up and bared her lips in a toothless smile. No one here, she gestured wiggling her thumb. She laughed madly as if delighted that the river finally belonged to her again and that there was no Reddy around. Someone threw a stone, not even looking at her as he did so, and she vanished, scuttling away into the bushes.

Where was he last seen? Asked the commissioner an hour later when he was apprised of Reddy's nonappearance.

No one would ever be certain of this. Everyone was somewhere else. Almost as if Reddy had timed it to perfection, knowing people could not pinpoint the moment he chose to go away.

'I was in my room reading, sleeping,' said his wife. The orderlies said nothing. They had too much to do, it was an effort to list it out, and the commissioner knew this.

'Someone must have seen him?'

'He was there near the river.'

'No, he had gone up to the roof, now I remember,' said Mrs Parida. 'He was adjusting the antenna.'

'Shall we go and look?' An orderly volunteered.

'Of course he won't be there, you fool,' burst out the commissioner. 'You think he would not have heard us, all the shouting and calling for him?'

Everyone was quiet before he finally spoke up again. 'We will have to check the theatres and the bus-stands.'

The madam burst into a wail of consternation. 'You are suggesting he left. Disappeared. And we treated him so well too.'

'I am not suggesting anything,' he said patiently. 'Just asking all of you to think. Did he give a sign, any possible sign of what he was going to do? Think hard.'

Mrs Parida just couldn't. She shook her head, and said, 'He was happy here. We did not even give him too much work.'

Her husband looked at her thoughtfully, 'Perhaps that was it. That we did not give him too much work.'

Everyone waited for him to return that night. I waited for the footsteps with an almost fervent expectation. At least that would tell me for sure that they were Reddy's as he clambered up to the roof, to check his comics or if it was too hot or just to see the stars. But that night, it was only the branches of the tamarind tree grazing the roof, or the wind scattering the dry leaves all over it.

The search for Reddy resumed the next morning. The hens hadn't been let out, they were already peering through their grilled cage, unable to give voice to their puzzlement. There was no familiar whistle, no cloak draped figure who sauntered down with them to the river. No frantic rushing back at the sound of his name being called, Reddy, Reddy, the driveway thudding as his feet struck the gravel, sending the stones skittering in all directions.

It was then that we knew for certain that Reddy had gone, perhaps never to return.

A week or so after his disappearance we were free to make up our own stories, reach our own conclusions about Reddy KV. For some days, a team of policemen in a yacht scoured the river. The boat was a bobbing black dot in the distance, its mast flailing like a man with ague. They were prodding the waters with their rods and batons.

When nothing came up, it was an orderly who spoke. 'He isn't going to come back. He had received some money from somewhere.'

My erratic heart began to beat up again.

Mr Parida didn't like the sound of it at all, 'I should have been told before. *That* was the motive, and behind every sinister act, there is always a M O T I V E.'

He spelled the letters out, wagging his finger in rhythm.

'It was a small matter,' it was Mrs Parida speaking up, everyone seemed to be remembering at once. 'A sum of six hundred or so.'

'And who gave it to him?' he asked.

The hammering in my heart, 'I did, I did' seemed loud enough for everyone to hear. Instead everyone looked at the floor, or at the faraway jungle-filled horizon and there was only the commissoner's mournful soliloquy. No one connected his late appearance the previous afternoon to his presence in our house; it was the time Maddy and Asha were at school. Those early days of Maddy's leaving were the most difficult. I always did think she would return from school and that I would soon hear the music in her room as I did every afternoon. A sound that drowned everything out, even the footsteps overhead and my irritated knocking on her door when the drumbeats got too loud. Even morning silences can be delusional.

There could be something suspicious about this, I should have been told, I should have been.

The matter of money gave a somewhat different complexion to the case. Or did it matter? The hens moved in a dazed, somnolent manner, looking up in surprise when a different voice clucked out to them. The rooster made a scene one day, refusing to descend from the pomegranate tree. Some unexpected, strange burst of energy had sent him flying up and now he did not know how to fly down. The orderlies gathered around the tree, making ineffectual noises.

Come down, you red-combed, damn fool idiot.

But the bird shifted and moved, and scowled down at everyone. And then just as unexpectedly, he flew down. Living for so long in that smelly, thinly netted cage, he perhaps wasn't used to looking down at the world from a great height. The tramp woman standing at the gate, watched the scene unfold and cackled madly before she was driven away.

'She would be scared of Reddy,' one of the orderlies muttered.

'Just throw a stone, she will go away...'

'And don't look at her,' warned Kerketta closing his eyes, 'she has a bad heart. I know.'

Kerketta classified women as having good and bad hearts, and considering he was a bachelor and likely to remain one, his faith in women's hearts mustn't have been very strong. But it was true, even a well-aimed twig sent in her direction would set the tramp woman hobbling on her way.

The first of the hens turned up at the Paridas' dinner table a few days later. Asha served her much loved butter chicken that was Maddy's favourite too. The leftovers of course returned with us, and Asha covered the dish with foil before putting it away in the fridge. But someone still managed to pry a part of it loose and taste the chicken, the soufflé and the lovely cottage cheese dish Asha had made. And this time I couldn't even tell anyone about it. For I was beginning to be afraid, worse, I could almost believe that Kerketta was right. That it could all be the work of a ghost with longings still to be assuaged, or perhaps with revenge still in his heart.

Reddy KV had of course never descended from the roof. He had walked to the other end of the roof, and climbed deep into the branches of the tamarind tree. Yes, I had heard it creak, had seen a black shadow move in its branches. The tamarind tree had grown right against the wall, and he had walked along the ledge to the post office wall, and then to other walls, past the Madnavati school where even the boys playing cricket did not see him, and then Modipara, the oil depot, still moving up and down walls, swaying precariously on his toes when the ledge got too narrow, jumping over gaps, crawling, till the wall led him to the railway station.

I had woken up with the sound of the train. It was moving with some urgency, its horn loud against the advancing darkness. It was the train that ran all the way to the north, ending at Delhi, not ever stopping at Brooks Town. Sometimes though it was held up at the crossing when the bigger train that ran between Calcutta and Bombay passed. It chafed impatiently as it waited. Once the barrier was lifted, and the guard at the signal cabin held up the flag, it surged ahead, its horn impatient. That was what had happened that day, though no one would believe me. Reddy KV, ticketless, without permission, had waited for hours, and then jumped from the wall, onto the culvert, over the ditch, and then had broken into a last final run to catch the train. Not a moment too late, for the train started up only seconds later. Its long drawn wail like a forlorn goodbye.

There are many nights, more of them since Maddy went away, when the silence becomes unbearable. So I go down to the gate, to the river, where the riverbed is dry in places and I sit, wrapped in the all quiet. Even a lone leaf stirs and falls with great reluctance. Far away, the clouds, in their various animal shapes, move in a steady, somnolent manner, always northwards, faster than a train ever can. There is often a star that seems to move too. A small, unblinking dot of light that moves in a straight path cutting over the clouds.

I had thought it was a shooting star, short-lived and ephemeral. And Reddy KV had, as usual his own explanation. It was a hot summer evening, and I had stopped to catch my breath on those riverbank steps. He knew it was me though he wasn't looking at me but at a plane that flew overhead. He had seen me often walk on the riverbank and that was when he tried to get too friendly. That time we had both watched that plane fly over our small, never-moving town, which even the express trains bypassed as they hurtled on their way to the big cities.

It's going to Burma, he said, his eyes alive with some anticipation.

He looked at me, his eyes dancing and very alive, 'Wouldn't you like to be able to do that?'

I looked at my leg, which was hurting unbearably from walking on the uneven stones that lined the riverbank, and said nothing.

Everything sat still below as the plane passed overhead. That night, after Reddy had left, I heard a plane flying overhead. I could tell it was the same plane Reddy had pointed out. It took the same route.

Many things had happened that year. A big country with its spaciousness, its ability to absorb, could swallow it all, but a small town couldn't handle it. A murder was unusual and someone had to be arrested first. And people would always remember Reddy going away and he became a terrible example to be cited, a dire warning. *Never hire servants from outside or those with no families, they will run away. That boy, he took money. Who knows, the way things are happening, it could be worse now.*

I had come from outside too, not as servant, but as wife. And became a different woman altogether. Not once but twice. A small town allowed that.

Part II

Three Years Later in 1992, February
Her Mother's Daughter

MADDY RETURNED HOME IN TIME for Raja Mohanty's grand party. He had finally had his way, and construction for that huge shopping complex in the prized plot of land he had eyed for so long, would soon begin. The plot included Dogra's house too, the one that had belonged to the maharaja, and with that any evidence of his murder would be truly lost.

No one protested, though Raja knew I disapproved of his plans for the land. Not because of Robert's family's association with it but it was just not the done thing to have a function so close to the cemetery and there was Robert's grave too, in the vicinity.

At times like these I thought with a pang of Soumen and he had been gone so many years, since I had last seen him sitting on that boulder on that road going to school, hoping to blackmail me. Or had he really? With Soumen, one could never tell. If he had wanted to tell the world my secret and Maddy's too, he could have picked any time to do so. He had the birth certificate with him always. So why did he up and leave so very suddenly?

I willed away any thoughts about him, but still he inveigled his way into my mind, in the way he would pop in and out of Brooks Town, all those years ago. There was that way about him. You let him in a bit, and he took up an entire roomful of thoughts.

Soumen, and I bore him grudges from the beginning, always had an innovative solution to everything. Even Dogra would agree. Soumen was Raja's uncle, they were related somewhat distantly. It had been Soumen who had offered Gautam Singh Dogra and his small daughter a home in Brooks Town when all doors had closed for them.

I wished, as I followed the preparations for Raja's party, for the years of bad blood between Soumen and me to vanish. Three years since Dogra's death and I thought now of Soumen's rakish looks, the wry lopsided smile and that glint in his eyes; he hadn't changed even as he sat in such a ragged state on the boulder. What on earth was he doing now? Was he still in Bombay, still struggling to make a film or had he moved on?

I remember that ill-fated party from the summer of a year in the sixties, and I was the new sensation in Brooks Town, one that would last forever. The older ladies marvelled at my pale skin and light hair and the men only looked. Soumen was young too, and perhaps had the daring the older men never had. He could have been forgiven for trying to ingratiate himself with me. The dancing was on in full swing, and couples danced to Cole Porter. Soumen had been everywhere at once. Attending the bar, keeping an eye on the bearers, and fussing over people. I noticed him hovering around me too, but I do not remember how the exchange really began. There I was alone on the loveseat, my hands still and waiting, watching Bob begin to make a fool of himself with one of the ladies and then there was Soumen next to me, and I turned my head away only to hear a voice close, 'Do you like the music?'

He was trying to get friendly. Shall I play some other music for you? Something that might be more familiar? He went on, and the dim light picked out his sharp, pointed, too white teeth. For a few moments, his face was close to mine. And while I had thought he had a vague attractiveness, now I was embarrassed to see his face so close up. He looked shy, but his breath had a touch of drink in it, and I saw the hall lights reflected in his warm, crinkly eyes.

I laughed then, the bright, tinkly laughter that made the dancers pause, stumble, laugh awkwardly before beginning again.

I coughed into my hanky. Sorry, you said something.

Now he was self-conscious. And he changed the subject, stumbling like the dancers some seconds before. 'Just hoping, milady, that you would let me know which film we could screen… the last one was not very popular.'

His voice shook on the word, 'milady' and my white lacy dress, reflected in his warm brown eyes, shimmered as a fan whirred too close.

Why not? It was a good film. I shrugged. Bob was still not back. He could have stopped to talk to anyone – Mrs Roy, Mrs Saaed, Miss Davenport, anyone. The touring film company Soumen had brought that very week to Brooks Town had only recently screened the old Raj Kapoor movie *Aag*, but most people did not like its passionate intensity. They preferred

Raj Kapoor as the Awaara, the comedian or the rogue with a golden heart.

Or perhaps you could ask… I stretched languidly as a bearer passed and I helped myself to another glass of wine.

Mr Hyde, Madam? He should be back. I will go and look for him. I made to raise a hand to stop him but they felt like dead weight resting on my lap.

His respect was now exaggerated. But he walked away, his face inscrutable, murmuring his excuse-mes to the web the dancers wove around him. Strange man, I thought, watching him move like a hypnotized moth, gliding away from the outstretched limbs, swaying hips. I laughed again. He had charm but was always clumsy especially in company. A cruel laugh that I would use again and again to good effect. All of us were drunk, and could not care at all for what the world thought. And I was learning all that would prove useful to me in the next few years.

But Bob had seen our exchange, the way Soumen had leaned over to speak to me, and on the way home we had another of our arguments.

You were away a long time too, I told him, and my teeth were clenched. Not that Bob cared. He shed all his nice English sobrieties when he was drunk.

I saw you having an intimate chat with him. The handsome good-for-nothing fellow. You are friendly with his cousin, that man Rabi Mohanty, too. Is there anyone in the family you won't let well alone?

That man… he just came up to me. And don't bring his family into it.

We both knew who he meant. Rabi Mohanty, Raja's father, who was more influential and powerful than poor Soumen would ever be. He was just too left out of things, or maybe the kind of influence he peddled had a 'use-by' date.

How come it's always like that? And Robert's voice had a sneer in it, How come it is always that someone or the other comes up to you, and you have these long conversations with him and these very interesting conversations happen just when I am not there? You told me the same thing last time when the other Mohanty, Rabi, was involved.

It's not that way at all, Bob. Please don't.

Please don't. He mimicked me, my hands over my ears. Those theatrics won't do here. This isn't London, where you could give your emotions a real workout.

That is making an insinuation.

The hell it is. And the hell I care.

He would walk off then to sleep off his anger in the library. God knows what the servants thought about all this. The sahib and the memsahib sleeping separately once again. No wonder there was no child, there was never going to be one. Kerketta knew this a long time ago.

Maddy only shrugged when I told her of Raja's plans. The land papers needed her signature too, and she was adamant about selling it. Raja had briefed her well. Still it had made her come back, and Asha and I were happy to have her, even if for a short while.

You can't lose her again. I heard Asha's urgent whisper in my ears as I tried to argue with Maddy. It is up to you, for god's sake, she said, more forceful. Here's a god-given chance to make up with her, Charlotte. You must.

And I almost laughed. It is not often that people called me by name. There were times I almost forgot I did indeed have a name. I could really be the rag-picking lady, whom no one called by name, no one even looked at and yet she responded every time, to every abuse that was hurled at her.

But to all my efforts and overtures, Maddy responded in one of two ways – either a disdainful shrug or a half-polite 'Oh' when she raised her beautifully plucked eyebrows.

The fashion had obviously changed. No more that thin, rainbow-like curve over the eyes, like a circle drawn by compass, the kind made popular by Farah and her sisters, Velayati's daughters. That style made everyone look so similar, so colourless. Maddy's eyebrows were thick but neatly drawn, giving character to the face. I would have told her so, but did not. She would never let me.

In these three years that she had been away, the distance between us had grown in several ways. The three of us – Maddy, Asha and I, only spoke of the shopping complex Raja had in mind. Everything under one roof. The café and the Archies store too. Maddy listened, her eyes on me, not on the women's magazine in her hand, only nodding to everything I said.

The three of us had a picnic lunch in the deer park one afternoon. It was a place that different deer species such as the barasingha, the chital and the barking deer had once frequented but hunting had culled their numbers, and it was marked by patches, their white borders still marked, where hemp had once been grown. The smell still lingered if you wandered too deep inside. The smell I associated with my early years here.

A still, unmoving afternoon that could have been borrowed from one of those long ago Sundays, when a day stretched for ever. A stillness broken by the buzz of bees and the rushing of butterflies. The air redolent with the smell of frangipani and in the distance, the sound of women slapping clothes hard against the rocks, letting off their pent-up anger. How I had laughed at Bob's remark then, one of those rare occasions when we could still tease one another, and share a joke. And in the end, it was he who had left, unable to handle his own rage, helpless against the storm of his own emotions. Pity, he might have handled Maddy far better than I did. But we were both so young then, and I only a few years older than Maddy was then in 1992. Besides, with every generation, the children only grow up faster.

We discussed Maddy's plans over lunch that day. Asha plying us with food she had slaved over but Maddy was still a fussy eater, picking at her food, chewing everything over too many times. I listened to her idly as she outlined her plans. She liked Bombay, she had made friends, and soon she would join the acting school. Asha's protest was a faint murmur, 'You cannot be serious. Acting is no child's play. To succeed in the film world, you need connections.'

I wiped my hands on the paper napkins Asha had so thoughtfully provided and thought of the stories Soumen had told me. Stories of how an unexpected twist of fate could change life altogether. How a particular actor had spent nights at railway stations, how a now famous heroine had been picked up because someone saw her face in a speeding bus window and followed her. You had to get lucky, just some acting classes would not do. You needed connections, said Asha, elbowing me in the way she had. She needed my support in her arguments with her.

You must speak to her, she said, again and again. She must at least complete her studies.

But since that night when Maddy had been taken to the hospital I no longer wanted the right to advise her. That night joined the long list of nights I wanted to forget and there were several of these – nights I waited for Robert to come home, and after he was long gone, all those other nights I waited, hoping someone would emerge from the only other house which had its light on late in the night. The nights I had seen a red dot of light dancing on the riverside and had deliberately and totally ignored Soumen's presence. But heeding Dogra's daughter's advice, I forced myself to watch television with Maddy, night after night, feeling Asha's eyes on me, urging me to speak, *to speak*.

You two are not communicating and both are getting moody. Talk it out and over.

It's not what you think, Asha. I did try but I cannot give words to what she wants or feels.

Between surfing channels and as we waited for the credits for a particular show to finish, I plucked the courage to ask Maddy if she wanted to talk.

Once Maddy gave me a fond, abstracted smile. Aren't we talking now? And another time, more irritated, she had said, What are we doing now? Aren't we talking? You seem to think talking needs to be a separate chore by itself, that one has to set aside time for it.

That was what Bob and I had done and we had done nothing but quarrel those last few days. We were both so caught up in our plans, plans that we developed on our own, thought over in secret, that we never realized how far apart we had drifted. Talking never helped, and soon we would quarrel bitterly, loudly and rancorously, accusing each other, our arguments all about other people. Names that came so very easily and tumbled off our lips, witnesses and abettors to our crumbling marriage. Bob was gone from me long before he actually left.

When Asha castigated me for not having made the effort, I was defensive. I have spent hours before the television, trying. And if she has made up her mind to do what she wants to, there is no way I can stop her now. Besides, it's best to learn from one's mistakes. Let her go to acting school and find out.

Secretly I was proud, Maddy was taking after me, after all.

Asha gave me a sad, kind smile. How little you know, how easy it is for you to speak that way. You must make that extra effort. Don't be afraid to rage, rant and even bulldoze. Life is not like one of your story books or even a Jane Austen novel.

Asha tried to speak to Maddy too. Late at night, she would tell Maddy dire stories of what happened to single young women, aspiring stars and models in Bombay. She had read about them in *Femina*, *Eve's Weekly*, and there were always the gory news stories tucked away in the inside pages of newspapers. Her scare stories, I was pleased to note, had little effect. It was in these unnoticed ways that Maddy seemed so very much my daughter.

Asha's efforts continued undiminished all through the time Maddy was with us. And that was how I found myself one afternoon in the café waiting for Ashok Parida, the commissioner's son. He too was back from Delhi for a break, and had grown into quite a well-turned out young man, if a bit too glib of tongue.

It was the first time I had been to that café, which I would always associate with the last time Subrat Mukherjee and Agamoni had met each other; the fracas over the letter had followed soon after.

Young Parida, at that time I could barely remember his first name though I remembered the kiss Maddy and he had shared, was late. He came strolling across to meet me five minutes after I had occupied a table and was assessing the menu for prices. He had been an unprepossessing schoolboy but now his curly hair was swept back, leaving a carefully maintained wave over his forehead. He had a foxy face, narrow almond eyes and a nose that twitched delicately as he took in his surroundings. In all, he looked like someone who was trying to fit himself to something else. I thought of long-suffering Mrs Parida and the possible plans she had for him, and I wished Maddy had made a better choice. But Raja Mohanty was a bit too old and worldly wise. And Jaspal hardly spent time in Brooks Town any more. I had heard he was more in Bangkok these days, looking to the supply side of his father's business. He never came back, specially after he was disowned for marrying a Chinese girl. It didn't matter, he simply set up his own chain of shops in Singapore, 'Jaspals' he called it. Some people could leave a town so effortlessly, Maddy never had this luck.

I was thinking all this and noting all of Parida's quirks as he came up. His nose twitching became more pronounced, his swagger more affected as he walked to my table. The tables near had fallen quiet, and I struggled to keep down my rising panic. I wasn't sure now. It was entirely by impulse that I had waved to him across our common wall, suddenly remembering the film script he wanted to discuss with me, that Asha had prodded me about as well. Use it as an excuse, you must, she had hissed, he can influence her, make her change her mind. He knows how these theatre people can be, he did plays and all that in Delhi. Maybe he can even keep an eye on her.

Little did Asha know how propitious her prodding would prove to be.

Those days with Maddy around, we had to carry out our conversations in low tones. But looking at him, I wasn't so sure of my plans. In his checked shirt, neat, finely creased jeans and the heavy made-up air about him, the film script seemed a put-on just like he was. And my fingers shook when he held my hand longer than usual and asked, if he had kept me waiting.

No, of course not. And I was looking around. It is a long time since I have been here, I lied.

My hands had never been held that way, not in a long while. And when he had let it go, I rubbed it, surreptitiously.

There was music playing now, and I saw the insect-eating machines installed in every corner. He allowed himself a smile, conscious of my self-consciousness, of the silence that had fallen and the girls who were watching him. A long time, he raised his eyebrow.

I waved his question away. You would not want to know. And I indicated the envelope in his hand, with a fluttery gesture, This was what you wanted me to look at, the script for the serial?

For the next half-hour we talked of everything but the one matter I had come to raise with Young Parida. You must ask him to introduce her to his circle, Asha had hissed. He will listen to you. And then she will have a different opinion of many things.

But the conversation we had went down an altogether different direction. We discussed the script, and halfway through it he lost interest. When he started describing his interest in films and the television world, he embarked on a long explanation and soon meandered, and then did not know how to proceed further. It wasn't that he had no words to describe them with but that he had never thought things out, had never had the time to do this. It was only when I found myself agreeing to his entirely ridiculous proposition that I realized how much I had allowed the situation to drift.

'Maddy might be a good choice for the role, don't you think? We need to shoot a pilot episode to win approval.'

He sat there looking so expectant and complacent about his idea that later I would berate myself, knowing I had only myself to blame when things went wrong. It was the same with Bob on board the ship, the romance so sudden and torrid that I was powerless to stop Tutul making his attempted suicide. In a matter of a week, my life changed. There I was, at 17, with my always too serious fiancé, and we were travelling to London to join my father and then there was Bob, almost as if he had been the permanent presence in my life and not Tutul.

With Dogra too, that day in 1971, as we placed black paper on all the windows, playing that ludicrous game with each other. I could not say no, or step in, and crush like a discarded cigarette butt a man's silly dreams. A silly man's silly dreams.

I thought of Tutul then as I let Young Parida's voice drone on. He must have read my stories, at least my middles, I hoped. Over the years, a few had appeared in the better known national dailies and women's magazines. I wondered where he was now, wondered too if my life would have been any different if I had stayed on with him. It would have been dreary, a perfunctory middle-class existence. Maybe sooner or later I would have walked out, mad with frustration.

Like Maddy had done. She must have felt the same too. Was that why she made friends with the oddest of people, Jaspal who had no need to finish school, Mahesh who joined the temple-destroying crowd and that long gone Reddy, with no consideration for the difference in class? Then why was I opposing her plans now?

Would you speak to Maddy about it? He asked towards the end, gallantly brushing aside my attempts to pay the bill.

I am much older than you, I laughed embarrassed, turning my head away. The deep wrinkle on my right cheek was then erased from his view.

Really, you don't look it at all! I wish Maddy were you, she is quite…

And there he was again, gesturing with his hands, cutting up the air, trying to shape the words that did not exist in his limited vocabulary.

I can't do much about Maddy. But really it is you who should take the initiative.

The initia…? He could not say the word, but his smile was charming and he held my elbow and escorted me to the door.

That is, you should go ahead and just ask her. Imagine she was me.

He threw his head back and laughed and everyone turned to look at us. If life were that easy, if only…

He was an unsure, charming schoolboy on the way back. He insisted on dropping me, though I saw that he was at the wheel of his father's official car and it was against the rules. But I was reckless and young again. The many empty, barren years seemed to roll away, as if once again I was cycling down laughing, all the way down to Exeter, leaving behind an anxious, blubbering Tutul at the very top, leaving behind the world that did not understand that there was simply no age for doing what you wanted to do.

'Do you think she will come for the party? I could ask her then?'

Who? I had been smiling, despite the ugly skeletal framework of the mall that was already coming up next to Dogra's rambling bungalow, encroaching on the cemetery and the deer park where he had hoped to train his students. Poor man. I thought, and poor Asha. I was so lost again in the past that maybe it was I who did not understand, for the two of them, Maddy and Ashok, would soon elope. That Ashok had used me in quite the same way as I, heeding silly Asha's advice, had hoped to use him. And then there was Raja who had been so clever in working out that neat little compromise with Asha. Right in the centre of the complex would be the memorial dedicated to Dogra sahib, the patriot, and the man who dreamed of giving his life for his country. Asha had been pleased. Utility – the one word that decides your space in the world, how freely you are allowed to walk in it. In that sense I didn't matter, and in retrospect that turned out to be a good thing.

There were many times Raja had turned up at our house in the evenings to show her the drawings, the planned model, the design of Dogra's bust by none other than Ramkinker Baij. He came with his special posse of bodyguards too. First, they followed his car on their scooters. But as television caught on in Brooks Town and bodyguards became more ubiquitous than the leaders they guarded, Raja's men climbed onto their motorcycles and roared up and down the town's few roads, preceding his arrival and departure everywhere, creating deep rifts in roads made only for sooty old Ambassadors, three-wheeled Matadors and of course for cyclists like the kind I had been once.

And last, Raja had acquired enough importance to write to the postal authorities using his own letterhead. He had put in a special request for a stamp in Dogra's honour, and had also appealed to the roads minister in the government to rename the road outside the grounds, leading right up to the forests, in Dogra's honour.

Once, many years ago, I remember noting the point where the forests began, just where the park and cemetery ended. The forests stretched away towards the low mountains, edging the same road I had once been driven down by Rabi, Raja's father. The trees grew thick and overwrought, thrusting themselves onto the road, so that at times, they fell forward, as vehicles passed, brushing past their windows and moving away shivering with muffled laughter. You could almost see the shapes that floated away, among the leaves and the shadows of the night, the sound mingling with Rabi's unmusical crooning as we drove along.

The forests have much dwindled now. In those few months I was away in the north, the months before Maddy was born, there were many trees singled out and hacked down brutally, the wood then taken away by the truckloads. Once the dam came up, the road broadened too, big as the river itself, with streetlights that worked alternate nights for some reason, and frogs that had once scattered themselves on a road that had been narrower now gave way to moths that danced in gay abandon around the lamps, some died caught against the windshield and the wipers. And now young Parida played the same tune on his tape, the song Rabi had sung for me those many nights ago.

It was the time Gautam Singh Dogra had just moved into the big house not too far away, along the riverbank. The house that he would live in till his death. It had once belonged to the maharaja, and Soumen without so much as a warning to Rabi, his cousin, who managed the former king's estates, had invited Dogra and his young daughter, to stay there. It was the way Soumen did most things, he wasn't held back by borders, by routine or even rules that included the need to ask permission. Rabi thought little of Soumen, except that he was an unscrupulous no-gooder, determined to spoil things for others, especially Rabi and his family.

'Just jealousy, you know, plain and simple jealousy.'

As Rabi explained, most of the royal property had all been divided by then, but the maharaja, doddering and kindly, had allowed the use of this particular house to Soumen, who had grand plans of shooting films in it. But so far he had had little luck. All he had was a film projector business that he travelled with all over the country, and that was how he turned up in Brooks Town often, to organize a film for us at the club. Soumen had met Dogra somewhere in Delhi and had struck up a friendship of sorts, which in turn led him to offer Dogra and his daughter the use of the maharaja's old house in Brooks Town, something that Rabi Mohanty had never liked.

I could agree. But Rabi had eyed the house for a long while and only Soumen knew how to deal with him on almost equal terms. It was strange that it was now Rabi's son, Raja, who would come by this house in a totally unexpected way.

For the most part that long ago night, it was Rabi who did most of the talking. Sometimes his hand brushed against mine, as he changed gears, and I allowed that. And sometimes he broke away from his crooning to look at me from the corner of his eye but it was after a long time he spoke, So what you think?

There was something in the manner he spoke that made some words unnecessary.

Nice, they have been looking for a place for a while, and the daughter seemed scared and out of place.

I didn't want to talk about Soumen, and so deliberately made it appear as if I had understood him to mean something else.

A place, but here. Then he broke off before beginning abruptly again, 'Even the man himself... something there.'

Looked out of sorts?

I had hoped once Soumen would offer me a film, till I realized that these were just fancy dreams on his part. All the hints I had dropped, in the few moments I had with him, about the plays and theatre work I had been involved in in London had been of little use. My opinion of him was beginning to veer around to Rabi's.

That you think, he was now saying, almost mumbling to himself.

Rabi sounded frustrated, a restless lion on the prowl.

He pulled over to one side and kissed me then. A rough, brute kiss, with the rough edge of his beard against my cheek.

He frightened me but the power in him excited me. As the executor of the old king's still substantial property, Mohanty had a lot of say now and money too. There was a strange animal glow on his face, the assurance that came with the knowledge that nothing would now stand in his way, nothing and nobody, not even that twerp cousin of his, Soumen, who operated on his own, reappearing every time he was in dire need of money or in desperate circumstances.

We broke apart when we noticed that light steadily advancing from beyond the clump of trees, making a wide yellow arc as it honed in towards us and then dimmed to shape itself into the twin headlights of a car. Bob, I gasped.

But Rabi did not seem perturbed. Simply pushed open the door and walked towards the front and there he was, standing under the bonnet when Bob drove up.

Rabi Mohanty, as I said, had an answer to everything. His son had that quality too. It was only his cousin Soumen who upset his plans.

What to make of it, uh? He was mumbling to himself still, as he bent down to look at the engine. He gets these people here and then tells me that they will be useful to my cause. This man Dogra will help you fight the government and for the king. What he thinks uh?

And the spittle flew fast and furious from his lips to graze the windscreen.

'It is that cousin of his who is troubling him again, and he wanted to talk to me,' even to my own ears the excuse I made sounded lame.

I did not dare look back as I drove away with Bob but I knew Rabi Mohanty was still staring, still muttering as he looked into the bonnet of his car. I was relieved to be getting away. There was that unleashed power in him that made people uneasy. His son had a more persuasive charm that allowed him to get things done.

'Soumendra plans to go to Delhi again, he is actually getting the documents retyped by a typist. He is really impressed by these people. You know, Dogra's father was once a minister to the maharaja of Kashmir, and there is his daughter too. He has plans to make a united front of maharajas against the government...'

But Bob did not see it quite like that. A man has his dreams and he is written off as a madman.

Little did I know then of the restlessness that Bob himself harboured. I did not even guess how strange the situation would be for him. He was now being reduced to a rarity, a strange commodity, a person who remained when all his other countrymen were making a choice. The Anglo-Indians were moving on – to Australia, Canada, and often back to England. But life had always caught him by surprise. His father had been in the railways and Bob assumed after the British left, it was people like him who would run India. But the plantation company folded up within a decade of his returning, jute and then nylon were more preferred than hemp for packaging. No wonder Bob often felt bewildered, wondering why he always found himself at the margins, like entering through the door and finding that the party inside was about to wrap up.

There he was in London, during the war, ostensibly studying for a technical trade but secretly working on a special code that would use tribal Ho characters, so that messages would not pass into the Soviet hands, but even at the height of the Cold War, that had never been necessary. Other codes developed by other people were used. And he returned to Brooks Town, and still found no takers. It made him even more disgusted with the inefficiency of the new order.

The corruption scandals incensed him, he wrote letters insisting men who robbed the country should be hanged to death. In calmer moments, he would argue that Bose might have been a better leader. He still exchanged some correspondence with the men of Bose's Indian National Army, whom he had shown his Ho code to. They were scattered all over – in Malaysia, Thailand and even the new country of Singapore. Maybe some of them still had their dreams and Bob was too taken with that to think things through. Once he had gone north towards Dharamshala, and returned full of even more secrets and bitterness, only to disappear some quiet bitter years later, and he had never returned.

And in the weeks I came back with Maddy and there was still no news of him, I had had a local church service organized, which Kerketta, ever the loyal, watched over. Poor Bob, at least his epitaph would have made him happy.

For Robert Hyde
who travelled far and wide
and had dreams aplenty

And over his grave in that space between our house and the Deer Park, I had had that magnificent gravestone built, with marble and stone, its smooth white face would catch the moon's light and turn into a serene, gentle blue oasis. He would have been at peace, I always thought, looking at the stone, a huge flat slab, that stretched, a long low platform. No more haunted by his demons, and that restlessness that made his long stint in this place an unending incarceration.

Young Parida dropped me home, then lingered long after we had finished coffee, and Asha had run out of small talk. We refused to leave the room, both of us, driven by our sense of decorum. We were not going to leave the two young people alone in that room, even if we could hear much of their conversation.

He had already had four of Asha's cookies, Maddy did not touch any. Her face was beginning to take on that pale, haunted look of someone who had been on a strict diet but I could no longer tell her such things. When do a mother and daughter find that they can no longer relate to each other? When do they realize that there is little either can do to bridge the irreconcilable differences between them? There comes a time when it gets too late to sort these out, the list of crimes by then stretches too far back in time so that it seems a futile exercise. And who has the time these days?

Asha made her feelings clear to Maddy once Ashok Parida had finally left, 'You can do better by choosing Raja. He is more secure and you don't have to worry about working.'

She added with her quick, nervous laugh, 'And you can continue to be friends with Ashok, like you are in Bombay.'

I waited for Maddy to explode. I had no idea of her friendship with Ashok but I realized how naturally inevitable it was. That kiss long ago, and he was going to be in Bombay too. But Maddy had big ideas of her own, of making an acting career for herself, of being financially independent. And I hastened to intervene, 'It's too early for things like marriage, don't you think?'

And I would tell Asha later, 'The girl has come home after a long time, you never know when her mood will change and there she will go, packing her bags up again.'

Not a question of time... began Asha now but Maddy interrupted.

'What will Raja get out of marriage to me? His family would cut him off. You know, Soumen his uncle has no children, and does not bother about the little land he has. And so Raja has even more to gain.'

I felt a grudging admiration for her. Love no longer decided everything. Every relationship had become a complex calculation, where you worked things out to your interest, and so I changed the subject. 'It is true what you say. And he will marry someone chosen for him. Things haven't changed all that much here. Do you remember what happened between Agamoni and Subrat?'

Asha waved her hand dismissively. 'He took things too much to heart. Left his sister and father to fend for themselves and went off to Indonesia.'

'But he does send money at least. Now old Mr Mukherjee no longer has to steal the old furniture from the club to meet his special expenses. No one seems to do anything for the daughter.'

Maddy listened to all this with interest before she got bored and directed a petulant glance towards Asha. I drew my breath in. This time the resemblance was so much more clear. How long could they stop the truth from staring them in the face?

In 1970 or so, I forget the month, Bob left home for the first time. For a long time, I always thought he had left for Dharamshala. For some years now Bob had been reading up on the Dalai Lama, who had escaped from the Chinese and made his home in India. I remember the angry letters Bob wrote to the newspapers that time and the clippings he kept of the *Hindustan Standard* which had published his letters berating Nehru for his cowardice.

I still have that piece, for I had rewritten it in parts after he had asked me to mail it for him. 'A man of peace cannot leave himself open to being cheated and Nehru makes himself vulnerable by his bonhomie with the Chinese. The Hindi and the Chini can never be bhai-bhai, as we have already learnt. Barring a period in its ancient history, since when have the two been close? And when Tibet needs our help, we choose to cosy up to the enemy but it is at our own peril. The Chinese in every way are like the Japanese. They plot in the name of friendliness. In every sense, it is the Oriental disposition at work.' The last two lines were my helpful addition. Bob never minded, he preferred thinking it was an anonymous if erudite sub-editor who had done so, and by then I was already in love with another man and did not care to correct him.

Prime ministers changed, on the other side of the border generals came and went, a new Five Year Plan came into place, but Bob's anger remained. It never changed in complexion and tone. His mouth set in stern lines, his eyes took on a secretive cunning look, he sat hunched at his table or looking out of the window at the distant mountains. And he never looked much at me any more. Staring at his square shoulders, his unrelenting self turned away from me, I wondered at the adoration I once had had towards him. The squiggles in a strange code that decorated his cabin in the ship that had first made him a mystery to me and then someone I could give up a settled life for. I stared over his shoulder at a window not too far away and thought of another man from the north, who had come to live among us.

Bob never noticed. He had withdrawn from most things by then and was becoming strangely morose and more violent. I avoided him much of the time. We usually met at mealtimes or when there was an occasion at the club. Otherwise the silence that set in and reigned till Asha moved in, ruled our lives. It was at dinner one day, early in 1971 that the radio broke the news of an Indian plane hijacked across the border to Pakistan. Bob always ate quickly and absently, one hand on the radio knob. That old Philips radio, big in those days like television sets now are, with its wire like antenna strung up like a clothesline on the verandah. In a trice Bob had jumped to his feet, the crimson spreading all over his face.

'That will show them up, they let a big plane like that go away.'

He strode around the table, sat down and got up again.

I knew it, I knew it.

Then for a few minutes he danced around the room, looking incongruous for his age but as gleeful as a schoolboy.

He sat down and then rubbed his hands, and then again, 'Every weakness exposed, every chink in the armour revealed. This is a country hemmed in on all sides by enemies and it doesn't even know how to protect itself.'

It was his bitterness, the fact that his carefully developed code, now twenty and more years in the making, had never had any takers. I knew what Bob didn't. He was a man who belonged nowhere now; a man who thus took pleasures in the strangest possible things, it was his way of getting back.

I put my fork and spoon down and said in my iciest manner, aware that the servant watched us, curiously. 'Do show some restraint, my dear,' I said, shaking my napkin insistently until the boy heeded my message and rushed away, to the kitchen, where he would regale the other servants and the driver with the master's latest peccadilloes and also, as an afterthought, tell them of what the Pakistanis had done.

I left my dinner unfinished, distressed as the All India Radio newsreader continued with the news in his sombre, grim tone. From my room, I heard the slamming of doors as Bob left, the rough banging as the car door shut, the swish of the car as it stumbled and then made a too quick departure out of the gate. The drunk guard hastily pulling himself out of his stupor. That night, when he did not return, I did think of these other details. For if he had to go the club, Bob would have rather walked. The paraphernalia of his departure should have provided me hints but perhaps quite rightly, there were none. Our marriage, by then, to all intents and purposes, was dead.

A few mornings later, a body was found dead on the railway tracks. A body so very mutilated that later the police gave up, and said it was a case of suicide. Nothing remained of the face, or much of the body either. It wasn't that a single train had gone over it. At night, there were at least three express trains that passed by Brooks Town. Trains carrying people to and away from Bombay, Calcutta, and Madras. It was night, the train driver had a schedule, passengers had climbed into their berths for a long night's sleep and who would have bothered to notice that in this lonely, neglected town in the heart of the country, there could be someone for whom life no longer mattered.

In the corpse's fingers, and Kerketta told me this some years later, was a skein of gold thread, something that had evidently come off a piece of cloth. After a pause, he told me with the strangest grin I have ever seen on anyone, 'It was not our sahib, madam, not our sahib.'

'Really, Kerketta, you say the oddest things,' I said, not knowing what to make of it.

I sat down hurriedly, unable to stop trembling and he held my hand in his crabby, wizened hands. 'Do not be upset, Madam. I picked the wrong time to say this. Years can go by and love never die.'

Little did he or I know that he too would pay for his ill-thought remark one day. But that remark stayed with me.

I looked at his bent head, his bald patch like the empty stretches of ground I had seen between the park and the forest, and he looked at my hands instead. 'But you will find happiness, one day.'

Snatching my hands away, I said as cold as I could, 'Kerketta, you've gone mad, to say such a thing, at a time like this.'

But I felt cheated, for the happiness I was soon to know would be short-lived. Love when it comes too quickly can be like that.

Asha was furious when she found out about Raja's proposed party and about Maddy attending it. He did not let us know anything about it, she sputtered.

What's in a party? I tried to soothe her, besides it should be fun for people Maddy's age.

Asha didn't agree. 'You will let it all go to her head,' she said as she flounced off. But she had nowhere to go any more. Her father's house, or rather the king's old house, was by now half-demolished, and it stood forlorn, the old pillars standing with nothing to support, the walls half broken, and the glass panes cracked in places. Only her father's study, where he had spent the last two decades of his life and where he had died, remained untouched as had been agreed. And once Raja's fine glass-fronted complex was ready, it would be shifted just as it was, and laid out in the room being readied for it, with nothing changed.

Asha took her handbag as she left the house, not bothering to tell me when she would return. The same frayed, hand-painted bag she took to school every day. It was ugly and needed to be urgently replaced, but she had carried it around for a long time, in just the same manner, as Dogra sahib had once told me, she had her mother's gold-embroidered blouse.

She was back in an hour. She must have walked through the rubble her first home in Brooks Town was now reduced to. Stepped over the stones, and into rooms now empty and forlorn, that stood naked in the sunlight. She must have stood at the very place she had once stood and paced around, looked out from the window, waiting for the rickshaw puller.

Later that very evening, her old anger forgotten, she arranged for Maddy's appointment with Farah, who ran the beauty parlour and who had once been her student. Maddy had pestered, pleaded, cajoled her into calling up Farah. Asha took her time agreeing, and I longed to intervene on Maddy's behalf repeatedly. Was this then the difference between a mother and anyone else? That it seemed to be me who realized Maddy's desperation more than Asha ever could? She finally capitulated, and only when a breakdown seemed imminent on Maddy's part.

'You promise to behave?' she asked.

And Maddy, nodded and smiled. No one could really tell who had won that particular round. Asha always fell in love hopelessly when she knew it would never be returned. Daya whose mind had learnt to go around in the same circles that the wheels of his rickshaw made, as he took the same roads day after day, would never think out of class. Maddy would never think beyond herself; and increasingly the love of the young would take on such contours.

'It's left to me to be strict and then I have to make up,' she hissed at me on her return. 'You should insist that she not carry on with Parida any further.'

'Carry on what?' I asked, almost pleading. Tell me what I should do, I really don't have an idea?

'Don't pretend. You are turning a blind eye to what she is doing. But people are talking. News travels. They have eyes to see with, ears too sharp for their own good and they will not remain quiet when they see what they see. He brings her home in his father's police car, they go for long walks down the river and now this party. It will make people talk like nothing before. You think it won't affect us, then speak for yourself. It might affect us. I teach in the school, do you think any respectable family will want to have me on, or even as a tutor. No. No way.'

I did not point out that she was the one who had made the appointment with Farah. She wanted so much to be Maddy's good mother. Maddy's good virgin mother, I thought spitefully. A virgin wife to every man who had desired her. I made you a personal appointment, she will make a home visit for you, I heard her say proudly to Maddy, who hugged and twirled her around. I saw Asha's face over Maddy's shoulder as they circled the old fireplace and the walnut table, with Bob's photo on it.

Does she do this with you, Asha's eyes seemed to ask and I smiled and joined the two of them doing circles around the sitting room till the table toppled, bringing Bob's photo down with it, and Asha was anxious the next one hour interpreting that as a sign of a calamity that would soon descend.

I am sorry, she told me over and over again. Should not have accused you of anything, I am sorry.

No, I did not ask her what she was apologizing for, or how far back in the past her contrition stretched. All those scenes in the past, all the cruel allegations she had made without knowing the truth, I could only replay them in my mind and check off Asha's apologies against each one. The times she had accused me of not caring, of being too absorbed, too distant, too…, especially not being too affectionate about Maddy. And it hurt more when she would philosophize almost in an undertone, 'But then she is not really your daughter.' Coming from a world of soaring mountains, cypress trees that shrieked when the wind caught them by their sweeping leaves and lakes where you knew you could never drown, Asha had come to Brooks Town and never could leave the small town that it really was. Her soul shrank correspondingly.

She would say things like this and never talk it over. She would never dare walk by the riverside.

While I struggled, never knowing whether to be angry or burst into loud recrimination when Asha made her sweeping magazine-read statements. What have I done that is so unnatural? I would ask, flipping through the diaries and the notes that I had written since Maddy went away. One could be most generous, most indulgent, yet never know what could happen next.

Farah was beautiful, a fluffy empty-headed beauty and she breezed in, her vanity box, scarf and cloak floating around her as if she had just flown in from colder climes. Once in she began discarding her clothes, laughing and giving Asha a breathless explanation at the same time. She folded her scarf and placed it next to her box, and then her cape, carefully untying its knots around her neck. 'It's too hot,' she said though it was four in the evening and the chill had just begun to creep in from the forest.

'You do not know what it was like to face the cold some years back,' I said.

She shivered at my words, squealed and rubbed her hands together. Ivory hands with pearl tipped nails. And her laughter gave an altogether different feel to the house. The two of us, Asha and I, watched Farah as she got to work on Maddy, her fingers working their magic as they felt, pulled, patted, rubbed her skin. An enforced intimacy that was designed to break down any reserve.

'The party, it will be big,' it was a question, not a statement on Farah's part.

'A small one, actually. And private.' Maddy giggled and then straightened her face.

'I got an invitation too and my father had a fit. He worried about it for a week and more, threatened to close down the parlour, lock me up in the house if I dared agree.'

She was laughing as she spoke. I wondered whether I should have Farah treat my skin too. I still had the scarfs and long-sleeved shirts to hide the bruises that marked my last years with Robert. Kerketta's magic potions had at best only lightened them. I could never go the parlour for fear of inviting too many questions.

'He sounds like a filmi father,' Maddy was saying.

'Oh, he loves films. In fact, he was watching a new Govinda video cassette. He adores Kader Khan.'

'He is very funny.'

The laughter sounded again. Asha laughed too, as she stared mesmerized at Maddy's face being expertly transformed under Farah's fingers. Later, when fingers were pointed at me, voices raised accusing me of neglect and of spoiling Maddy, of course, I would blame her as well as Farah for being key players in the entire elopement drama.

The elopement happened soon after and overshadowed the resounding success the party had been for Raja. The scale on which it had been organized was something Brooks Town had never seen. The band that had come from Calcutta, the food served by a five-star catering company from Calcutta too, all had Raja's stamp on it. He was now truly his father's son. A small town has its own hierarchy, set in a scaffolding of stone.

A day later, as strewn bits of paper and plastic rollicked in the flattened grass, there were some who came to verify, to wonder, shake their heads at how much things had changed. The next evening, Raja sent around the photos, and the cake too. It should have served as a sweetener but the photos said everything. I saw the two of them dancing and I saw the grave too, the flat oblong stone I had had laid in Bob's memory, and that now served as a makeshift platform for the dancers.

Asha couldn't have enough of the photos. She was determined to accost Maddy about them. But she had slept late and complained about aching limbs. 'They wouldn't let me be. They insisted I dance ', and she stretched languorously but Asha would have none of it.

'It is a disgrace, you should not have danced with him that way,' she said.

'Everyone was dancing. Really,' she insisted, 'and it wasn't just me on the gravestone. It was too crowded, there was that hard to place smell, and we moved away. It is just that they took my photos and not of the rest. Even Taj's two daughters, they came in their rickshaws, and proceeded to dance with reckless abandon. But Raja would not let their photos be taken.'

'Don't try and blame Raja, Maddy. Look at the shameless picture you make.'

The ghostly smell of hemp that one could still come upon unexpectedly; sometimes under your feet, you could still see the crushed serrated leaves. They would appear when you thought all was gone, burnt down. The past surprises you by choosing its moments of reappearing, if you learn to let go at the right times, that is… But Asha for now, was too caught up in the immediate past.

'But there was Ashok too there with me. No one seems to be asking him anything.'

This is where I pitched in, 'As a woman, Maddy, it is up to you to ensure your own respectability.'

'And that, I suppose, means doing what everyone else expects of you?' she asked.

I could tot out every explanation I had made to her over the years, only to stress the point. Ladies behaved in a certain way. I stopped myself many times from telling her that I did not want her to end up like me. Already I could foresee where such scandalous, unapologetic behaviour could take her. You would be lonely, frustrated, devious – everything I saw in myself – and I did not want it to happen to her. But I did not, could not, tell her all this. It was Asha, who wept, bullied, demanded things of Maddy, insisting that had the relationship between the two of them been any different, none of this present state of affairs would have resulted.

For his part, Commissioner Parida's response was first a shrug. It was just a party, his son had been invited as had several others by Raja. 'You should be asking Raja these questions, as to why all these photos were taken, and not me.'

It was the memory of his face when he said that, self-satisfied and unmoved, that came back to me when he came to my house two days later. Maddy and Ashok had already left, and no one knew when or how. And I leaned back and repeated his own words back to him.

'What can I do, these young people have a mind of their own, they do what they want.'

He was left spluttering. 'You think I do not know about your ward? She led my son ashtray.'

But I couldn't really laugh at his mispronunciation, while a teary Asha stood by.

Raja, for his part, laughed a bit too heartily when I accosted him about the elopement, and the photos. If he had any inkling, why hadn't he let on?

'I had no idea that things would get so serious. They were just dancing with each other,' he said. 'I noticed they were friendly, and people don't elope to marry just because…'

He shrugged, laughed and then spread his hands wide. 'People get close and friendly, there is no reason to rush into marriage.'

Asha darted stern looks at me, before intervening, 'People also talk when you get close and friendly. You should never allow that. It was your fault, Raja. You should not have let it go so far at the party.'

'I had a lot to do, really,' he said, in that charming schoolboy manner of his. 'I could not keep my eyes on them though yes, Maddy is a good dancer and it was difficult not to keep one's eyes away. But…'

But Asha was insistent. Her vehemence surprised me. 'You could have Raja, stopped it if you so wished. That man Parida is here every day thinking we had something to do with it.'

'Is that all?' He was now his usual assured self. 'No, I shall explain things to the commissioner. He needs to handle this better, and he shall. The two of them are adults. He can't just keep barging in all the time.'

He had to leave, and Asha turned her ire on me. The extreme reactions her love had invited could have prompted her to behave in the same way. We are schooled to love in a particular way.

'Instead of worrying about Maddy, you are more concerned and angry about the disrespect shown to Robert's grave. You left the photos in Raja's office, marking things out. And a letter too.'

'The photos… they put an entirely different picture to things,' I said lamely, 'they had been dancing on his grave.'

That would lead her to level more vile accusations, 'You would care more for a dead person than for any other person, even if that person is almost your daughter.'

And this was where I burst into laughter.

It was some time later that I returned to the post office to send off another story. The postmaster was on the phone, staring at his table, looking mournful and angry in turns, trying to explain things to a presumably irate caller.

When he had finally returned the receiver to its holder, he stared at it as if he expected it to pounce on him again, and then laughed sheepishly. Sometimes one had trouble picking Nautiyal out in the streets. He carried all the time a frayed leather bag under his armpit, the same one displayed on his table every time I saw him at the post office. His face now looking across the table at me seemed very young, vulnerable, and he was prone to blushing every time a silence fell. His legs, visible through the folds of his thin pyjama, were however those of a much older man's, thin and reedy, with an old man's shoes, stitched and re-stitched several times.

Now he blushed and complained, his hand waving over the telephone. 'About this Speed Post, madam, other people just don't understand, that it does take time even to deliver. The government says one day time only, but they don't understand. One day, one day, they keep screaming… even if there is only one day delay, they sit on my head.'

It was nice to be talking to him. He seemed oblivious to the elopement and all that had happened. It was nice to sit there, under the hum of the old lugubrious fan, hearing his voice shake as he talked again of the evil days the Speed Post had imposed on them at the post office. His voice trembled also as he thanked the boy who served tea in clay cups, as it did when he handed over the keys to my postbox to an obliging clerk, instructing him to bring up whatever was inside. The clerk nodded and withdrew, staring at me unashamedly. The way people looked at me now had changed after Maddy's elopement. There was a glee mixed with pity. The clerks knew what had happened, everyone did, except of course, the ever harassed Nautiyal.

In all likelihood, Mr Nautiyal, who had had two daughters in quick succession, had perhaps not even heard the matter of the elopement. His increased loquacity dispelled any fears that I had.

He was talking to me about the magazines he received and then, I could sense it coming, the usual blush came over his face. 'I have been thinking of a story for a long time. Do you have the time?' But he did not wait for my answer. He had worked up his courage with some difficulty. He leaned forward and the shiny varnish of the table on which the silver fan moved as dully as before, took on the reddish hue of his blush. His small self had squeezed into the old, battered paperweight that perched on his table. 'It is a bit romantic.' Like the quivering image in the paperweight, I squeezed in some enthusiasm on to my face, 'Do go on, that's very interesting.'

'But it is not the usual kind of love story.' He looked around and lowered his voice, and I leant forward too. His smell caught me unawares. Not just of the snuff that he must smash hard in the palm of his hand, before smearing it onto his gums, but the smell of his unwashed vest, the hair oil he used, and the smell of the post office, that had seeped into him over the years. Of old letters, gum bottles, burlap sacks, of things unchanged. 'And it is a true story.' I saw myself in the twin circles of his spectacles and found myself caught in the same past, locked with him together in the paperweight. 'You would know about it too. But it is a love story, with villains, all the politics that goes on in a family, everything.'

He held my eyes and then blushing a last and final time, he said, 'They are still exchanging letters. The two teachers from the school. Do you remember?'

'Agamoni…'

His hand fell over mine. Papery and hard, like a postcard itself. His hand stayed over mine, as he whispered the next words urgently to me. I longed to pull my hand away but his had an unexpected strength.

'I know airmails come from Indonesia for her. Even before, she would come to my house to pick up her letters, written by that Physics teacher. Then I had to ask her to make alternative arrangements. I asked her to, I have two daughters and the wife was getting curious, she said neighbours ask too many questions. She is married to someone else, you know, she told me. So I explained it to her when she came. And she understood, was very airy about it.' He released my hand suddenly and the air from the fan had a decidedly chilly touch as it rushed in over my now exposed skin. Even so, the hair on my arms rose, and I felt in me, the rising excitement. 'And what did she say about the letters?'

'Nothing. But she knows every detail about them. She checks the postmark and gets anxious if a particular letter is missing. But she is a very nice woman. She understood, she knew the risks I was taking. This,' he pointed towards the bundled up envelopes in his hand, 'is all private property, I am not allowed to open it unless some authorization comes. I am only the custodian.'

He had become expansive. His shawl fell away as he raised his arms to encompass the entire office, the shelves with their chalk painted numbers, the huge wooden tables around which the clerks spoke in muted whispers, the guard at his stool near the door, the sun straying through the bars and the skylights broken and chipped high near the ceiling.

'And she explained the problems she had too, about her husband being busy and her in-laws too strict about her outings, and left saying someone else would come for the letters. Someone she absolutely trusted.'

He looked at me closely for several moments, as if he expected me to say something. But I listened. Something made me feel this was important.

'And so her friend, the other schoolteacher comes at a particular day and time. The one who had that thing with the rickshaw puller. Sometimes the rickshaw wallah came on his own. The teacher now comes on her own, every day. She comes straight here and holds out her hand. As if she knows too that there are letters waiting to be picked up. It is a totally unique system of communication. Imagine a love story, that communicates through the mind, and across the ocean too. Imagine the countries that come in between... Burma, Thailand...'

'Depends,' I said drily, 'on the direction, sometimes only the Andaman islands need come in between.'

'Yes, but even then, imagine the distance. This is what I call true love.'

I saw my many faces, two locked in the shiny glass eyes of his spectacles, another spread-eagled on his glass table, splattered and broken up by the odds and ends on it. 'There is a story there,' I said, 'but as a love story it might not work.'

We had shared so much the last few minutes I felt a pang in my own heart as his face fell. 'There is just something you need to touch up.'

He looked puzzled, signing hastily on a form held out by a peon and staring hopefully at me. It was a face I had never seen on him before. He was not blushing, but everything in him had worked together to produce that intense expression on his face, that left the rest of him shrivelled, drying up before my eyes.

'I can read it and let you know.'

He seemed to be waiting for that. With his gaze fixed on mine, he pulled out a file tied with red string, a stamp affixed on it. He laughed, looking far younger than I had ever seen him before. Perhaps this was the face his wife saw, the devilry in his eyes, merriment all over him, the post office and its smells far away. Men and their hidden selves, and he had fathered two daughters in quick succession.

I patted his hand as I left, smiled encouragingly. He began blushing once again and his goodbyes remained unsaid.

It was a long time since I had such an idea as this. I could barely contain my excitement, and longed to sit somewhere in absolute undisturbed silence and read the file through. It was the anticipation that at long last I could finally write the story I wanted to. One, that would be contemporary, modern but still have echoes of all the traditional emotions such as love, respect for old norms, etc. Words that editors would always toss at me, when they rejected my stories for being too daring, too revealing, too expressive. One of them had written, 'You cannot write of a woman in those days having such naked sexual feelings. It's not on.' Now if I told this story well, there was no way the *Imprint* magazine could refuse to publish it.

This was the reason why Maddy's letter and its contents did not register at first. There I was, on the stone steps that led down to the river, away from Asha's prying eyes, and her terrible inquisitiveness for she knew Maddy would write sooner or later. 'She has to, it's like her. And besides she can't burn every bridge behind her.' She looked at me before throwing that last statement.

I ripped her letter open and ran a quick eye down it. Maddy's usual hurried scrawl, riddled with the accusations she had hurled at me before. That she had tried one more time but now she had to get away, for good. She could not make a future in the narrow, one-street town that I had chosen to live my life in. That she was now more suffocated than ever, almost dying of claustrophobia, and besides she had found a couple of roles already. Not the lead ones but she wanted to begin with the small ones.

A letter from your daughter, I heard the voice clearly, gravelly and slow, laced with the laughter I remembered.

Then I recognized the face from the past, the face that had vanished so unexpectedly from Brooks Town, someone who had still his boyish thin figure but a face now much older and wiser. There he was, at the bottom step, a gun poised against him, like a third leg, his eyes barely visible within the matted, browned locks of his hair and there was his voice, cracked and broken, breaking off into laughter every now and then. Oddly enough, I wasn't frightened by the gun. Later I would remember thinking that even at that moment, I couldn't picture him raising the gun, his hand on the trigger, aiming for a kill.

'Sorry to disturb you,' he said, waving his hand, smiling. 'But you were sitting there so long, and I watched.'

'Where had you gone?' I asked, remembering the stones that had made him run from the boulder. A decade had gone and the anger had long dissipated. I wanted to apologize but despite the silence that stretched, the words didn't come. They would need too many preliminaries, and perhaps necessary follow-ups and with him that had never been necessary.

Here and there, he replied, or maybe nowhere. I had forgotten this place till I recognized you sitting here, just like yesterday. He could see through me, like he always did.

'Will you let on now about what I did? After so many years, when the man himself is no longer alive? It would destroy my daughter...' I looked away unable to finish but there was no answer. I heard him sigh, and looking back, I saw he was no longer there. I hadn't even asked him about the gun. Was he too a part of a play of his own making, just as I was the tramp lady who walked on her own by the river? I had heard the land he had so shamefully neglected was being eyed, and by members of his own family. Had he come back finally to claim what was his?

I heard his steps crunching the stones across the riverbed. Something about that sound, the light deliberate steps made me stop and watch. Footsteps made for silence. I thought I had heard them often in the night, and then I couldn't be sure. Footsteps that walked alone, that would never belong anywhere, no matter the claims on him. And then he was gone. The man from my past had vanished in the way he always had. Some things never change.

I had nowhere else to go to, and that setting was strangely peaceful, making me forget Maddy's letter. I sat there, holding onto it, knowing I had to read it once again all over to understand, thinking too of the story the postmaster had told me and wondering if it had really been the man from my past I had seen? And why was he back?

In the same manner he had come back all those years ago, and sat on that boulder, the one we passed on our way to school, till Maddy had made him leave. *Leave my mother alone.* Those words so clear, her voice innocent. I could forgive Maddy anything because she said that once.

I got up, feeling a sharp pain in my knees and tears in my eyes. I rubbed my hands, they felt dry and papery like Nautiyal's and I looked away. I was getting old and I really couldn't keep worrying for too long.

As I turned to walk slowly back up the steps, the sunlight on my back gentle as it had always been, I wondered if I dared pass off Nautiyal's story as my own and send it to a magazine? Nautiyal's ideas were vague and scattered; if I worked on it, gave it strength, an atmosphere, wouldn't it be truly mine? After all, a writer gets her influences from varied sources.

You have never cared for me. Maddy's words danced before

my eyes still. *Too busy in your world. You only wanted me for the company. Now you have no right to tell me what to do. I do have a future in acting. And Ashok and I might be getting married soon.*

I crunched up the letter till it was a small pellet that I could hide securely in my palm, then turned and threw it away at the river. I had lost her already. There was nothing I had to hide anymore.

The tramp lady would perhaps retrieve the letter later. She had appeared in more recent days, the sunlight catching the end of her gold-embroidered blouse. Asha had thrown it away, tossed it carelessly on the lonely riverbed, that torn half blouse her father had carried with him for so long in his wife's memory, had finally meant nothing to her. I ascended the steps to the gate, not knowing what to think, clutching the postmaster's notes. It was his notes I was more interested in. And I met Asha's hope-widened eyes, her desperate curiosity with a casualness I did not really feel.

'Nothing from Maddy?'

I did not reply, and heard her voice behind me, 'Maybe you should try and get in touch with the Bombay police?'

'Parida's father must have done that. Besides, they are both adults now. We just have to sit back and wait for the news.'

This time she rushed ahead of me in the corridor so that the two of us were facing each other.

'Is there anything you've ever done for love?'

Here was my chance to berate her for her foolishness. What good would it do to either party, Subrat and Agamoni, if their affair continued in its straggly, ragged way, and her efforts in it all? He had gone away to forget, she had a new life. Some love stories have a short shelf life. I wanted to tell her too of my visits to the prison, the food parcels I had once left for Daya in her name, the visits that stopped the time Maddy found herself in hospital. Maybe, she was right after all. In matters of love, I had never been persistent, had simply given up in the face of hopelessness. An enduring love story had to take all such things into account, paper it over, even things like one's silly ego which made put-downs unbearable. Perhaps love allowed this. I was mulling over this unexpected realization and said nothing.

'You don't really care, do you? Do you?' she said, working herself up to a bad temper.

'Now, don't get melodramatic, Asha.' I pushed the door of my room open, and she flounced off and I knew we would not be talking to each other for a week or so. I was happy. I had a story to work on. Far away, as I drew aside the curtains, I saw Soumen again, among the boulders. He was picking his way through the dry bed, crossing over to the other side. Where was he going now? Or had he ever really left? Why hadn't I stopped him? I was glad I had thrown the letter away, it wasn't a good thing to have lying around in the house. The written word granted a permanency but it could leave lasting scars. Asha would never understand. I cared for Maddy enough to tear her letter up. You need to go looking for love, that it takes as much time as making other life decisions, and I for one, wasn't going to stand in Maddy's way. I knew the other side too well. And Soumen, a man totally on his own, always knew: you had to carry a gun for your own protection, never to kill others.

Love Stories from the Past

When Agamoni made her request that first time some years ago, Asha simply could not turn her down. Agamoni Gupta was a colleague and friend and helping her out by acting as intermediary between her and Subrat was a way Asha had of rebelling against her father, keeping alive her own lost love story. And after a gap, it continued even after Agamoni's marriage and Subrat's moving to Indonesia. The thought of being an accomplice, an aide to love always excited her.

If Dogra sahib had not been on such angry terms with the Iranian Velayati, Farah's father, who ran the STD booth, there was no way he could not have known. All that waiting for her when she was late from school yielded nothing up for Dogra. Instead it was Velayati who really knew all that Asha was up to. Having made a complete round of the city in Daya's rickshaw, picking up her magazines, Asha would then ride up to the phone booth to inform Agamoni about the letters she had also picked up for her from the post office. It was the timing that made Velayati suspicious. Sometimes if her father waited for her at the gate, she would sneak back within the hour to call. Not later. Everything was neatly timed, every move so perfectly synchronized that it did not take him long to find out.

He saw her face in profile through the glass pane. Noted the silly precautions she took, and his STD phone booths were the most modern of all installed across the city. Not for him, those bulky black telephones on their yellow stands outside a shop on the main street. He had had built three separate glass panelled booths, complete with comfortable stools with table fans. Asha Dogra did not linger. She did not sit on the stool nor did she put on the fan. She pushed her lips as close as possible to the receiver, muttered a few short words he couldn't pick up, and left, placing the two rupee coin before him.

Perhaps Velayati would not have made those sly remarks to Dogra sahib if Asha had been nice to him. A smile or even a thank you would have helped but Asha carried her secretiveness too far. When he put everything together, made a thorough analysis of the calls, the timing, the duration, Velayati reached some definite conclusions. Yet the lady still kept up her pretensions. It was that which drove him mad, irritated him thoroughly.

It was just another afternoon, that the two men came to blows. While Dogra sahib stole anxious glances at his watch, padded up and down in front of the grilled gate before his house, blew his nose, Velayati watched him, one eye idly watching the stream of callers who came to use his phones. Then, at a less crowded moment, he walked out, ran a finger down the front window of his glass booth, strolled around again, saw how Dogra sahib avoided his eye, and then shouted those words out, words that were designed to provoke.

Waiting for your daughter? She is late again.

There was no reply at first, Dogra blew his nose but the insult only egged Velayati on.

Funny. It does seem to take her so long, and my daughter is here over half an hour ago.

Dogra still did not deign to reply. Never before in the last eight years since Velayati had moved in, had set up his establishment right under his nose, had he ever had a conversation with the Iranian. Having failed to stop him from setting up his phone booths, Dogra maintained his distance. The curtains facing the garden and the road outside were always tightly drawn and the gates firmly padlocked, the keys in the cavernous interiors of Dogra sahib's pockets.

This does happen too often. If I were you, I would keep her...

But he never finished the sentence. Dogra had crossed the road, in a trice had hauled Velayati up by the collar and shouted into his face, You mind your own business, you bloody Irani.

The other man had not resisted. He was known to suffer from high blood pressure and had a weak heart, part of the baggage that had hurriedy left with him from Iran, the very day the Ayatollah Khomeini had returned to a tumultuous welcome at Tehran. Velayati's face had now gone red, but he managed to hold out a hand, blustering that he was only joking.

Your kind does not joke. They have always had an eye on our girls. Don't I know better?

One of Velayati's daughters and Farah's sister who ran the beauty parlour with her, came down and tried pulling her father away. There were others who now circled the duo, but Dogra's fury refused to ebb. Asha noting the commotion from afar asked Daya to take a left turn that beckoned invitingly and would lead in some time to our house. It was there that she called Agamoni, and the two of them rang up Farah, to ensure that between the women there was no bad blood.

And as they giggled over the fight between the two men, I noticed how Agamoni sat, hunched forward, her fingers protective over the letters that Asha her friend had picked up for her from the post office.

'Sometimes a little of anything can cause a lot of harm,' She tried to explain the quarrel away.

'I mean,' she said, brushing away the wisps of hair that floated loose over her forehead, 'your father being so protective, he just did not find a suitable groom for you.'

I could have stamped hard on Agamoni's pretty toes. Didn't she realize how insensitive she was being? Or perhaps in the complacence of her soon to be wed status, in the conceit of basking in the love and adoration of another man, she had developed too thick a skin?

❦

Dogra Sahib, for that is how in the earlier days I called Gautam Dogra, always said that it was never his intention to hurt me. In those early days, he said sorry a bit too much. It made him a bit of a blundering buffoon. It was this overwhelming and very charming need on his part to apologize that left me blinded to everything else about him. His hypocrisy, self-righteousness, all his double-standards, his boorishness later... but I stopped myself abruptly. There I was doing it again. This habit of seeing something bad in a person once adored is hard to get over. It had happened with Bob before. And besides, both of them were dead. What good would it do me, or anyone now?

The first time I saw him was during the debate called to decide once and for all, the name of our city, then and even now called Brooks Town. Bob had refused to attend. He had been drinking far too much but he said it was an affront to even contemplate the idea. It was the hemp plantations and the Brooks Town company that had brought fame to the city, rescued it from tribal oblivion. 'Why, if you have to change the name, give it a more appropriate name,' he suggested in that mocking way he had, 'how about Hempel? Or Hemp-pur or nagar? Or even Ahemp?'

The irony of it struck me too – that we were debating the matter of renaming the city in the very precincts of a club set up by the planters, the very usurpers and the exploiters, who had, as was written in our pamphlet, enslaved the kingdom, reduced the status of a once free people to colonized subjects.

Bob didn't want me to go either. He left me with those marks around my wrist that I had to cover up wearing ridiculous cloth bands like an Amazonian warrior, and when I left, he watched me darkly through a parting in the curtains as the car that Rabi Mohanty had sent arrived to pick me up.

It was a secret I painfully protected, terrified of drawing Bob's ire. For it was me who had written, rewritten, corrected the leaflet that was circulated, read avidly by everyone who attended the meeting that day. The crowds spilled out of the hall and there were many who had draped themselves over the banisters, occupied the window ledges, and even strayed onto the garden from where they followed proceedings through the open windows.

It was at first a one-man show. Rabi Mohanty read out the speech in his monotonous rumble, loud enough to drown most things, so I missed at first the soft whisper close to my ears. I turned around some time later and there he was, the estranged cousin, Soumen, by my side. He had a thoughtful look but smiled on seeing me. It broke his face up into crinkles, nice ones, some wedged deep into his skin, others that spread lightly around his eyes. He looked older but still unchanged in many ways.

'You are back,' was all I could say weakly, hoping desperately someone would come to my rescue. I was sure he had returned with yet another madcap scheme.

'He is now doing social work, my brother, he needs all the encouragement. And so I came,' he smiled and his face changed instantly. With his lackadaisical foxy looks, he had a charming smile too.

He spread his hands wide and the watch jangled and slid down his wrist. I looked towards Rabi but he was still reading out from the paper while Soumen had now inveigled himself between me and the crowd, so that I had little way of escaping.

'My brother... he always sees the writing on the wall well in advance, but you think the government won't see through this?' His voice was a soft murmur in my ears. 'But at least he is keeping his hands off my friend Dogra.'

'Or maybe the government has other things to do,' I said deliberately pretending not to understand.

'Such as fighting with others in the government, taking over banks, shutting up one royal house after another, and trying to work things out with the Sheikh in Kashmir. The lady, our wonderful prime minister, sure has her hands full…'

We actually laughed together, the watchfulness vanished from Soumen's eyes and he visibly relaxed. Rabi was still droning and the audience was now restless, distracted and doing polite things with the paper handed out to them. The paper with Rabi's speech on it, the one I had written, and corrected, recorrected, proofed, slogged several times over.

'You are away now most of the time.'

'I will be killed if I stay too long,' he laughed. 'My brother has it in for me, the property is not enough for the two of us. Besides, I am doing some important political work too.'

'Really?' He looked down at me, and smiled at my disbelief.

'Yes… and my dear cousin, my brother in other words, doesn't like it. The small-time maharajas here want a party of their own, something that will fight for their privileges… The rajas of Rajputana are really…,' he shrugged, 'agitated'.

But his explanation was broken midway, someone from the back had stood up and wanted to ask a question. Someone had at least paid attention, the question would stop Rabi in his tracks, he would not ride roughshod now over everyone with his audacious plan. But that someone who was now calling for attention made me draw my breath. As would happen each time I saw him again. Someone who was tall, burly and with the leonine features that reminded me of Shammi Kapoor, the brooding younger son of Prithviraj Kapoor, who I had seen in a recent film. It was Gautam Singh Dogra, who had moved in the year before, and was staying in the Maharaja's old house, after Soumen had expressly invited him to do. Only three houses away, and sharing the same view of the river as I did, and I had not even bothered to notice him till now.

He stood up, smiled, and biting his lips, introduced himself, 'Gautam Singh Dogra'. He paused, looked around, lost. Did he expect applause or some sign of recognition? It was at these instances of uncertainty that I found him most attractive. I would come to understand only later that he was a man whose past defined him, a past that exercised such a pervasive influence that he found it difficult to understand the present, and was confused, even enraged, by it.

I looked at him unable to look away. Perhaps Soumen must have noticed my flush, the feverish, hungry excitement in my eyes, for it was after a while that I realized he was no longer talking to me, but just standing, frozen by my side. There were some words he said that hung in the air between us. 'I knew someone who could make me look like that too,' I thought he said, before Dogra sahib's voice boomed out over a hall that had fallen totally silent.

'Yes, thank you. I have just one question, Mr Mohanty. Why this name in particular? Any significance?' Dogra asked.

'I beg pardon…' And I heard Soumen snigger by my side. Rabi Mohanty, usually so assured, looked like a gargoyle, his mouth agape, unable to comprehend that someone had actually raised his voice.

'That is tradition, the old name.'

'And who decides that?' It could have been a contest between two booming voices, and Rabi was easily outclassed. His voice heavy and guttural was really not as impressive and in the audience there was nervous laughter.

'It has been decided. Mrs Hyde please come here.'

They turned to look at me then. All of them, those in front turned, while those at the back and farther away craned their necks to look at me, as did the man from Kashmir, who looked down at me from where he stood. Even after I knew his name and could call him by it, I would still refer to him this way, at least to myself.

I heard Rabi call out for me again, his voice more guttural, and I can still remember, running up to the stage, breathless, blushing at the sudden applause and then clinging to the dais as I made the necessary explanation.

'It was, we thought, a unanimous decision.'

I drank in big gulps the glass of water Rabi held out for me. At once a buzz went around the room and I knew I had fuelled speculation all over again. He was just giving me a glass of water, I would have shouted over the mike instead of the explanation I was now being asked to make.

'It is the name of the traditional deity of the town,' I began, clearing my throat, more loudly each time so the buzz went away.

As far as I can remember, my explanation was well received. As for my questioner, he had lost interest as soon as I had started speaking. He fidgeted, shoved and then meandered off and I noted that Dogra sahib was the first in queue when the food was being served. And when Rabi pointed this out to me, I said, nonchalant as ever, and feeling sorry for the man, standing apart for all his handsomeness, 'At least he spoke up and that's something.'

Later we would acknowledge each other quietly, he nodding and taking off his cap when he met me on the road. I had stopped going for my walks in the deer park and insisted on taking the road. Bob made his usual sneering remarks when I set off the first time but stopped when he saw he was having no effect. 'Think you need company, eh? The same loneliness biting you, again?'

People did stare, they did cross over to the other side of the road, rickshaws tinkled their bells a bit too loudly, passing on coded messages to each other, but I walked on stolid, unbending, my heart beating fast, hoping I would run into him.

But other than that, he barely spoke. He walked, head lowered, his big coat flapping by his side. It was much later I learnt about the half-torn, ripped, gold-embroidered blouse he carried all the time in one of his big pockets, the only remnant of his wife he would ever acknowledge. Once he almost stumbled, and I saw him turn beetroot red. A week of this and he changed his schedule. I realized though he was still taking his walks when I asked Asha, who had also enrolled in my special Saturday drama classes, about him. She was a a rosy-cheeked, shy girl then and I gave her the lead role, which she was really no good at. But it was one way to get to talk to her, and about her father too. Those days I had such power and could dispense my largesse, give them roles that made them step out of their small town lives, whether it was Jaspal or Asha. Both had little need of it.

Giving her an abridged copy of *The Merchant of Venice*, I had long sessions with her on Portia. This was that glorious period in my life when I was in love anew, before Asha left for hostel to get her education degree and the time when acting was considered a serious art. It would be another few years before the acting classes were suspended. No more could I use the school premises for licentious activities – a phrase first used by Manjit Singh, Jaspal's father; it gave the school the licence to stop the only thing I ever really liked. Parents insisted the classes were a bad influence on their children, filling them with no-good ideas and the principal and most of the staff agreed that academics was what really mattered.

And no one could ask me to leave considering who Bob had been, the money that had been sunk into the school by the Hemp Plantation company. And so I became the crafts teacher. Anonymous and unobserved, it left me alone, to do my own thing.

But that year when I was Asha's teacher, I asked her as casually as I could, when she brought her script to me, 'Does your father go for his walks still?'

And she, naïve in the way she would always be, with her father's fine forehead and full rounded cheeks, had replied, 'No Ma'am, he goes a bit late. Does some exercise inside only.'

'Exercise, why? Is he well?' Oh, my wasted acting skills, how I had put them to use once.

'Oh yes, he is, very much so. But he says other exercise besides walking is also important for the health.'

'So he does walk too?'

'Yes, he does.'

She blushed, looking down at her script. And I tried to hide my trembling hands, unable to accept the fact that he was avoiding me. It was the first exchange that we had about her father. I hoped she would tell him about it, how later father and daughter would discuss me. That pretty, fair lady with the delicate and lonesome looks. Dogra sahib did turn up once for the annual play where I became the cynosure of all eyes for I wore my formal black skirt and the white shirt with the puffed sleeves. I had spent weeks sorting it out, restoring the fine silk lace around the collars, and refixing the silver buttons that I bullied Mulji Tailors into ordering from Calcutta.

I heard his booming laugh down the corridor which set off a wild beating in my heart. And then I saw him approach, his daughter holding his hand, an identical blush on their cheeks. Our eyes met and I rose to welcome him but he stepped back, into someone else, his cap fell off, and there he was looking for it on the floor, stammering that it was getting late or something equally incoherent, while I looked on, unable to hide my hurt and bewilderment. As for Asha, she looked at both of us, and there was none of the confusion or shyness on her face. She had understood.

She had grown up too fast, motherless and too suspicious. When she returned with her degree in education, she had already the glowering expression, those stray rebellious strands of hair she kept brushing back from her forehead, and those ever narrowed eyes. As for me, I could no longer approach her. That look of silent accusation stopped me dead in my tracks.

We would run into each other at the club, when Asha and her father would turn up for the fortnightly film screenings but they soon stopped, as war happened again, and Gautam Dogra became obsessed about training the country's youth and setting up his military school. And the movies that were screened were soon too outdated and old anyway.

Over the years, by the time Soumen and his two man crew arrived, the movie might already have appeared on television or else people had seen it on a rented video cassette. Though the club had always screened films for viewing pleasure, citing it as entertainment expenses in the accounts, it was really becoming a non-profit venture. Poor Soumen could not understand. He would explain that he had been touring all over the country and everywhere he found good crowds to see his films, and he was rightly bewildered when I told him that his films were dated. For all his ambitions of making his fortune in films, he just hadn't the luck. Or perhaps his luck extended to his living out life as a low-level operator, moving from being a political fixer to doing odd-end jobs, such as a guide or a casting agent in films, but that was it.

'Dated?' he asked now, his eyes blinking, his smile once charming, kept fading with the years, often pathetic in his attempt to cajole. The three of them, his two assistants and Soumen himself, looked caught in a time warp. While moving around the country, its small towns and wayside villages, picking up and showing ten-year-old movies, they had forgotten how much life around them had changed.

He now fanned himself with his doffed cap watching me uncertainly while his men set up the projector on the table and the white screen cloth stared on expressionless.

'Soumen, do you think people want to see films like *Pink Panther* and *Breakfast at Tiffany's* any more, when new films are coming here as fresh as baked bread? Your movies are just getting older and older.'

'They are classics, classics that make you dream. That is precisely the point. These films are ageless, their stars are people you could lose your heart to.'

He looked at me and grinned, 'A bit like you, my lady Charlotte.'

He still had his old persuasive charm which I could almost like and which had made Dogra too move into this forgotten town, leaving his home in the mountains and a more active life in Delhi. The charm that made him so hard to place.

'No, Soumen, things are different. You must understand.'

But he refused to. These last few years, all he had been doing was touring the country, showing his films. One day, I knew he would simply fall dead while turning his projector or would probably be choked to death by the swirling film reels that his assistants, in their gloved hands, were meticulously now rewinding and numbering before putting them back in their special aluminium boxes. And here we were, putting them up in the club, and footing their food bill. I felt sorry for him too. He was a kind of friend. That was how I had always thought of him. A friend, sort of. And now even his cousins, the Mohanty family, had little to do with him.

'You show us new films.' And I corrected myself, realizing I was talking like him, 'Why don't you show us new films?'

'New films?' It was only now that he turned to look at me, amazed and shaking his head in disbelief. 'New films, they are just for the front bench stalls. I am showing you films that will never die, that are immortal. Tell me, will people ever get chance to see Peter Sellers, Gregory Peck… to see Amitabh Bachchan you simply have to go to Bombay.'

I gave up arguing, hoping that the dwindling crowds would convince him. The Sunday film on television was now the staple leisure-time activity. The truth evident to me when the only audience for my plays were the actors and the extras and Kerketta who could make his voice as loud or soft as you wanted it and his applause travelled over the walls, across the road, into any ear that refused to be convinced. When Soumen screened his old films, only the first four-five rows were ever occupied; there was an ocean of vacant chairs between his table and where we sat, and yet Soumen could not be bothered. I saw him, a lean wiry shadow, sitting in the very last row as the reel unspooled, chewing his thoughts and watching a film he must have seen a hundred times already.

'*Magnificent Seven*, brand new film,' he told me proudly this time. 'And it drew big big crowds in Kolar, Ooty, Coonoor...'

But Soumen didn't really have much to worry about, while we constantly thought of ways of drawing in more crowds. Every movie screened brought in a neat sum as well as the mandatory bottle of whiskey. He had no family to support and did not care much for his wealthier cousins either, except to embarrass them once in a while. He lived in a cottage that was little more than a shack, in Bombay's Juhu area, very near where the director Chetan Anand and his muse in later life, Priya Rajvansh lived.

'I breathe films, that's all I need to survive,' he once told me in what I thought was a rare moment of confession. 'I travel around the country, showing movies, and then moving on. I love it.'

He might have said the same thing about politics or the mountains too, one time, I thought. But there were also times when I would remember what he had whispered in my ears those many years ago. A hint of love and what it could make a person do. The time long ago, when we had all gathered at the club to petition for a new name for the town. He had whispered in my ear as I stared and stared at Gautam Singh Dogra.

'Someone can make me do that too,' he whispered. 'Only you,' I thought he said that but it was too late. I had already fallen in love with Gautam Dogra, the first time I saw him.

When I did look at him a while later, he had that dreamy look on his face, a smirk and then he raised his glass to say, 'To lost love.'

He might have always had that prophetic streak in him, Soumen. And he always left too soon, always.

He stayed in the outhouse of the club for the two days that he was there, that time. Every time the lights were switched off or there was a power cut, I would see his cigarette in the darkness, roving and moving in a highly erratic manner, as he walked by the river. There was that night I remember when I saw the tiny red button of light moving out of the gate, down the steps towards the riverbed, that stretched brown and grey under the moon's waning light.

As the light faded away, distinct voices came in its place. Soumen's low wheedle and someone else's long, gravelly monotone, a voice I loved. Dogra and Soumen were greeting each other like old friends but of course they had known each other for a while now. Then as my eyes adjusted to the darkness, I saw their heads turn towards me. The world around me went still in degrees and I moved back into the shadows. A lone crow returned flapping back to the tree, the branches fluttered and then went still as if some invisible hand had been laid on it. There was no wind, or if there had been it had shushed itself and was looking on, at those two men, by themselves on the dry riverbed. The grave shone grey and empty. I could even hear the cold rippling through the iron of the window bars, the stiffness of the curtains, and my own soft breathing.

The yellow circle of light from my lamp made a small patch, and the sea of darkness stretched outside my room. And if I looked out, I would notice that for the first time in many years, the light in Dogra sahib's room had not been switched on. And then I saw the two of them begin to have an argument. I knew it from the way Dogra shook his head, the way Soumen's hand waved with the cigarette in it, in the maddening, nonchalant way he had. The next moment they were rolling on the ground, the two of them and I heard Dogra's harsh, rough grunts, Soumen's muffled screams – and the sudden rustling of the branches as the disturbed birds tried to make sense of it all. There was this about Soumen, I found myself thinking, while I worried about Dogra and his temper. He had fallen out with almost everyone he once knew, whether it was his cousin, and now Gautam Dogra. Why had I been the one exception?

The men wrestled on clumsily, trying hard to keep their voices low. It was never really going to be a fight to the finish. Little wonder that years later, the murder of Dogra would shake things up, much more than a murder rightly should, and ensured a likely killer was found in Daya Sharan, more so because he was apt for the part. The fight, if it was one, was interrupted by a sudden high piercing scream, broken by the sound of the last express train of the night going over the bridge. By the time it had passed, and the rattling of the bridge had eased, there was quiet all over too.

I never saw Soumen again in Brooks Town after that night, till the time he reappeared on that boulder, on our way to school. And Dogra, as was his usual way, did not reply to my neatly written, politely worded note.

I understand you were the last person to see Soumen Mohanty before he left. I am referring to events of August this year. I would like to meet you to discuss this further.

I saw the letter still in its fancy envelope in all the stuff he discarded, that Reddy picked up to dispose off later. That he handed over to me with his all knowing smile. Gautam Dogra had by then too much to occupy him and I too was a thing of his past, a past he wanted to deliberately and cold-bloodedly expunge.

Reddy found that letter along with others Dogra had been receiving the last years of his life from groups as diverse as Hum Hindustani and the Akhand Hindustan Mahasangh. When Dogra was appointed the city's chief fundraiser for the temple being built at Ayodhya, he received many congratulatory letters too. That must have made him happy. It was after several years that he greeted me across the road, waving the rolled up pamphlets he had just received. He mattered once more in the world's scheme of things. He never waved like that to me again.

The first letter Subrat Mukherjee wrote to Agamoni from Indonesia came with the new year's card he sent her. After Agamoni replied, he sent her even more cards, and more letters that had less restraint than the ones he had sent before, when they were both teachers at the school and saw each other every day. The distance gave their hitherto long submerged love an intensity even the two of them had not known about.

They talked about the school, Mukherjee asked about the new Physics teacher, Agamoni mocked him, they talked about work pressures, she complained about the television, and they exchanged notes about the indifference of students everywhere. Not once did they ask after each other's families, not once did Agamoni ask if Subrat Mukherjee ever intended to get married. Some things were somehow just assumed.

But how long could some questions be kept away? And three years on, the questions only became more insistent. The ones other people asked her. Isn't it time, Agamoni? Three years already gone and where are the children? And her parents who had spoiled her beyond measure soon found that they did not have the answers. Long time friends, nosy neighbours, short-term acquaintances heard Agamoni's silver laughter, the sound of her laughing anklets rushing up, down the stairs, and they began asking too. And they asked the questions that could only embarrass and silence the listener. Why is Agamoni at her parents? And where are the children, it has been some years since the marriage, hasn't it?

Agamoni had at first blushed, or tossed her hair away in the manner she had, hoping that was enough to change the subject. But with time, such tactics no longer worked, and she had to look for new answers. She said, he, my husband, keeps very busy. That he, her husband, travelled a lot. Also that she had been unwell. But such answers never work. Busy, but husbands were meant to be busy. Where would they get the money to support you, to run the family otherwise. Not that Agamoni needed anyone to work for her. She was a teacher in her own right and her father a wealthy man. But childlessness was a sin and she could not compound it with other faults – of pride and arrogance. And other men travelled too, everyone told her, offering her several examples, of the Anglo-Indian train driver who fathered nine children, of medical representatives and travelling salesmen, who all managed to have children and still kept on with their travelling.

And far away, Subrat Mukherjee read between the lines of her every letter, followed the dates between every letter, made his own calculations and speculated, allowing his own hopes to rise too. He knew she was teaching still, he knew where she spent her holidays and he realized soon enough she did not have children yet. The love rekindled again with the distance and over time, sustained by the emptiness in both their lives. And Agamoni's flightiness in turn was giving way to an older woman's snappishness, her behaviour became stealthier and she was suspicious of others, and as she dropped out of company she spent more time with us, Asha and me, where in my study, she wrote her letters to Subrat Mukherjee. It is strange how love can fester and thrive even in the most unfriendly of surroundings.

In the winter of 1971, rumours circulated all day, and only at night, gave way to fears. Night that set in soon after sunset. No one put on any lights, even the streetlights went off, and Brooks Town huddled in darkness.

One day, night came in earlier than before. It was an afternoon and the mist that had settled over the river since morning refused to lift, cutting off from view the jungles that ranged over the mountains. We could have been marooned on an island, ringed by smoke and that hazy mist. And it scared everyone. *It was the enemy's doing,* they said, not afraid of being laughed at. *They sprayed some poison clouds, don't open the windows as precaution.* The club had not opened for some days, the milkman and the gardeners came early and finished work well in time. No one wanted to be caught out in the open when the attack happened, though being at home did not necessarily make it safer.

The mist swirled against the windows, leaving behind a smoky imprint. As if someone had peered in and left a trail of fingerprints on the glass. It hid totally the view I had from my window of Dogra sahib's house. Through the morning, I had seen the faint phosphorescent glow of light through the white smoke and even that was soon eaten away by the raging mist. I sat in half darkness, though it was afternoon and I could make out little of the study table or even the tiny letters of the book I had in my hand. I had already made a tour of the house several times over, shutting and bolting the windows and doors more securely than before. And I looked out of the window, saw myself enveloped in a swirling greyness and called up the club. Only when there was no answer did I try Dogra's number. And despite the cold, I felt the heat rush over me, and heard the tremor in my own voice.

The telephone operator manning the old exchange was the one with the grumpy voice, he sounded old. I had never looked forward to him, but his surliness was a blessing, for there was no meaningful silence, nor an interested 'oh' as he took down the number I asked for. I imagined that he too was perhaps alone by himself in that room, with his headphones and cable-switches, on duty when everyone else had taken the afternoon off. So I thanked this grumpy man, and he grunted in reply. Then said, from a long way off, It is my duty madam. Your call please.

'What's your name?' I asked.

'George Singh,' he said, and then, 'please speak here.' It was a name I would encounter many more times.

Dogra sahib picked up on the third ring. He might have looked at his instrument, when it jangled into the silence of his room. I wondered what he must have thought as he reached for the receiver. His voice was cautious, hesitant. I had the feeling then that he had expected my call. That there might have been days when he had looked across his own window and seen mine. Moments when he must have had the same thoughts that I had.

'This is me. Me Mrs Hyde.'

'Ha, yes, hello.'

It is a strange thing about old conversations. Sometimes you remember the pauses in between sentences more, the sighs, even the expressions, even if you cannot see them.

There he was, at the other end of the telephone, three houses away, a poison mist in between and it was his rusticity, his huge rudeness that I always liked, and so I was smiling, a bit less nervous as I asked him about Asha.

'She is at her friend's. Thought it best for her.'

'So you are alone?'

'Yes.'

There was a long silence and it was in my haste to end it, to hear him again, that I plunged into areas I would not otherwise have.

'I thought you would not be there either.'

'No,' a short, gruff laugh, 'it's best I sit here alone. Whether an attack comes or not, we will be killed, wherever we are.'

'No… no you mustn't say that. Not at all.'

'I do believe in destiny.' A short heavy silence, something dark from his past had slipped into his mind making him deliberately cheerful the next minute.

'I have put black paper all over the windows, over the glass panes,' he said then, 'If you go to the stationers, you might find their supply exhausted.'

'Black paper… you are really well prepared.'

'In some senses… only. Maybe at night, they might miss me, otherwise…'

'Yes,' I said dryly, matching my mood to his, 'it would be difficult for them to miss your sprawling bungalow.'

We had never spoken to each other so much before. It was as if the unexpectedness of the situation, the unexpressed fear, the pent-up silences of the past had been erased, the floodgates thrown open, and we were talking to each other. Perhaps it was best we could not see each other's faces.

'I hope you done the same.'

He had swallowed up a word in his nervousness.

'No…' and I remembered to be cheerful again, 'it won't help much now will it. The stationery shop will not have black paper.'

'Oh yes,' and he laughed, a short gruff, very embarrassed laughter, maybe he regretted his sudden cheerfulness. And I plunged on nevertheless, 'and then, as you said, it does not matter really. If I am doomed…'

'No, no, you mustn't say that. Let me see, I must have some black paper left. Asha had some. I will check and maybe…'

'That is most kind. My house does draw attention, the red-brick colour and the roof does catch the sunlight.'

Of course, I was babbling, the black paper would prove useful only at night, it wasn't very much of help during the day when notwithstanding the colour or the roof quality, the planes could drop their bombs anywhere at will.

'Let me see,' he said again. He had not caught on, or maybe did not want to. It was the ambiguity about everything, this moment given to us, pulled out of everyday life, that made me push on. Maybe it was with him too. I heard him next, 'I could come over and get it fixed in no time.' Did I hear his sharp intake of breath or was it the wind in the trees?

'That is very kind of you, very kind indeed.'

He came after an hour, an hour in which we both worked on our appearances. I was in the floral skirt I had got from Calcutta, and he came complete in a dashing sweater and bowler hat. The strain was there already, his steps faltered as he neared, and I watched as he fumbled with the riverside gate. There was no one who saw us, only the two of us looking on at each other, at our other selves that seemed to be carried away with emotions let loose after ages. He would not run away this time, cross over to the other side. I would have no need to fumble, to scheme, to be falsely decorous. We would acknowledge what had always been there.

An hour later, the house was absolutely dark but for the sunlight filtering in through the skylights. He could not reach up there, and I did not insist. He had worked quickly, and I had followed him, helping him, extending the scissors, the gum, trying to keep the conversation from dissolving into silence. The last room was the study, he had looked around the room with its books and papers strewn everywhere and had smiled in appreciation. He liked me then, I knew it. He had realized how wrongly he had judged me. I wasn't another of those pretty, flighty, silly women. I looked at the two windows, one of which offered a clear view of the river and his house and hoped he would not stop to enjoy the view. I feared it would bring him to his senses, and I wasn't looking for mine anyway. I saw his eyes swivel over the river, stare across at the mountains ringed by their forests and then equally swiftly and abruptly he turned away, too deliberate, before his eyes moved towards his own house. The next moment, as we rolled the paper over the glass, and snuffed away the last stream of sunlight, we found ourselves in darkness. Not saying a word, not even breathing, we automatically reached for each other.

For ages we must have stood there in blissful silence, in a quiet world where no sound existed, just the two of us. His heart beating against my hand. He was bulkier than I had imagined, he smelled different too. And after those first few moments, when we heard the rustle of the leaves pushed against the branches, a vendor's shout from across the road and the cawing of crows near, we became frantic, increasingly anxious. For the world was intruding in once again, erasing out those few moments in my life when I had known what absolute beauty was.

We could not see much of each other. His breath was hot on my face, when he laughed, his chest heaved under my fingers. He held my breasts and then clumsily dropped them, and I felt the heat rise to his face, and so placed my hand over it, wishing away and yet wanting this shyness that was part of him too. For all this fumbling, we must have moved to the bed, knocking off a book from the table, stopping still in momentary shock, laughing softly before beginning again. And then it was miraculously all right. I held my finger to his lips and his tongue swirled around it. His tongue on my neck and shoulders, and lower, so in my fingers, his hair felt springy, falling apart the more I tried to hold it, and him. Mine tasting the hair on his chest. It was madness then, but for everything else, I would not have changed one moment of it.

I had never been more conscious of another person's breathing. We did not know what to call each other, perhaps it was deliberate. Do that, he said when he liked something I did. While I limited myself to a yes, and a yes, and sometimes an oh of surprise. We knew each other's names and that it would only bring reality hurtling into us, and I would rather he was mine, these few moments. There he was, as I will always remember him. He was breathing hard, his breath sweetly heavy on me, gasping, as frantic as I was and I matched my breaths to his, as if the slightest let-up on my part would make him change his mind. I touched him, and my fingers left a fiery trail on his skin, as they took in the exquisite softness of his shoulders, his bare chest. His face in the crook of my neck, his shaggy crop of hair on my lips, and then the pain so far inside that I didn't even let myself scream. Even this pain was mine, a secret.

His name died on my lips. What did I call him? Or did he really hear me over the silence? We held onto that silence, till we both heard as one, the rough scraping sound as a bit of paper slipped from the window and a warm sun looked in on us, nudging its way in more and more. And I saw his pale shoulders, the wisp of hair falling over his ear, his cheek, and the grey stubble.

He lay next to me, our breaths at first mingling and then separating, moving away, till we became two different people, strangers again. He rose, quickly, and now I could see him, a shadowy, heavy figure stumbling over, locating his hat, fumbling with his clothes, pushing back a piece of a gold-embroidered blouse into his pocket. Those minutes might have been the longest I ever knew. I looked for the right words, tried them out but none seemed right. Not even when he moved in a dazed fashion to the door, remembered to take the back gate, and then let himself out, very deliberately, not looking back even once. What happened could just as well never have happened. He would never speak to me again, not even when I left abruptly for Dharamshala six months later, to return with Maddy.

An exchange of letters could be as hallucinatory as a few minutes of darkness. The truth you imagine is very different from reality. It could have been Dogra sahib but only I thought so. The minute his breathing eased, in that second's silence when neither of us spoke, one side of the truth appeared to him, stark and terrible, an accusing finger that blotted his clean, unblemished life so far, a truth so terrible that it made him rise, turn away and leave without another word, not looking back once. He returned to his usual self, the one he had lived with for so many years. I had always understood his concern for Asha, but he chose from the very next moment on, as he walked out of the wicker gate that led to the riverbank, to have nothing to do with me, shunning the club, all contact with everyone till the itch to return to the limelight returned and cost him his life.

Wait. I must have said that at last, as he walked down to the gate.

Wait. And I heard my voice, cracked and breaking and it didn't matter if he heard. Those moments of happiness, I told myself, they would last me. But one is never as brave as one imagines; and your memories break down your courage.

But I did meet Soumen again, and by then, I had a secret I didn't want anyone to know. Six months later, the snow lay heavy on the highway and my bus had already been delayed by three days. I was travelling up north from Shimla to Srinagar, but now all my carefully set plans looked set to go awry, all due to the weather and the rumours. There was to be a meeting in Shimla between the Pakistan president Zulfikar Ali Bhutto and Indira Gandhi and till the last minute, it was believed the ever mercurial Bhutto would change his mind and the meeting would never happen. There were barriers put up at the exit and entrance to Shimla, the road to Srinagar was heavily guarded, and the snow meant only the military vehicles could pass with some ease. And so I moved to Reckongua instead for the remaining period of my pregnancy.

Our cars crossed each other at the Mall Road. She was in a jeep seated front, and I was in the Ambassador. There was just a gap of two windows between Indira Gandhi and me, for just a few seconds and she was gone. That flash of a second, when our eyes met and she smiled, I would carry with me through the rest of my stay at Reckongua. She was at the height of her power then. The days when nothing could go wrong for her. She had just won the war with Pakistan, a new country had come into being and she had returned to power with a big majority. She was the empress. Seeing her and the first glimpse of Soumen whom I stumbled upon in the lobby in a most unexpected place were the only things I remembered about that colourful little town by the hillside. Soumen was just the same, was dressed like a local too, with the very colourful skull cap the locals wore, a leather coat and knee-length boots. And he looked more cheerful too – the same smile that left him with perpetually crinkled eyes. Perhaps it was simply being away from Brooks Town that made him happy.

'Fancy running into you here and you look lovely,' he said when I noticed him looking at me for a long while.

I was discomfited, I had little idea that I would meet the travelling projectionist, the no-gooder, the wild dreamer in such a faraway place.

'Come on, I do travel, it's part of my job. And then you could call this a coincidence. A lovely coincidence,' he said. It is only now I realize that he talked so much just to put me at ease.

'And you?' he asked, as he stirred the sugar into my tea. It was just like him to notice my trembling hands. It must have been the cold.

'I needed a break,' I lied smoothly. 'I keep having nightmares over Bob, month after month. It's telling on my health. Water retention, poor sleep and all that. I needed to get away, even friends and my doctor said that.'

And he believed me and was solicitous in every respect. The man who helped me most was the man I had scoffed at all the time. Soumen doubled to combine several roles here, in the small town of Reckongua. Besides showing his films to the tourists and the Tibetan refugee community, he also served as the guide who turned up early in the morning at the doorstep after I had expressed a wish to the nurses that I wanted to explore the mountain passes that lay eastwards. I was by now tired and bored of being cooped in my cottage, the valley was aflush with flowers and the drabness inside was a bitter contrast to the riot of colour outside. I wanted to see from up close the buntings that rose up and down with the undulating hills, hear the bells that chimed all hours, and watch the boys playing football. There were no letters from Dogra, not even a message. It was as if he had managed to swipe me away from his mind by simply turning over, getting up and walking down the stairs, out of the door, forever out of my life. I should not have pushed things, and I have told myself this so many times already.

Soumen assessed me with his sharp narrow look, and his ever-present smile. The nuns said he knew a lot about the mountains and the passes that led eastwards. He kept going through them, into China, Tibet and Mansarovar, several times.

He was not very talkative, as he led us up the paths, stopping to show me bits of stone, patches of rhododendron bushes. When we stopped at the old Tibetan teahouse for butter tea, we sat quietly and he did not ask many questions then too.

He asked me if things were the same in Brooks Town. And if Dogra was still around.

The mention of his name was enough to startle me and I pressed my hands hard on my cheeks to stop the blush from spreading. 'It is very cold suddenly,' I said laughing.

'Are you nervous?' he asked me in turn, and I shook my head.

'There is something about your face, I read faces,' and he laughed away his explanation. Too easily, deliberately, but

I had noted the second in which he had watched my face, waited for my reaction. The blood had drained from my face. But I was lucky, my pregnancy did not show, enveloped as I was in the voluminous folds of my robe and perhaps he did not understand such things. After all, he had never been married.

'It's all right, really, a man like me always on the move. I have learned how to tell people. Dogra never seemed to want to stay on there, at least not when I first told him about the place. Still he has. Pity about his wife, though. She simply disappeared.'

Soumen spoke deliberately, as if he had rehearsed the words, but I got up abruptly and turned away. I didn't want to hear of Dogra's wife or anything more. The nuns had told me other things about him, his itinerant ways, his habit of disappearing for days and then reappearing all of a sudden. He is like a butterfly, flitting in and out, you never can track him down, they would say. 'Heaven knows who he is with,' they would titter and look away.

'We must go,' I said, 'it is late.'

He remained sitting where he was, on that low boulder, looking away and so I had to ask, 'What do you know of Dogra's wife?'

'I knew her once long ago.' And then he told me how he had tried to help her escape from Srinagar but there was never space for her in the Indian planes. Then it turned out she was from the other side, a village caught on the wrong side of the line, and the government refused to sanction her papers. And he took her to Bombay, promised her roles in films, 'There was really nothing for her in Srinagar. She was a proud woman and wouldn't take pity from those who knew her. But Dogra never forgave me for doing this and never would he have her back again.'

I held my breath, hearing about a woman I had never known about, who was yet important in every way. He was quiet and it seemed he didn't want to talk any more. But he did, and when he did, his voice was rough and cracked, and he wouldn't look at me.

'She stayed with me in my cottage in Juhu. She had bit roles in the Prithvi theatres group… they were to come here too, but it never happened.'

I turned my head away, reading my hands. That was why they had fought each other to the ground those many years ago. He loved his wife and didn't want to see her again. He didn't give her a chance to explain either.

'Did he think there was anything between the two of you?'

His laughter was sudden, loud and not his own.

'As if…'

He looked at me, and shook his head. 'It's not as sordid as you think… she was…'

I didn't let him finish, not knowing the truth is sometimes so much better. 'I didn't think at all.'

I touched his cheek then, and he flinched but he let my hand stay. I saw his eyes darken and his jaws tightened. The snow on his chin I blew away from my fingers and laughed. My breath moved like a small white cloud onto his face. He breathed it in, in turn. Then he smiled, pressed his knuckles gently on my cheek and the moment soon passed. It was beginning to get colder and he insisted on seeing me safely home. We didn't talk on the way back, but I sat on the pony and he led the way, holding the ropes, and I felt almost as safe as I did when I lay in Dogra's big, strong arms. It was on the way back I told him the story of the baby I intended to pick up, and take away with me. 'Quite dramatic,' he said and laughed, 'that will shake the whole old town up.' Soumen's truth, like his fleeting appearances in Brooks Town, always came with his short bursts of laughter.

The voices at the riverbank I had heard, years ago. Those lonely nights when I had been all by myself, and with no news of Bob. The two of them, Dogra sahib and Soumen arguing and then rolling over with each other to the ground. Soumen's muffled shrieks and Dogra's own furious shouting. And then the report of the body found on the train tracks, part of a gold threaded blouse trailing in its fingers. The torn half, which Dogra carried in his pocket all the time. A man who knew how to love, after all, except that he was afraid of it as well. The dead body that Kerketta had also looked strangely at.

But it was the guide who was speaking up again, 'There is your past waking up again. When there is a fair at the boarding schools, I have a stall too. A crystal ball gazer. Pity, I should have taken you to Bombay, I could have made a heroine out of you.'

I remembered my own old desires, thought of the child I would have and nearly burst out crying. Oh, the cruel games that destiny plays on us.

I laughed instead, he said such funny things that were of use no more and the day was beautiful. A soft blue sky with the moon still visible, the chinar trees like proud soldiers marching all the way up and down the hills, the fragrance of the pine cones that rolled right under the feet, the lingering warmth of the tea cup I had held around my hands, the low mumble of other conversations that came to us with the wind.

'Brooks Town, still is a small town, I can tell. Once there was a plantation but now it is just a hillside town. Once a very British town. The manager, your husband. He too died very mysteriously, didn't he?'

I looked down at my feet, my heart taking on an erratic beat. But the next moment he said very casually, 'But I could not be sure of course. It is all the news I pick up here and there. And really I could be wrong,' he said again, ruefully.

We laughed together. He was harmless, I thought. And when I asked for the guide next, he had disappeared.

I remember now the many details I had forgotten. Simply because they were too flimsy compared to what happened next. How I left in the heavy rain to make my way back to Shimla, where Maddy was born. I had spent too much time at Reckongua and at Shimla the British hospital had a good reputation. Though nothing could be done about the theft that happened when Maddy was brought back to me and I slept in deep exhaustion. Waking up, I knew my room had been pilfered but I couldn't be bothered. A new baby is hard work. And so it was much later, only after I had returned to Brooks Town, that I realized that the birth certificate was the one thing I had lost during my time at the hospital in Shimla.

I was never really a good mother to Maddy. The night she was in hospital, Prem that young doctor consulted his notes, pored over his old medical files and finally announced, sounding so very uncertain, that Maddy's problems stemmed from the largely psychological, and that it was due to, (poor boy he stammered and hesitated so much), inattention in the crucial years of childhood.

'What kind of inattention?'

He didn't know that. 'It says not too much love.'

'Too much love.'

And there was Asha by my side, consoling me, patting me on the back, 'There, there,' she said, 'everyone knows how kind you have been to Maddy. She had no one in the world when you got her, and then you do so much for her.'

I was weeping then. Sobbing my heart out as Maddy lay in the hospital bed. Angry with the world, with Maddy, and with that man Dogra. It was as if he was determined to punish himself for those few moments of weakness. For the next ten years, he would withdraw himself into splendid isolation. Rarely venturing out, and his daughter Asha bore the brunt of it. There he stood, outside the gate, monitoring her every movement till he paid the price for it, with his life.

Only I knew what had gone wrong. Stabbed to death by a sharp-edged knife that was not found anywhere in the scene of the crime. And my own Tibetan dagger, that I had picked up from my time in Reckongua, was missing. Someone had simply come in and helped himself to it, someone to whom the mysterious footsteps belonged, and it wasn't Reddy. Of that I was sure. Three years after Dogra's death, I had still no idea where the knife had gone, or if it had been misplaced somewhere, or who could have taken it.

My other secret was the tramp lady who sat on the river boulders, who never drew a second glance from anyone. Even if anyone as much as glanced at her, they dismissed her as the same one who had been evicted from near the school cricket grounds by Subrat Mukherjee one Saturday afternoon. It is strange how if one is or looks old, poor, scrawny and ugly to boot, you are simply wiped off the earth, your existence of no concern to anyone. It gave you an anonymity, even freedom. So I walked up, down the riverbank, sometimes looking in at every gate, and one afternoon, entering Dogra's house with the key I had stolen from Kerketta many years ago, a Tibetan dagger in my hand, I drew no one's attention, except of course Reddy's and so I contrived to send him away.

In my time, I had been a good drama teacher.

~

Love just needs the smallest encouragement, nothing else. A glimmer of hope, the possibility of a dream, will still allow love to thrive in the most arid of climates. At least Agamoni had her letters and she could read them many times over, imagine Subrat's hand as he wrote the lines, the expressions of his face. And the waiting afforded a delicious pleasure too, for they knew a letter was on its way even as they waited. But there were bits and pieces that the letters nevertheless left out.

Agamoni did not tell Subrat that she was pregnant. And Subrat never bothered to tell her his plans of coming home because both father and son had finally given in. He was going to get married, his father was getting old and there would soon be no one to look after his unfortunate sister, who still ran up and down the 108 steps of the Budhiraja temple. His father had agreed to sell away in part all the furniture he had gathered over the years. It was a quid pro quo. If I do get married, Subrat told his father, there has to be a place to bring the bride to.

She can't climb over the hoard of furniture that the house is full of and I am not going to marry a circus acrobat.

A trapeze artist, I would have corrected him.

The years apart had given him a new boldness, and the letters he wrote made him more articulate. He said things out fearlessly when earlier he would have sunk into quietude and depression. It gave him hope and too many new ideas.

The postmaster knew of this, of course. A long gap between letters meant something momentous was going to happen, something scandalous and he could barely contain his excitement. As did Asha, who faithfully collected the letters that came and passed these on to Agamoni. But Agamoni's schedule now included a visit to the doctor every second day which meant that for some days, the letters were at home and I would see Subrat's spidery, painstaking handwriting on every envelope and be assailed by too many feelings.

The letter he wrote her to tell her he was coming home I read secretly, when I could hold myself no more. A thick envelope that had come only a week after another thick envelope. Asha had not had time to meet Agamoni, who had taken some days off school for her attacks of morning sickness had got too severe. It was as Dr Prem Agarwal had ordered.

Subrat was still formal in his letters. But there was vehemence too, in his formality and it took me a long time to read it through. So when Asha returned unexpectedly, I had perforce to hide it, and that upset Asha. She had never lost a letter she had been entrusted with, before.

'She will kill me,' Asha sniffled, and I worried about the letter, secure under the mattress, hoping there would be enough time for the gum to settle down, before I could produce it triumphantly.

'Don't be silly. It's only a letter.'

'But an important one. She really looks forward… she likes receiving letters…'

'Don't let her husband know about it.'

'Oh him, does he ever have the time…'

'Well, he does seem to have the time, especially for an important thing like a baby. And Agamoni seems happy to have gone through it. She has been very occupied.'

Indeed she had been. That had been Subrat Mukherjee's anxious query, the moment he asked after her health. *Have you been taken up with other activities now? It would appear that there is too much on your mind at present. I do hope it is not something disquieting.*

'Does he know about her condition?'

'Of course he does,' replied Asha, her eyes everywhere but on me. She looked up as if she hoped the letter would come floating down towards her. 'He has been visiting every weekend.'

'No, I mean Subrat.'

'He must.' People can be very obtuse especially when looking for things they have lost.

'Would she let him know?'

'Why not?' She looked at me strangely, 'Why would she not?'

'I don't know,' I shrugged. But it was entirely natural that she had not had the time to let him know. A woman when pregnant has too much space to occupy and too much to occupy her. Even as you take on more space, fill out and acquire a presence, a heavier one, you are no longer yourself, your real self is enmeshed deep within all those other demands that pregnancy imposes.

In every para Subrat aired his concerns, as if he were haranguing her. And towards the last, he did break down and finally tell her that he was thinking of returning. The pomposity, the reserve had finally given way in that last desperate para.

My father has been asking me to return home. I am seriously considering it. I do hope we can meet. The last occasion seems a long time back. That café, you told me, is no longer there. But there are other places. I hope you will let me know. That might give you reason enough to write.

This was sarcasm, but would Agamoni read between the lines and understand. She was too full of herself.

My father thinks it is time I settled down.

Ah! Here it was, the sly, barely disguised attempt to emotionally blackmail. To make a last assertion. He must have agonized over this. Wondered, pen in hand, looking out of the window, in a strange country, how she would take it. He must have thought it over, rewritten it several times before writing down what he did. It wasn't what he but what his father wanted.

'And it is time too.'

'Isn't Subrat going to marry?'

Asha shrugged. She was looking through the books, under the table, and her raised shoulder caught the edge. She rubbed her shoulder where it hurt and then retreated to her room, to rummage through her medicine chest for the bottle of Iodex. Asha was vain about her fair skin, hated the slightest blemish. The petty vanities that haunt the smallest of us. I slipped the letter behind the sofa, to make it appear that somehow it had slipped through the cracks. But Asha forgot the letter as she administered to her own pain. And so did I, the moment I had covered my tracks and all evidence of my crime.

In disjointed letters, using a childlike hand, I had written to him:

Don't come, Subrat. She's going to have a baby. There is no point. Get married if you must, but forget her.

It was the kind of anonymous letter teenage girls once wrote to spite each other. And with usually devastating consequences.

It was a tragedy then that I might have been responsible for. A week after Agamoni received a letter that broke her heart, her spirits, the rains descended and for a week again showed no sign of letting up. The sluice gates of the dam were finally opened and the river's waters long hemmed in, burst through frothy and furious, onto a river already bursting at the seams.

The child born that terrible night when the rains lashed down on us, locked inside that hapless town, was born impaired. Agamoni, childless for three long years, was thrust with a child who would remain dependent on her, for life and perhaps she welcomed that. Subrat never came back, not even when his sister got married.

I could well have read his letter, understood his crazed desperation and simply sealed the letter back to its original shape and waited for things to resolve themselves. Now I look at Agamoni's child, playing by herself in the garden, or sometimes on the dry riverbed where she accompanies me on my lonely walks and I tell her, sorry. For things I don't understand either. And little Phalguni only smiles.

Other Deaths

Grieving happens in unexpected ways. Even six months after the inexplicable death of Gautam Singh Dogra, his daughter baulked at the thought of baking cakes. Even if she tried, the cake would spring its own unpleasant surprises. It would refuse to rise, and lie flat like a pancake, cherries and raisins resembling erupting summer boils. Else it would inexplicably burn, leaving one side charred sooty black. Sometimes, the cake would show false signs of being completely done but would be half-baked inside.

She moped over her cakes, though Maddy and I insited they always tasted divine. And sniffed in the aroma with much pleasure too. But she would peer through the glass front of the oven, slide in her knitting needle repeatedly, sniff and peck off a crumble here, there, but her diminishing ability to churn out cakes of the highest order – cakes that had once been a rage in school fetes, that still drew an unknown intruder into the house – distressed her.

And it was in times like these, that she wept bitterly thinking of her father.

'He had an uncanny ability to sense when it was done. Simply by its smell, or by the way it looked.'

But a few weeks before his death, Dogra sahib had lost his love for cakes, and what went uneaten or leftover, was simply given away. The aroma outside the house had its own magic. The boys at the paan store or the crowds that gathered at the Iranian's STD booth refused to disperse. There were also packs of ugly, stray dogs that began gathering on the street outside the Dogra home, rummaging in the bins, refusing to disperse. They came up by the riverside as well. It was terrible to come across a hungry dog especially by accident.

And that one afternoon a hungry mongrel had bitten sharp into my ankle, leaving me hobbling in terrible pain. Luckily for me, there was no one out on the riverbank, and so no one heard. And Reddy who had seen the tramp lady that afternoon, was not there when I walked home by the riverbank.

'I should have guessed,' Asha wailed. 'His loss of appetite was a warning. He was falling sick. Perhaps it was his heart. Instead I went on baking cakes and…'

But he hadn't told anyone that either. Bent with his pride only a little to ask Kerketta for his special medicines. But his happiness those last few years perhaps made him ignore this pain, or his other needs, and much as I grudged him this, even me. That last year when he had little time for cakes, Gautam Dogra had thrown himself heart and soul into the task of building a new national army. An army made of youth who would be idealistic and brave, to defend their religion and their motherland. I should have been happy for him; that that last year of his life was so fulfilling for him, when the memory of his old glories fused with the new opportunities he had been given.

For Gautam Singh Dogra had never made a secret of his illustrious past. He had, just like his father before him, risen to be minister from a mere sergeant in charge of the Dogra troops, a contingent personally committed to the safety of His Majesty, the Maharaja of Kashmir. It was he who had made that crucial phone call, though there were others who claimed to do so as well, before the lights went out all over Srinagar, and the stillness broken occasionally by the frantic barking of pie dogs, descended all over the town. For that one phone call, Dogra sahib had to accept a lifetime of anonymity, lost in the dry interiors of India, to remain until the very end, on the very periphery of things.

It was an ordinary night. People had gone to sleep early, the moon looking down on everything, not missing a thing. Everything had died down, even the whispers from the forest. That was what made everything stand out. The advance of the tribal army moving in determinedly. The returning steps of a woman, Dogra's wife, from the maharaja's palace, where she had gone to handover the stitched clothes. Dogra Sahib was polishing his gun, watching over his sleeping daughter. It was then that the town was plunged into darkness.

Dogra sahib stopped, startled. He walked to the window, only to be greeted by the utter quiet and the eerie darkness. It was a darkness that oozed out from everything, from the ice dripping slowly from roof to ground, from the rustling of crows in the branches, the slow barking of the dogs, a child crying somewhere, then stray shouts and then footsteps. He saw the palace too, a black hull of a ship inert under the moon's gaze.

Robbed of its lights, its laughter and everyday liveliness, it looked shrunken, a stranded creature of darkness just like all else around it. He called up Delhi, yelling the name out to the operator. Prime minister. Give me the prime minister.

The operator hesitated, he took his time. They were used to dialling hotel numbers in Bombay and Delhi to make reservations for the maharaja. He had never spoken to anyone senior enough. So when Gautam Singh Dogra announced himself with due pomposity, the night duty operator at once knew someone was very drunk or else playing a prank.

'The prime minister. Sir, it is really very late.'

'I know that, it's urgent.'

There was silence again, a few clicking of keys, the dial being pushed around to the very end and then back again. And then back again. 'No,' he said finally. 'Not able to get through.'

'Get through to someone you idiot, before they cut the phone lines.'

It was to VP Menon's office he got through, in the home ministry. And the explaining in breathless, gruff tones that followed, his suspicions of what must have happened, forgetting even to identify himself at first, forgetting the essential preliminaries without which a political city like Delhi just cannot begin to function. Menon sahib, he was told after nearly half an hour, was already in Srinagar.

Dogra sahib's humiliation began from that minute. A string of humiliations that added onto each other like a chain, broke his heart, made him for many years a mockery of his old self. It made him twice as hearty and bluff as he really was, just so he could get away from his old self, his remembered humiliations.

All his efforts had been for nothing. His wife giggled over something silly she had done. 'Gave the wrong blouse, I hope they don't make a fuss. What to do, too much to do… if she tries it on, it will very likely burst.'

She held up the original gold threaded blouse she had stitched together beautifully for the maharani.

'Stop your giggling, you silly woman.' Of course, he had to be harsh and rude because she could not see him. Shock led to silence once again, and now there was something sinister about it. The silence watched them too, just as they too waited for it to break. And they heard the throb on the floor tiles as Dogra sahib stomped across the room in his tension. 'The lights, what's wrong with the lights?'

He understood, for something made him blow away the candles as soon as they were lit. 'No candles, silly woman. They will see.'

There was something wrong, that he could tell. But perhaps he read it in the fear in his daughter's face held in the last frame of light before he snuffed it out. Her large eyes brimming over with fear, her hands holding onto her mother's chador. 'Pack a few things, fast. We may have to leave right now.'

What has happened? His wife kept asking and all he could say, would say, that dark night, was let us see, who knows, anything can happen. But he knew it could not be natural. Never before had they been without power for so long. This was the most privileged part of Srinagar, nothing had ever gone wrong here. And the sudden plunge of darkness meant something was afoot, still formless and vague, something that still made him bark out the words, using all the force at his command, almost as if he were commanding the regiment he had strived to set up – a special posse of men to guard the maharaja.

Some things like destiny you cannot stave off. What has to happen, will occur. It was odd that at these moments of dark uncertainty, such philosophical notions should come into his head. But they did and alarmed him more. It surely meant that something of deep significance was imminent. What had been the point of all that he had done? Had his being at this particular juncture, in this very place of all others, served any purpose? He waited for something to happen, for the phone to ring, as he thought all his thoughts. What should he have done? Had he been a good husband, a good father? And in his irritation, he shouted at them, snapping at them to hurry up, hurry up (for what, he did not know) and then repenting. It was an uneasy night they spent, all in darkness.

They would not have known of the plane had it not been for the servant. He came running in the morning with the milk and this vital bit of news. He was late and the tea had not been made. Morning had broken hesitant and fearful over the town, and though the usual people appeared on the streets, there was a watchfulness about them, as though the town that had once been theirs, had suddenly become a strange place for them.

'The plane ... sahib ji, a special plane has come from Delhi. They are saying maharaja is leaving.'

He still remembered the force with which the statement hit him. Everything seemed to have been riding up to this moment, the dark hour in which even the maharaja would leave the city. 'He has given us to Hindustan, sahibji. To India.'

He felt it hit him again. That load of bricks that he was trying to lift, falling off and hitting him on the chest over and over again. Where had his old skills gone? The ability to fend off blows thrown at him from every corner. Maybe he could still stop him. Ask the maharaja to reach some kind of compromise, to fight. It was better to fight than to flee in such a craven manner.

'Everyone, everyone, sir, from the palace is leaving. There is not a moment to lose.'

He heard the stifled sobs on his wife's part, saw the look of bewilderment on his daughter's face, the look he would come to hate, for he would always from now on associate it with the way he swallowed his pride, humbled his ego and joined in the rush to escape.

'I tried to convince the maharaja not to run away,' he would tell people later, once he was ensconced in his Brooks Town house.

But it was a feeble attempt at restoring pride. Pride lost despite his best efforts to restore it, and now as circumstances changed, pride that became little more than bombast.

It was a sight that made him weep later and then laugh. The maharaja rushing towards the plane that was waiting for him. There was a threat to his life, the aides said pushing everyone aside. The Indian soldiers guarded the runway to the plane. Dogra's wife still had the blouse with her, lacy-edged, its threads of golden silk catching the sun, and he could hear her sob, he is going, he is going. What does this mean? And there was his daughter tugging at his sleeve lisping as she asked the same question, where is he going, papa? His helplessness rose like bile, like the weeds that clogged his beloved Dal Lake.

The maharaja did not look back once as he climbed the three steps into the Fokker aircraft. There were his two leather suitcases with him, others that stood in the runway to be taken by a later plane. He did not once look back and cry at leaving his beloved Kashmir behind, Dogra used to think later, and bitterly. Little wonder no one was saddened when he left. But then how could he have known that things would take such a drastic, irrevocable turn. Just as half of that fancy blouse his wife had stitched remained with his daughter, frayed and half-torn though it became over the years. He carried this other half in his pocket after she got bored with it. Then one day, years later, it was she, his daughter, who gave it away to the tramp who roamed the river every so often. He sat at his table in his study, a room in the house he had borrowed for a while and then stayed on, looking out on the dry riverbed, imagining a different time, of himself in his clubhouse verandah, looking out at the Dal Lake, at the houseboats, swaying gently even on windless days.

He did not know if it was deliberate, but the gold gleamed still those many years later, in the old, fraying blouse, as the tramp lady tried it on, sitting on her boulder in the middle of a dry river. It covered only one half of her, and it puzzled him. Where had the remaining half gone? Was there some truth to the story of a gold threaded piece of cloth being found in a corpse's hand, the one killed in the rail accident, those many years ago? But he wouldn't think of his wife at all. And whatever else he thought was interrupted when he heard the tramp woman's laughter that came to him from across the half-dry river, over the walls, along which he could see the dratted servant boy, Reddy, walking as usual. She was mad, everyone said, but he thought even madness was merciful, it made you forget, did not leave you with a mind that made you look into yourself, and berate yourself always for what could have happened.

He came to know only later that she had never left; when the maharaja's luggage took up too much space she agreed to leave on a different plane. Bewildered, and trying not to show it, he boarded the one plane that stood on the runway. While his daughter could show her excitement readily, he could not, neither could his wife. It was she who broke down, blubbering as she sat down on her haunches on the cold runway. He looked on disinterestedly, smiling absently at his daughter and the sweeper at the far end, sweeping the hangar, looked across and noticed the terrible incongruity of the situation. He saw the shrivelled weeping lady, her skirts spread wide, around her. She did indeed look very much as if she was defecating. When she rose, the blouse snagged against a stray nail on the runway, but she did not notice. The two halves of that torn blouse remained with the two women who together had once been part of his life.

He remembered the daze in his daughter's eyes, the way she clung to his arm, as they heard the rough Indian soldiers barking rudely at her mother, 'Hurry, hurry up, this is a runway, no place to sit. Come on hurry.' They saw her as she got up only to sit down again a little distance away, her ungainly self bunched in the back with the other pieces of luggage. They never said goodbye to each other.

'She gave me this,' his daughter said, showing him the blouse and when he did not answer, she tugged at his hand, repeatedly, 'it was Ma's and now she is gone.' He had roughly pulled it away from her, and stuffed it into his coat pocket, the one with the flapping sides.

She who had been so close to him, whose every smell, change of expression he had been familiar with, was now a mere blot in the ground. He remembered the noise the plane had made when taking off. How they were shooed away, his daughter clinging to his hand. It was like the earth opening up and swallowing up Sita. They could still hear the whirr in the sky and then nothing. And there was another insect on the ground, where the plane had been.

'You all, get into that one, quick...'

Terse commands were barked at them, and into wireless sets.

'Ma left this. And left.'

He would remember the tender smile on the soldier's face as he rushed them in. 'You can give it to her when you see her, bitiya. Now hurry.' He had a daughter too, somewhere far. Dogra could tell that, in all this suddenness of leaving. A leaving, rendered smaller and even meaningless in the context of all the big events that were to unfold, the battles that would be fought, a war that would never end, not in his lifetime, he was sure.

She had smiled all through the short journey then. Clinging to the blouse, pulling it away from his pocket like she would always do, smelling it, hurting him each time it brushed roughly against him. But he could not tell her to put it away. Perhaps it brought her mother closer. The soldier waved to her through the window and she waved back. Sometimes he saw his daughter's face just as it was when she was younger, the way she, then a five-year-old, had looked at the soldier through the window. Perhaps she had lost her heart to him right then and could never again give it to anybody else. How much we lie to each other, he thought. When she screamed at him for lodging a complaint about the rickshaw puller and then blaming him for her unmarried status. When she told her friend over the phone, sounding mock-tragic, 'If I marry, who will look after him? And he cannot adjust to things any more. After my mother died, he has never been able to forget her.' He heard her and could only laugh.

He laughed bitterly and loudly, and often helplessly, through the window, late at night, so of course, everyone laughed in turn at him. Velayati did, as did most people at the club. That Dogra, still dreaming of his maharaja and his regiment. They asked him the same question, many years after he had settled down in the old maharaja's guesthouse. If you were so close to the king, how come you ended up here, of all places? Don't you miss your mountains, your Kashmir?

He would repeat the same story, that over the years became more and more the truth. For he knew that in the remaking of his own life, he had to give himself a different history. There they were, in the hotel Imperial in the heart of Delhi, Dogra and the charming, crinkly-eyed man who called himself some sort of middleman.

Two men, now with no place in the new order that had come into being. Call me Soumen, not Soumendra, the other man had insisted, though no one had ever listened to him. 'It's no use looking to the British,' he reasoned, 'they have just fought a war and that Patel and Nehru and the Congress party they ran were just too keen to get power. They would allow nothing to get in the way. Nothing.'

'But I am planning to meet Nehru,' Dogra ventured tentatively when they were well into dinner and there was a pause in the conversation.

He laughed deprecatingly at himself, belched and then laughed again. His daughter was nearly asleep, but she was still with them at the table. Now he wondered what to do with her, and more importantly, with himself. 'And what do you think will come of that?'

'Nothing,' the man cracked his knuckles. 'Nothing. All the kingdoms have come crashing down. They are promising to build a new India, and for that there have to be villains. Our kings and we who serve them have no place in this new order. A new independent country, where there will be governor and a prime minister. And already these people are moving around like the royalty of old. Nothing has changed my friend, but some people pay the price.'

It was thanks to Soumen some years later that Dogra moved into this house, that had once belonged to the maharaja. In the years he spent in Delhi in that small seedy-looking hotel off Janpath, and watched his money slowly run out, it did seem he had been waiting. Waiting for an appointment with one government official or the other, while in Srinagar, with a new dispensation in place with the heir and son anointed as sadr-e-riyasat, there was no place for him.

He hung around, thinking how circumstances made one do things one would never have had otherwise. There he was among the refugees, the rehabilitation camp men, some others dressed as holy men, all of them waiting for Krishna Menon and all his assistants would ever say was, 'Minister sahib is with the prime minister, he has no time.'

Finally at the end of the third day, when they were getting restless, the crowds pressed into the garden and that was when the police were called. He remembered how tightly his daughter had held onto his hand, and the way they had run before he slipped and fell to the ground. How he had shielded her from a policeman's lathi, grateful when the man had put it away and only shouted at him, rudely. They were quiet on the way back. Walking back, stopping to buy peanuts for the girl, he was thinking how doors were abruptly closing in his face. Here everyone was busy with the refugees, but how about refugees like him? Wasn't he some kind of a refugee too? He wondered how many refugees, apart from the ones created by Partition, had really come out of Independence.

Soumen was waiting for them, impatiently, in the lobby. And Dogra was happy to see him. In other circumstances, he would have avoided him; he was not the kind to have for a friend. He hobnobbed in strange company and was given to much boasting.

'So you met him?'

'He was busy.'

Soumen only laughed, and ruffled his daughter's hair. She smiled back, any tender gesture, even a smile could move her, as it still did when she was older. His poor motherless little Asha. 'And so you will keep going back to him tomorrow, and day after…'

He shrugged, 'Let's see.'

They sat in the creaky cane chairs, derelict like the hotel itself. It was peaceful with a tired sun flickering its way through the leaves, giving the lawns a striped look. When the shades of brown and yellow changed it looked as if the grass was lolling too, turning over and over to give itself the sun.

'You have to decide fast, you know. You should decide what you must do now, you have to think of your daughter.'

They talked long into the night, his daughter asleep on the cane chair beside them, and by the next morning, his new life was ready and waiting for him. He simply had to board the train and by the next night, he would have a place to stay in, for as long as he wanted. 'Don't worry about how long, stay there in the bungalow. It is the maharaja's and he will not mind. We can work out a strategy of what to do. How to return to Kashmir and sort things out.'

And the man himself had not turned up at the railway station. They had waited till the first warning horn had been sounded and he was still confused. It was his daughter who had decided things for him. 'The train is leaving, Papa.'

For some bleak things, there were blessings too. On reaching Brooks Town, no one asked them any questions, he produced Soumen's letter, made his explanations but none were needed. The caretaker at the outhouse handed over the keys and showed them around the house.

Among the first things he found out was the way to the post office, a sprawling tin-roofed structure on the leafy broad avenue, with government bungalows on either side, that reminded him at times of his beloved Srinagar. The river that he looked out on was different though – it had a dry, ephemeral feel and it never let him feel at home. He came to the post office almost daily, collected a parcel or two and then he walked to the club and back again.

The post office people however had enough of him after a

while. What he received puzzled them – religious magazines, newsletters by martial arts organizations, history journals and then there were lurid horror comics. But they never understood why he had to turn up to collect them in person.

The postmaster would endeavour to explain, with an ingratiating smile, 'We will deliver your letters to you, Dogra sahib. There is no need…'

But Dogra turned red in the face, and growled, 'I just come here and wait for my letters, is that a wrong thing to do?'

No one had a reply to that. Of course he had every right to be in the post office. Was it everyone else who made him feel an 'outsider'? I was a frequent visitor too, after I had stopped trusting anyone with my stories. But his presence was discomfiting, even as it was strangely exciting. He glowered, frowned, chewed his lips, and never once did he sit on that chair that was offered to him. Instead he stood over them, and watched over each of them, at the same time. All of them felt his eyes on them and it left them feeling scratchy, or at times, with a sore back, all from sitting up straight, to meet his gaze.

Nautiyal babu had complained to me more than once, under his breath.

'He expects to get a letter everyday but is that possible? All he gets are these magazines and other newsletters. He does keep asking if there are letters, chitthi, chitthi, and does not believe me. Sometimes I have even turned the entire post office upside down at his bidding, in case we had missed seeing his letters, but no, nothing, no letters. And we are left with a mess to clear up.'

Asha always thought he waited for a letter from his wife. They had heard nothing from her, except the news that had reached him right in the beginning that she was still somehow in Srinagar. But after that he had come up against a blank wall, just like the many others he encountered during those terrible days in Delhi. Perhaps in her way, she had made good her escape too, from a family, a husband and daughter she no longer wanted to see. Asha saw her father's agony and her own despair for a letter from her mother but this never came. I thought of her holding onto one half of a gold-embroidered blouse and never told her what Soumen had revealed to me once, as he sat on a boulder overlooking a valley in Reckongua. I never told her either of a strange exchange I had once witnessed in the night, the rumour of a dead body caught under a train. In a sense, because she waited too, she understood what Agamoni and Subrat went through, and that was why she did all she could to help them, even taking foolish risks in the bargain.

It might have made Gautam Dogra a very happy man had he known that besides a memorial in his name, there were many of his students who refused to let his dream project perish. The grounds where Raja's complex came up were vast, and one Sunday, as I hobbled outside, I heard the shouts ringing out, military style. Sometimes, from my window, I saw them clearly: a band of boys I had never seen before, declaiming loudly, hands on their hearts, another hand stretched towards an orange coloured flag.

Some more days would elapse before I caught sight of Mahesh. It would be the first time in quite a while since I had last seen him. There he was skulking at the back, hoping he would not be seen, but what I cannot see clearly, my mind decides for me, sometimes quite accurately too.

They became more vociferous by the day. Every day they marched in a procession down my house, into the park where they stashed their banners onto helpless, flailing branches, stuck them into the ground and raised their slogans, for they knew I could see them well from my study. They marched into the Paridas' bungalow next door. The commissioner was away at work, he was to retire some months later, and he too would never leave this town, which had made him important and embarrassed him in equal measure. It was his wife who appeared on the portico to always bless them, putting that vermilion dot on every forehead and a marigold flower or two. Ever since her son went away, and the commissioner forbade her to contact him, Mrs Parida only emerged when the temple boys, as they came to be called, marched by. Bowing profusely to her, raising slogans in her name, 'Mataji ki jai', the boys then marched through the town. I was told they pulled up the municipality workers, the shopkeepers, passers-by and the younger people for their shoddy ways, their copied lifestyles and their pitiable ignorance. As for Velayati, he shut down his booth whenever he heard them approach; their vociferousness meant he always had advance notice.

Mahesh had lost his earlier lisp and his speeches at the park soon acquired a rabble-rousing fervour. I know because I heard him. He read out from a piece of paper, enunciating every word carefully, looking up every so often in my direction, knowing the words carried to me, knowing I watched from behind the silk drapes. His English was still broken as ever, but still Maddy had imparted to him some of her brazen confidence. I didn't grudge him that.

It is time we arm ourselves to protect our country and religion. Centuries of oppression have made us into cowards, making us bow and bend.

Mahesh was cheered and applauded heartily for this.

That year, it was all about anger and suspicion but I did not own a television and so misread the signs. There were young people everywhere, all over the country, who seemed suddenly very angry, who would do anything to listen to small-time rabble rousers, who were determined to march to Ayodhya to save their history and culture. But I had smaller, more immediate goals. To get the boys off the grounds and to get rid of Kerketta, for I had already left it three years too late. After Reddy who knew all about the tramp lady, it was Kerketta who could give me away. That he still hadn't done so could be because he was biding his time, like his voices must have told him to. Besides, I did think he had the knife with him. For it was only Kerketta who had access to the entire house at will.

I had desisted in my plans for so long only because I knew him too well, as he did me. He had been around since time immemorial, weeding, planting, watering every garden along the riverfront bungalows. He had the keys to the outhouse of most houses and you could hear them jangle as he worked, or whenever he broke into his funny jiggling run as he moved from one house to the other.

But it was a plan I had worked on meticulously, and it was the most perfect thing I had ever done. I stayed poised and calm before Kerketta, my hands clasped firmly on my lap, so he wouldn't suspect a thing as he always could. And the letter

I wrote, which Kerketta translated for the local paper, proved his undoing. He went about it painstakingly, peering with his threaded up spectacles, making me explain and define every word so he would be able to translate it correctly.

When I sent him to the post office with it, I told him, smiling brightly, 'Let's hope it gets published, and because it is more your effort than mine, I have sent it in your name. Lawrence Kerketta… nice sounding name too!'

It did appear in the space of a couple of days and the anger in it drew everyone's attention. It talked of a host of things – the indiscipline everywhere, especially among college students, their fascination for the idiot box, the rudeness in the air generally that made even the leaves wither and dry in the wrong season. The old order must change, I wrote, but not in such a fashion that it leaves everyone fearful. This is not eastern Europe with its history of suppression, and we did not deserve it.

Kerketta brought me the paper and read it out. A glazed look came over his eyes after he was done, and there were tears in his eyes, 'No one pays much heed to a humble gardener, and for my healing abilities they call me a quack but, but… (and he held the paper up) with this, I have now become a writer.'

As I surmised, he went to town with that letter. Showing it off, displaying it to everyone he came across. Taking it out, already crumpled and folded many times over, from inside his shirt. His keys threatened to damage the letter he had cut out neatly from the paper, and so he took to leaving the bunch of keys in my safekeeping. And that was when I seized my chance and in relief put back the key to Dogra's old gate. There was always a chance Kerketta would soon come to remember the exact sequence of events that had led to his first losing it. Just as suddenly as he had forgotten about it all. With Kerketta, the unexpected was always possible, and I was saved by a happy coincidence of circumstances, that otherwise could be very disjointed.

People he knew, his fellow gardeners, the clubhouse electricians, the peons, took it all very good-naturedly, 'Why do you sound so riled in this letter, Kerketta sahib?' they asked. 'Seems as if you have been badly stung.'

Velayati at the phone booth was surprised to see him. He had only seen Kerketta occasionally, when he had been summoned to the house by his daughters for his quick-fix remedies and the special ingredients that elaborate beauty treatments required. And now Kerketta wanted to make a call, an STD to his village. His name had finally appeared in the papers, and made him, as more and more people came to believe subsequently, a perfect target for murder. A murder that was never solved. Besides, you could arrest 600 or more men for a crime, but where was the space in our jails?

For that was what the police believed. To them it was a question of the hundreds of young men who entered our small town over the period of one week to receive special arms training, before they left again, making up as big a crowd as before on a train to Ayodhya. There was to be a big ceremony at the proposed temple site next to a 400-year-old mosque. From the crowds that had gathered, some staying on the riverbank with little creature comforts, you would think almost every young person in the country was headed for Ayodhya.

But there was someone who got left behind still, who had to take a late train because life for Mahesh Agarwal was always ordained thus. That he would always arrive at the end of the action, as the last sequence in an act that had already played itself out. Besides too many people had seen him threaten Kerketta when the latter turned up at that park, already teeming with hordes of overzealous, overeager young men who would make mincemeat of anyone who looked and behaved different, or had a name too obviously different from theirs. There was that madness in the air that decided everything.

But no one had actual proof of whether Mahesh actually did strike Kerketta and then just vanished. Besides, Mahesh's family was well-known in the town, and then as the police said, it just did not add up, all the evidence was circumstantial. Commissioner Parida had the last word: A person could go missing even if he had not committed a murder. Two disparate things need not be connected.

Here is what happened, from what I still remember of the circumstances. I will now repeat it all. It is not the usual detective story, for Kerketta's death was not really a murder. He was a victim, as police records and the newspaper put it, of a communal riot. A small one compared to the many others that broke out elsewhere in India following that terrible December day of 1992. In Bombay, Kanpur, Jamshedpur, Meerut – the tally diminished as one read down the order, and there was Brooks Town towards the end, victims two, several wounded. For those two victims included the murder victim and the murderer, Mahesh Agarwal who had gone missing ever since he missed the train carrying the first load of young men to the ceremony at the temple site in Ayodhya.

His family had long given up on Mahesh. Prem, his brother, busy as ever, had no time to think about him. When he did, he would frown, remember and then shrug him out of existence. His family never recovered from the embarrassment of his friendship with Maddy.

But a sheep however black belongs to the flock and his family came rushing to his aid when his name featured in connection with the riots, and Kerketta's death.

As Mahesh's family established with some vehemence before the police commissioner, the young sergeant of Rama's army, as the young men called their contingent, was indeed in Ayodhya at the time of Kerketta's death. He did not miss the train but had taken an early one which took a circuitous route to Ayodhya. Kerketta's death was unfortunate, they said, Mahesh had no role in it.

The police reports as a quick investigation revealed said that Kerketta had tried to foment a riot. He had rushed in with his wheelbarrow, that torn piece of paper in his mouth, intending to upset a meeting of Rama's army, just as Mahesh Agarwal was making his speech.

The crowds that practised, camped, held speeches, were particularly raucous that day. Mahesh had brought them in by the truckloads and for two days, everyone in Brooks Town had seen them, standing up in those bumptious, terribly maintained trucks, tridents brandished in the air, shouting slogans, and leering and passing lewd comments at the hapless women and the girls who happened to be on the roads at the time. They set up camp in the pandals that had been erected, a huge colourful tent that flapped as the wind pushed its way in and out and all day long they sang their tuneless, sonorous bhajans and their speeches filled with such hate and venom that my fingers tremble even now as I write this. No one, no one it seemed could stop them. When I rang up the commissioner, he hemmed for a while till he admitted that he had been instructed to do nothing. This was a cultural activity, of immense significance to the young people who had gathered.

It might be too late by then, don't you think? I could not resist asking.

It is never too late for anything, madam. The instructions will come, you see.

And later that day Kerketta was indeed murdered and by then it was indeed as the police admitted, too late to do anything.

Kerketta had been foolhardy, he had brought on his own death in a way, the police explained. He had tried in vain to keep the grounds clean. He was yelled off, abused and threatened by everyone, even Mahesh, though as his family insisted, he wasn't there. Kerketta was only doing what he had done all his working life, as a gardener in the public works department. He did not pick up the scattered bits of paper or even the remnants of firecrackers strewn all over but with his face half-covered in his scarf, and his wheelbarrow, he weeded, watered, and pruned, ignoring the men who pursued him, their faces contorted by rage, anger and sheer irritation. How could someone be engaged in work like this, when they were engaged in far superior acts of devotion, they had asked one another.

Kerketta, oblivious to this, basking in his new found glory, continued with his work, not noticing the crowds growing agitated around him. The drumming took on an insistent, throbbing rhythm, cracker bombs went off at repeated intervals and on a mike, I could hear Dogra's disembodied long dead voice again, recorded in a tape among others, exhorting them to repeat after him, Jai Sri Ram. Interspersed with cries of Har Har Mahadev.

It was an excitable, volatile crowd, running all over the place, was all the police said. Those who were caught unawares, were simply trampled down. And why did Kerketta have to go in there knowing that emotions were running high? And why did he have to foment disharmony, try and lecture them?

As it happened, they did find that incriminating letter on him. That letter that had somehow turned his head, filled him with an ambition and arrogance that had come to him too late in life.

They put him down as a victim. Brooks town's first victim of a communal riot. A dubious distinction, everyone agreed at the club, though they seemed very pleased about it too. It seemed we did have something in common with the rest of the country.

It was Raja Mohanty who drove up a few days later. I heard his car squeal to a halt outside, heard the gate opening brusquely which gave away his presence. 'Can I get a piece of cake?' he asked, his wry smile lighting up his face and pushing against my defences.

Well, Asha has not been baking for a while now.

He threw his head back and laughed, So you have been quarrelling, and I thought sweet aunties did not do that. And more seriously he asked, I hope you find things quieter now?

He meant the crowds of course, that had moved onto Ayodhya, barely a day after Kerketta's death. He had been crushed to death, the keys in his pocket the only thing that remained in shape. I shuddered at how Parida had described it, the whole town had heard him for he had unintentionally spoken into a megaphone, that had been discarded but still worked.

We stood in some moments of pretend silence, and then Raja could not help it, he rubbed his hands in glee. He was really such a boy in many matters. It was a big task, getting all these men together for the temple mission but we did it. We got a special mention too from the World Hinduism Council and Dogra sahib will be felicitated.

Why that should make Asha happy, I said.

Indeed, I was hoping to tell you first, so that together we could tell her.

Raja Mohanty was ever the diplomat. He did such things because he was able to, and it earned him a lot of goodwill. It hadn't taken him much after his old friend, Doctor Prem Agarwal called him to ensure that Mahesh was sent out of the town quickly soon after the murder. He had after all been seen by many people including me, as part of the mob that attacked Kerketta and I could easily identify him. So Raja Mohanty had his car drive him at breakneck speed to Jharsaguda where he took the train to Ayodhya that he had missed. It was all so neatly worked out. What did it matter what the police was told; as long as you arrived safe at your destination, did it matter if you took a late train or the one that had left before?

Mahesh never returned. It would be one day a month later, as he danced the death of destruction over a mosque that had been destroyed, that his face appeared on all television channels. But it could have been any other face, as his nervous family claimed. In this way, Mahesh Agarwal for long a victim of a poor fate, became a hero to his family.

The Floods, and What Happened Later

THE PHONE RANG AGAIN, INSISTENT and cranky. I had complained to the telephone department but the calls kept coming. The frazzled old operator, George Singh, who had since become supervisor greeted me effusively and blamed the blind calls on the birth pangs. 'The new automated system, madam,' he said, 'it will take time to settle down.'

'Funny, how it is that the wrong numbers and blind calls come to me?'

'Heh, heh,' he laughed. In all the years he had connected me to those I spoke to, I had never heard him laugh. Now it burst out of him, crackling with all the tension of overhead telephone wires.

He looked at me, with that speculative look that presages a bolder, more suggestive comment, and we shook hands, his grasping mine unctuously.

'I am George Singh, remember we used to speak on phone, and now we meet finally,' he said. 'Next time you come directly to my office. Am here very late.' He shuffled towards the gate with me.

'That's all right,' I made to say but his name interested me and I held my patience till he told me his story. The one tale that he had about himself, like all of us do.

'No family left here now. I came here first twenty years ago, moving from place to place as phone exchanges moved from the manual to the automated system. Other people moved on, to desk jobs, comfortable and in nice offices, but I missed the voices, those that asked me for a number. From those few words, only one at most times, I played my own games. Imagining the person, the kind of house he or she lived in, what he or she was like. They thought I was mad and stupid to continue, when I asked to be transferred. From Phalodi, to Shillong, Ooty, Chickmagaloor and here, there is not a single part of the country I have not seen. But my children's education was spoiled. They grew up with their mother, and in boarding schools. And all gone now to Canada.'

'Well, at least you don't have to worry about phone calls to them?'

'But the time differences, I can never get it right. Am on duty when they are asleep. And people are not themselves when they are just woken up.'

It would have been an interesting conversation but he spoiled it by a second hearty handshake, gripping my hand longer than I liked.

'Do come by again, and I hope, not with a complaint.'

I was sure I would not and knew his old rheumy eyes were on me as I walked back down the hill, where I thought I could still hear the thump thump of Maya as she ran up the stairs of the temple, and I did not ever once look back.

The calls came at the same time around afternoon. But no one would speak at the other end. Asha was not around these days for in the afternoon she would leave to oversee the work on her father's memorial. And I rushed to answer, thinking perhaps it was Maddy, or who knows, some other voice from my past.

'Hello,' I said and then said hello again. It was a child, it had to be a child. In the two months that I had received the calls, I could now make out the confused snivelling, a hiccup and a prolonged, frightened silence.

Reader, I am getting old and all that I have written about may appear mixed up. But I could have just sent two letters and ended it. I could have written to Asha and Maddy explaining the true relations between us, but till my death who could I entrust this document with? Not Raja, as I learnt with poor Dogra sahib he could find ways of using my trust against me. Asha never caught on to him, she was swept away by his charm. And I was too lonely and only too glad to have her in the house.

Such a convoluted explanation, will anyone ever believe it, and could it ever be written down?

I could leave it with Nautiyal Babu, the postmaster, in the vain hope he would not access it and write a story about it. He could try, and try, but never get it right. He would slave over it day and night, till his illiterate old wife would call in the quack, tearful and worried with the new madness that had gripped him. 'He only sits at his table, scribbles and scribbles. I don't know what. Some love letter…'

I could have turned this into a story myself but have been occupied the last year writing all I can remember about myself. I still have a feeling I have left it too long, but all my adult life, I have lived in a small town, Brooks Town, and my ambitions only grew larger, more than the town could ever handle.

If you have read so far, you must have got the connections. How I had once stolen the gate keys from Kerketta's pocket for only then could I enter Dogra's house at will, unseen even on that last and fateful day. Kerketta never realized how very close he had come to the truth at the police station as Daya was being interrogated. There was the dog that had bitten me sharp and deep, and it had taken all of Prem Agarwal's newly learnt skills and ingenuity to make sure the injection course, 14 in all, was painless and delicate. I had also made sure Reddy was gone and was no longer around to go snooping around in his usual spiderman manner. For he would know, he had seen me walk along the riverbank for so long now. And Mahesh too would never return. He had seen me on the riverbank too, and perhaps realized that there was really no difference between the tramp lady and the woman he had known all this while as Maddy's mother. But the dagger had gone missing and I still hadn't found it. The one I had found and couldn't take my eyes away from at the Tibetan market in Reckongua, on my evening out with Soumen, and it still wasn't where I had always kept it. On the fireplace. I had hunted the whole house down for it, and still it had not materialized. As the weapon of murder, its loss was always a worry.

It has rained the last two days, nonstop. All I can see is the silver sleet outside the window, and the drizzle makes a steady, uninterrupted sound, like a phone line with a bad connection. The sky had been grey for days before, a thick grey glove pressing down on us, spreading a heavy heat everywhere. Every window left closed for a long while was now left open. As those hot silent days raged, I had a clear view of the river, the boulders like prehistoric animals frozen in time. The trees had begun to look withered and dry, the leaves stiff and stuck on with gum. Even the gravel over the driveway sizzled, barely minutes after they were watered.

So when the skies opened and the rain came, we were glad. I heard it outside my window at night. The same unchanging sound, the rain's gentle drizzle and the smell of wet earth. Asha asked me about the tramp lady then. Where had she gone in this rain, she asked over dinner. But Asha has also been preoccupied of late. Agamoni's pregnancy was in an advanced stage and she was confined to her home. Bored and spoilt, she always sought Asha out, and Asha, obliging as ever, spent her nights there.

I look out of the window and it is still raining. I could have been alone in the world that night, for there was the darkness and the sound. From the farthest window, that had been Maddy's room, one had a clear view of Raja's mall coming up over the cemetery. But the rain had eaten this up too, the silver lines of rain could well be the skeletal frames of the building, now moving and tottering in the thin wind.

It was at night, just before Asha was to leave that the phone rang again. It was Asha who answered, but handed the phone to me after her first hello.

'For you.'

'For me?'.

And the voice I heard on the phone came from my life many years ago.

'Charu, it's me.'

I could not speak. My lips must have moved but for the first time no words came and I who had been so good with words. No one had called me for a long time now. It was the same voice I had once known, the voice I knew I would never hear again after my irresponsible, terrible behaviour over a period of one week on board the *Queen Mary II*. At least thrice he had come to my cabin, asking me to open, with those words. And now I heard them again, unchanged, in the same even tone. I wished as I had not wished then, to see his face, whether his face was as expressionless as his voice.

'Hello.'

Through the reflected window, I saw Asha turn to me. There was something in my voice perhaps and she stayed, sat herself down on the sofa. A magazine in her hand, her attention on me.

'This is a warning. The dam gates will be opened at 11 p.m. later. There is too much water in the reservoir. You need to move to higher ground, at once. Please listen to me.'

'Why? Where are you?' My voice was dry, I held on to the phone and I saw myself in the mirror, wondering how much I had changed since the last time we saw each other. And his face came back too, startlingly clear to me. His square, honest face with the soft eyes behind the thick spectacles. Had there always been something I missed? Had he forgiven me?

'Tutul…'

'Do as I say. There is not a moment to lose. I should not have done this but I have.'

His voice rose and fell as he spoke, a sign that his attention was distracted. And I heard the same snivelling and a childish voice too. 'No Baba, leave that alone. Alone I said, not for you.' The phone went dead the very next second. Was that child his? I smiled at the thought. Children have a way of doing that to you.

There was Asha by my side, curious and demanding.

'What happened? Who was that?'

'A warning, we have to get away.'

We would have one of our arguments again, but I did not respond, did not want her voice to intrude into that voice that had returned from my past. I returned to my room, looked outside at the rain, smiled airily at Asha as she followed me into the room, and said I had to go with her. 'The dam gates will open at 11 p.m. tonight.'

'And you got a warning on phone?'

I shrugged nonchalant. It was so easy to return to my everyday self, to the present, to tease Asha into jealousy.

'As it happens, I did. And now I am afraid, you will have my company at Agamoni's.'

'We can't just leave the house like that.'

She looked horrified, as she sat down on my chair, and the table shook as her legs trembled. I felt the sound gather around me, somewhere in them a mocking laughter. Several times the trees had bent for a closer look in through the window. I thought of Tutul or Dibyendu as he was formally called, and his dry, careful voice, the same voice he had used in the long conversation we had with Robert Hyde.

There he was, sitting by me, as the sun beamed down on us, and sprayed itself out across the Mediterranean. Earnest and careful as he explained his reasons to Bob, who in turn was smiling and assured, his attention not really on him. It was a situation I had witnessed several times already, and I cringed, embarrassed for Tutul. Why did he have to go on so much at length? It sounded subservient and equally boastful in turn. And Bob, lounging in his tennis trousers, and the towel, was all attention. It was the smile he gave me at the end of a sentence that washed over me with utter humiliation. I flushed and looked down, and heard Tutul speak of his visit to the Hoover Dam. 'Those are the kind of things we need now. The railways were what you did, now it is up to us to build these temples of modern India.'

'That is wonderful, they are all doing it. Indonesia, and even places in Africa. Wonderful.' That was how Bob was, ever the born-again aristocrat, never letting on that his forefathers were all servicemen, and drivers with the railways.

And Bob raised his glass to the two of us. 'To your success and India's.'

I called up the dam control room as Asha hurried to get her things together. There was no answer. I tried again and again till Asha looked in, 'Aren't you leaving? Who are you calling?'

'Just checking. It could have been a prank.'

'No, there has to be some truth. None of the gardeners came today. If you look through Maddy's window, Parida's house is in darkness.'

'You would think they would have told us?'

She was dragging me by the hand before I could wash them again, and we were out of the driveway, running through the pouring rain when I swear I heard the phone ring again.

'Let it be, we must go.'

Asha looked back at the house, it was already hazy, the rain had claimed it absolutely. The trees swished towards the window and back again, like a witch dancing in glee, as if she had finally found her victim.

It was Agamoni's driver who drove us through the pelting rain, the streets that looked like swelling grey rivers, the streetlights that had swollen to purple balloons. We had barely climbed the hill towards her house when the lights went off. The town drowned instantly in darkness, and looking back, I saw the darkness where the rest of Brooks Town had once been.

The driver laughed nervously as he switched his headlights on to full beam. 'Never rained this way before. You were lucky I could come to get you,' he was turning his head to look back at Asha as he drove, and the car lurched, as if flinching from the pelting it was receiving from the rain. 'The train is late, I had to get sahib and I have to go back again.'

'And your madam, is she okay?'

But he had stopped the car, the water gushed down the window and the wipers flailed and pushed again and again at the glass. He shook his head, wrapped a towel and opened his side of the door.

'Where are you going?' I screamed. He was already leaning against the bonnet, wiping furiously and when he returned, he was shivering and wet, while we had forgotten about Agamoni.

'I will have to drop you and return to the station,' he laughed. 'No rest from the rain.'

When we turned into the driveway of Agamoni's house, we sat still in the car, hearing its shuddering engine die away, and the rain falling outside, drumming on the roof, shimmering past the window, like a curtain holding back something always. It was then that the driver turned his head back to tell us, 'It's not just the rain. The police station and the jail have been opened, for there will be no help once the waters come in from the dam. All the prisoners on the loose somewhere. Imagine…'

He shuddered, and Asha and I did not dare look at one another. If Daya finally found himself free in this raniest of all days, would he still remember what freedom felt like? Or did he find more freedom in simply standing, walking around on his own in the prison, than forever bouncing up and down, his feet clamped on a rickshaw's pedals, chained to a rickshaw behind him?

On the ship soon after, I had remonstrated with Tutul in his cabin, protesting at the manner he had behaved, and the reasons for his detailed explanations. Bob had been bored. Tutul's guarded reply was that he needed to be told all that he had heard. 'Those British think that they did us a favour by going away. That they helped the backward, uncivilized savages of the east with a push. They will never believe that in the end they were forced to leave. That they were defeated and limping.'

I laughed, 'Don't make it sound so grandiose. We were just at lunch with him.'

'We happened to be at the same table. Don't make it seem as if we were luncheon guests.'

I had given up, turned away to hide the expressions on my face. He was technically correct but it was I who had inveigled our sitting together at the lunch table. I had just had a swim and it was cold and I shivered and laughed as I made my explanation to Bob. His cabin was at the very end and I passed it every time I had to go to the swimming pool or the library. The first I had seen of him was his golden hair all lit up by the sun, giving him an odd halo as he sat in his rocking chair doing the crossword puzzle. I did not know then he was playing with the code that was his life's work, in a way. It was something he would do all the time and would irritate me later, for he never seemed to want to do anything else.

And later after lunch, we had met again in the library, where I knew he would be, reading the news of the cricket match between England and Australia. But he wasn't reading and it was a few minutes later that I collided with him between the twin rows of book shelves. We moved then to the tearoom and he asked me where my very serious fiancé was.

'He's just sleeping, doesn't take to the sea very well.'

'I gathered,' and though his voice was dry, his smile remained as welcoming as ever. The smile that had once made everyone do his bidding. 'Why does he have to get so serious about everything? I admire what he is doing, it is what every Indian should be doing.'

Was Tutul right or did I miss the condescension in Bob's voice? And Bob was still speaking in that persuasive soft voice of his, 'But it is not true that we are the villains that we are made out to be. We defended India so bravely in the war, Japan was a real threat. My father who was in the army, he and his men had to escape under the cover of darkness from Burma, when the Japanese closed in.'

'And...?' I was breathless, he smiled and I blushed as I put my cup down. I had been holding onto it like a nervous child.

'Got them into a special boat with the British soldiers, they came to Madras, safe and well.'

'You make it sound so very easy, when it must have been difficult. I mean there were so many people wanting to leave and...'

He shrugged, 'We know how to do our duty. As simple as that. And there is no need to broadcast it either.'

He raised his glass to mine as I smiled awkwardly, embarrassed and furious at Tutul for making a fool of himself.

It was still raining and Agamoni's pain had only increased. The baby was going to come early. Agamoni was moaning and it matched the sound of the wind howling in the branches, looking for a way out. It wasn't the usual Agamoni, her wailing was beyond her need for attention. But it was fear, a raw and very real fear and looking at her, the rest of us felt that fear too, creeping up, laying its cold, icy hand on us. Asha shut the windows, drew the curtains and took charge. But Agamoni shivered, she lay, a mass of quivering fat, on the couch, her head raised on a pillow, moaning as she clutched her stomach. And I stayed as unobtrusive as possible, out of the picture. Later they switched the radio on, and the ever happy sounds of silly conversation and canned laughter did little to diminish the chaos that threatened to besiege us.

I was dragged back into the room by Asha, for Agamoni needed all the help that was needed. Not with the radio on, I protested, but the radio voices went fainter and fainter till they vanished completely, leaving us entirely on our own.

Agamoni shrieked and I heard Asha scream to no one in particular, 'Get some candles now quick, quick. It is much darker now.'

I heard the flurry of activity. The swish of running feet, the draught of a breeze as the door opened, its slamming shut, the stillness, the striking of a match, the smell of wax, and overlaying all this was the sound of the rain, monotonous and even, in the background. It could have been almost peaceful but Agamoni remembered her wailing again. I heard the creak of the chair as I sat down, an angry cat got up where I sat and no one heard my frightened shriek followed by the hastily smothered giggle.

The candle turned us all into ghosts. Four of us, for Agamoni's mother was there too, looking at each other, glad of the faint, flickering candle for it hid our expressions. And Asha ever so often would go to the window and look out.

'We would have known if the car were back,' she said vaguely to no one in particular.

'And besides it has been only 20 minutes,' Agamoni snapped. In the faint light, I could still make out the huddle she formed.

'There there, my sweet,' comforted her mother, 'you should not be agitated. It's the rain, he will get here in no time.'

'If he does, has he ever had the time?'

And it was Asha who raised her hand this time and with no explanations needed, we fell silent. For a moment, the lashing rain reentered our thoughts, took over our consciousness, ate into everything. She turned to look at us, her hand raised, her face pointed towards the darkness outside the window, and then we heard the latch turn. The window was open and she stood outlined in the darkness.

'Listen, listen.'

It was the dying end of a train horn, that came to us through the silver drizzle. The wind clutched at the open window, determined to claw it out of Asha's hands and the train horn came again, louder, more pitiful.

'That's the train. It is on its way.'

Agamoni broke into loud sobs as did we, our tears mixed with relief and happiness.

But the horn we heard was the train's last cry for help. The water released from the dam rushed over very close, and in minutes had gushed over the tracks, and the train, with a relentless, heartbreaking pull of its brakes, ground to a complete halt. As the water swirled, gurgling grey under the wheels, the cabins plunged into darkness. The power lines had snapped.

The first class passengers were quiet for few seconds, then there was the harsh grate as doors were pulled aside, the sound of running voices, a man's thin voice calling for the guard.

He had always had a thin voice but now it was breaking with a terrible anxiety. 'The train, why has it stopped?'

He was met with a deathly silence. It rose from the tracks, and seeped inside, muffling everything. Everything had stilled to give space to one voice.

He ran down the entire length of the carpeted corridor with its curtained windows that swelled into his face as he neared. He reached the door, and pulled at the levers. It opened so suddenly that he almost fell out, but the depth of the silence shocked him. Broken by the ceaseless, even buzz of the insects, the faint rustle of still awake birds, and the creak as the wind caught in the branches. As he waited, breathing in his surprise, forgetting his anxiety, he was yanked off the train by a strong hand, and it was his scream that froze the other passengers. It was an unnatural sound, that burst high into the sky and the rustling in the branches increased, as the two men wrestled on the ground. But it was an uneven contest.

I was woken the first time then by that scream. I thought I had dreamt the sound up but the awakened sleepy voices around me assured me that I had not. What was that? A high piercing noise that zagged its way skywards and into our dreams. And there was Asha and Agamoni's mother looking at each other, at Agamoni's fidgeting, her body swollen with the child in her, shifting uncomfortably and her mother then sighing in relief at the probability that she had not heard it, she had fallen back to sleep in sheer fatigue.

I lay awake as the others drifted back to sleep. All of us in the darkened hall of Agamoni's drawing room, a room reserved for special social occasions. It was spacious and airy, and all of us had to be near each other, she said. A place that could hold all of our fears and still be roomy enough to hold more. Till the lights were on, the servants had transferred the statuettes and figurines and the many flower vases to another room, and then in the light of the candle, they had laid out Agamoni's bed and arranged our beds on the floor. There were still a few figurines left, their polished skins and stone set eyes taking on a life of their own in the darkness. Long after the scream had died away, the metal figures still tingled, as the sound of the scream sank in deep and left behind a faint hum.

'Just someone in the rain,' said the mother, patting Agamoni, soothing the hair away from her head. And then I heard her muttering her prayers. A scream isn't an auspicious sound in the least, not when a child is expected.

'It must be that beggar woman on the river,' said Asha, arranging the blankets that Agamoni had overturned in her sleep.

'She's not…,' and I held my tongue at the last moment. It was the weather that seemed to portend doom, that made me want to confess. But I would not give myself away like that. There had to be more drama. All the years, the care I had taken to live a strange double life, moving around untroubled on the riverbank, scrimmaging in people's backyards for their stories, making friends with the dogs, I was sometimes more a rag-picker than myself. How many things we throw away, not just stuff unwanted, but even the most precious? Did Asha remember how carelessly she had forgotten about her mother's gold threaded blouse? Did she know of its torn other half, the half that tragic lady had in her hand as the last train ran over her? She had nothing more to live for, her husband thought she had sold herself for her bit roles in Bombay and first she killed her memories and then herself. And I had that half blouse, picked up when Asha herself had carelessly thrown it my way from her open window.

'I haven't seen her for a while, though,' I heard Asha speak up, as in those moments she had, when she could guess my thoughts.

'Shh... don't mention such things,' said her mother and the silence fell down again, muffling all sounds. Yet I knew Asha wasn't asleep while the rain hadn't let up a bit.

And in the silence, her voice came to me again in a whisper. 'The house, is it safe?'

And as I dreamt, I thought of the house, where I had lived in since I was 20, still standing firm as the waters rushed out from the open dam gates, as Tutul watched, his hands rigid by his sides, his eyes fixed and staring at the dials before him.

When the gunshot rang, it was morning, and mercifully, the rains had abated. Agamoni still slept and we, relieved at having lasted through the night, were having our first cup of tea, laughing nervously at what we had gone through, at the tales the servants had to tell. They trooped in one by one in the morning, each one looking abashed, and forcefully solicitous, inquiring about Agamoni's health and then sitting down on their haunches, saris arranged carefully under their bent legs. 'The waters, they were so high,' their hands flitting around their knees, or a bit higher, 'it even entered the old hospital compound and your garden too, memsahib.'

Asha and I were both thinking of the house, while Agamoni's mother drew the servant aside. Nothing must disturb Agamoni, especially that her husband was still to arrive, his train that had blown its horn plaintively for some long minutes had fallen silent. Perhaps he was still stranded, the driver had not yet returned with the car. And it was then that the gunshot rang out.

A sound none of the others had heard before, but I had,

drawing me back to the days of my childhood in Calcutta, when suspicion was in the air, and Muslims and Hindus were always at each other's throats. Independence had come more than 10 years ago but had solved nothing; the refugees who came in from one side of the new border told their own stories. It was a time when the end of the world seemed near. Tutul would still be hard at his studies, closeting himself in his room while I would do my best to disturb him, creeping up to him by the louvred windows and blowing, my hands around my mouth.

It was Asha who admonished me, using the same tone of voice, as had Tutul, 'You can't be smiling at such a moment. That sounded like a blast.'

The maid rushed in through the door, tears streaming down her face, her hands to her head, blubbering, 'It is the time for destruction, the dam has burst. Pralay, Pralay.' The word for destruction, it sounded as if a high priest somewhere in the heavens had smashed his cymbals with some venomous finality.

She sat down on the floor like that, the tears running unabated, while I smiled. This was what would prompt Asha to later tell me that I had no feelings. That I had laughed my way through a poor old woman's fears. But then a dam could not just burst like that.

Asha would talk about that laughter later, in spite of all that happened. How Bindusteshwara turned up at the gate, just as they were taking Agamoni to the hospital and how terrible he looked. There he was, holding his limp arm, his clothes awash with his own blood. The exhaustion was written on his ravaged face, the pimples an angry red, swollen with the effort he had taken. He sat down on the flagstones by the driveway and could walk no further. And so it was that I made two trips to the hospital, driving the two of them separately, Asha sitting by me, anxious and nervous as first Agamoni's moans and Binduteshwara's constant imprecations to the almighty made me only clench my teeth and press hard on the accelerator.

They would laugh about it later, when all I would remember was my own frightened heartbeat and my prayers as I drove to the hospital. I did not want to be held responsible for any mishap, for the car took on a life of its own, as we took the downhill turn, and swept past Dogra's house. There was the gate at which he stood, waiting for his daughter, the same daughter who turned her head away as we passed. We jostled over the uneven road, and Asha held onto the dashboard while Bindusteshwara groaned aloud, calling for death.

She said I had been rude to him, told him to shut up. Her recollections of that night, which always began on a grim note, inevitably ended on a lighter tone, 'You were really on your worst behaviour that day, Charlotte.' She giggled, and that I suppose couldn't be a bad thing.

But for many days and weeks, Agamoni refused to speak to me after that, she had discovered a new love for her husband. The baby Phalguni born with a harelip somehow united them in their sadness, gave them a love they had not known before. And Agamoni has not had another child yet, for all her desperate attempts not to let Bindusteshwara out of her sight ever, accompanying him on all his tours. He became very god-fearing after that night when the train stopped in the middle of the heavy rain and he had made his escape.

It was this, his only act of heroism, that convinced Agamoni of his love for her, that cured her of her madness. We learnt too that it was in the pouring rain that the contractor, Manik Ghosh's once wayward son, Dipankar, had pulled Maya, Subrat's sister, into his jeep and had driven her home, after wrapping her carefully in a shawl. Now that is the love story I should have talked about. Instead of getting all wrapped up in a story about unrequited love and a murder.

The house did not sustain damage at all. The waters had damaged the garden though. The flowers stood wilting, clinging to each other, drooping flat-faced on the ground like dead fish, and everywhere there was a stink. The smell was inside too, sinking deep into the carpets and the mattresses. There were the two of us lugging the carpets and mattresses out, taking it out into the terrace, to spread it out, beating it hard so that the sound rushed across the river, to the distant mountains that after that night of terrible rain seemed denuded and bereft of all plants.

I looked across the river but there was really no sign of anything, of the man who Bindusteshwara had sworn, had pulled him off the train. He had been left without several teeth, a deep gash on his collar and on his upper arm, when he had wrestled with the man on the railtracks. 'We were both exhausted fighting,' he said, 'but still we would stop to draw breath and begin again. It was strange, the two of us fighting like schoolboys, refusing to give up, until I sensed something familiar about his face. It kept appearing at me in a flash, and his hot breath blew over my face, and I asked him where he was from, while I kicked him hard, on the ankles and he retaliated with a vice like grip around my throat.'

'More than you, I belong here,' Binduteshwara had told the man, his teeth gritted against the pain, 'this place is mine, my wife is here, my child too, who is not yet born.'

They had paused, stretched against the tracks, the fishplates wet and pressing against them.

'I am from here too,' the other man said. And Binduteshwara shrugged, 'I accepted that though I could not place where I had seen him before.'

Binduteshwara said, the other man was dark and much too thin, had a deeply cut up wrinkled face and his hair fell rakishly about his face, hiding his eyes. He did not have to tell any more. I knew who it was instantly. The man who kept coming back had come back again.

It was what Binduteshwara said some minutes later that convinced me. The manner that he said it, so casual, almost like an afterthought made me long to scream at him in frustration.

'When I challenged him, he did tell me,' Binduteshwara went on, rubbing his still sore arm, twitching his lips into a distasteful grimace, 'of the houses that lined the river. He asked about the mansion, the Englishman's house, which meant your house,' he nodded towards me, 'and then the commissioner's house, the maharaja's old house where Dogra sahib was murdered and also the club. He did remember everything in detail.' He stopped but his gaze full of malicious pleasure, was directed at me.

'And then he yawned, stretched and walked away just like that. I saw him pick up his gun, fix a long knife back into his belt, and walk away,' Binduteshwara concluded, his voice tired and dazed.

'He could have easily killed you,' said Agamoni, her eyes wide in admiration.

'Doubtful,' the bravado was there in his voice, but spasms of pain ran through him and he spoke again, in a quieter tone. 'He didn't want to. He just smiled and walked away, tossing that long knife into the air and catching it in time. I had to leave too. I had other priorities.'

His wife blushed while his eyes met mine. But there was no way he could know more about an 11 inch Tibetan knife that only I knew about. Did Soumen have it then, all this time?

Still one could imagine the fight between the two men, that it hadn't ended quite so suddenly as Binduteshwara had described. They were both breathing heavily at the end, their clothes torn, wet and blackened in equal measure. But it was the other man who rose first, and he bent down to straighten Binduteshwara's trousers, remove the dead leaves and the mud from his shoes. He did not look up once to see the sneer form on the other man's face. The superior smile was on Binduteshwara's face when they shook hands as if they had just signed a business deal and he only stood and watched, and there was nothing said, not even a thank you, or no expressions of profound gratitude.

It was that which made the other man see red. And he pulled the knife out and slashed Binduteshwara's arm one more time, tearing off his shirt and gashing his arm. It was then that Binduteshwara's poise snapped, and he screamed that thin, high-pitched girlish scream and made a dash for it. He fell not once but twice, and it was again the stranger who picked him up, pulled him through a mile or two before they were out of the forest.

He was alone with his thoughts as he pulled the other heavier man through the mud tracks. He knew these forests well, since he had been a child, had moved in them for most of his life, and there were other thoughts to occupy his mind. And when the track broadened, a thin gravelly road stretched out to join the main road, he pulled the man roughly to his feet.

'You can go and tell your own story, I really don't care.'

Binduteshwara now relieved, half-groggy had stumbled down the road, tottering and falling, still hearing the other man's footsteps in his ears, screaming in relief as he reached the gate.

Perhaps Binduteshwara hoped to frighten me, that the man who had bragged about all that he knew would return, to the mansions and bungalows that lined the river. But if he could, he would have done so earlier. Perhaps his earlier complexes still held him back or maybe he had learnt something in all his years by himself. That he preferred staying in his domain, and there was no place he would ever really belong to. And I leave the window open still, in Maddy's room, where the ivy has grown back again, and I wait for his footsteps, the soft catlike jump as he takes the wall, the creak of the window. And for a long time there has been only silence.

And then the other day, the car drove up. Not what I had been waiting for, though the phone had rung several times in the morning and I had responded. There I was, vainly trying to get someone else to snatch the receiver away, cajoling and coaxing in turn, but it had been a hopeless effort so far. There had been the giggles, the absent-minded one-sided conversation, the plain foolish baby talk that I never had patience for.

Tutul however had a wasted drive. There was really nothing we could say to each other, and there was Asha in the room. Much as I wanted her to leave the room, I wanted her to stay too.

I could tell Maddy if I had the chance. That there was never any drama in my life, the moves I made all backfired and I lived with what anyone would have called mistakes.

'I came to see how you were,' he said, when I had managed to hide my surprise and he, his embarrassment. He was still as stiff as ever, he wore his stiff starched collars and those black oxfords.

Asha smiled and settled down more comfortably, crossing her legs. 'We were frightened. It was one crisis situation after another. We had moved to a friend's house and she was expecting a child. But why did you release the water?'

And Tutul, I somehow realized that now he was more Dibyendu than Tutul to me, laughed, crossed his legs in the same manner and talked about the heavy rain, unprecedented in this season, leaving them with no option but to open the sluice gates.

He and I never spoke of the things we should have. It was a very polite conversation, irreverent in some ways. He could have been a college friend, not mine but Asha's, who had dropped in.

I was glad, mine was a story I couldn't share with anyone, even Maddy then. Now I must. It wasn't only Bob but also Dogra. The wrong men to fall in love with, men who had fallen in love with past ideals and could not look anywhere else. And it left them embittered and disillusioned. I might have done better to stay on with Tutul but it will always be too late to undo a summer sea cruise and its youthful moments of madness.

It was me who got the tea, while Asha spoke about Phalguni, the baby born on that terrible aftermath, who emerged trembling and silent from her mother's womb. It was Asha who still shuddered, the experience of it all giving her a new loquacity. She shook her hands, her head, and said it was terrible, the entire process of giving birth. 'Here you don't even know what to do with yourself, the things that can happen and you have to take responsibility for a new child and poor Agamoni.'

It was over the last week that Agamoni had metamorphosed into poor Agamoni. Asha took it on herself to explain all that had gone wrong, what Agamoni had undergone the few hours before the delivery and then the rains and the power cut. No one can do a thing in these circumstances.

The circumstances decided things for them. Perhaps that was a good way to let things happen. I decided on at least three occasions to do things on my own – my running away with Bob, and then my pursuit of Dogra, and then deciding to have Maddy. Either way, life would have still been boring for me. I would have lived a secluded, quiet life, though Bob left me richer and lonelier.

'Did you know he has a son who is like that too?' Asha told me when he had gone. And she elaborated all that she had learnt when I was away, making tea, and like before I wiped my hands clean before I touched anything. And Asha told me of Tutul's son who was a bit slow, like Phalguni.

'How old?'

'Twelve. And he has the mentality of a three-year-old.'

'He told you all this?'

'Yes,' said Asha, 'when I was upset over what happened to Agamoni. The rains, if they had not affected the power to Prem's clinic, the baby would have been normal. And afraid of the things beyond our control. And his son.'

'But such a young son?'

'He married late,' she giggled, unable to bear more the oppressive seriousness of the conversation.

She and I do speak about Tutul once in a while. I do want to call him but now I desist. I do not want to make the same mistake again. He would think I had repented, and it would cause recriminations, break open old wounds and that would help none of us.

Agamoni moved in with us. She knew what people said about her, about the punishment she had received for her long neglect of her husband, for indulging too much in her secret love, and now here she was, saddled with a child. The three of us, and little Phalguni. She is a quiet child, looks out at the river and plays with the phone. The calls still come and then Phalguni and Tutul's son have one of their strange conversations. Sounds in their own special language, strings of a song she must have learnt, long ago, perhaps in another birth and they laugh. A not-always-human sound but welcome still. It belongs to things that are fast disappearing.

But there was that one time I did call up Tutul. To find out about his son, and a woman answered. It was a tired voice but an educated one. Someone who fell silent after the initial hello, as if she had never heard another voice ever. While I looked for an excuse hoping she wouldn't understand. No, she said there was no one by the name Dogra here.

'Sorry, wrong number,' and I put the phone down and looked out across the river. It was the same but not quite. It had returned to the quietness I remembered earlier. When I had run away with Bob and come here, I had fallen in love with the place, and not him, never him except for those initial days on the ship. The tramp lady too had disappeared, but then after everything, she had to.

That 11-inch Tibetan knife is still with me. If ever Maddy does come back home, she will find it. Over the kitchen fireplace.

It was returned to me as I sat alone by the riverbank, on the steps now covered with green moss, and as the branches of an old peepul creaked overhead providing me company. If I looked carefully in the distance, I could see the trucks moving away from the forested hills, their headlights like giant glowworms devouring everything that came in the way. Now you could see brown patches in the hills where there had been only green. That night was a night of the full moon and everything was lit up a ghostly white. There were the sounds of Brooks Town behind me, the cars and the television noises that broke through every time a silence fell, and so I missed the other nearby sounds.

I should have heard his footsteps, me who used to listen for them all the time in the past. But Soumen was always the deceptive kind.

'You still sit here, aren't you scared the river might run rough again?' He came up to me as he always had. Sideways, a sly grin on his face, the wrinkles on his face deep and abiding as the trunk I suddenly found myself leaning against.

Of course it was him. It was Soumen, the man who came back, time and time again. And for what? When he looked at me like that, that old familiar smile crinkling his eyes, I almost knew.

'You looked very pretty,' he went on, 'so I wondered whether to disturb you. But I had to be on my way, you see. They are ripping up the forests so fast,' he said looking in the distance, and in the quiet between us the roar of the distant trucks sounded menacing. 'I am glad I never got attached to this place. True, it was a town where nothing happened, but I would never have been able to stand all this.'

I nodded. He sat by me, and for a few minutes there was quiet again.

'Why are you here?' I remembered to ask him, 'Why don't you come in for a while?'

'No, no, don't you think that man if he is here will recognize me,' he laughed. 'I only fought with him, but it could have been worse. He refused to let Daya travel in the train, a train that could take him away. How else would Daya ever get away? And then, the man's wallet didn't really have much and what use do I have for stuff like credit cards?'

He threw his head back and laughed. A soft laughter, meant only for me. Funny Soumen, the Sydney Carton I never knew, coming to the rescue of people when he had no need to. He would never tell me what happened that night with Daya. Had he seen something in Dogra and his lost daughter those many years ago that made him do what he had for them? I felt an ache settle deep in my heart as I thought this.

'It is a far far better thing you have ever done,' I misquoted those immortal lines unashamedly, 'but aren't you old to keep doing this?'

'Aren't you too?'

I flinched at that and I heard his laughter, gentle and mocking wash over me. 'You are still the same. Vain and utterly pretty. Spoilt Lady Charlotte.'

And then he took my hand in his, and raised it to his lips, looking at me in the eye all the while. 'You are worried aren't you? Here you are then.'

He took my other hand too, and held them, for a long while. Hands that had once known perfect love, hands that had spilled with blood and to me looked forever smeared by that blood, hands that were old and trembled as he held them in his old hands. He placed them back in my lap before taking the knife out from his pocket very deliberately.

The man who knew all my secrets – from my time in Reckongua, who knew it was me who had murdered Dogra, who knew of the disguise I had lived half my life in, and the time I had spent on the river – was this man I had never thought much of?

'Life is no big deal, my dear. It never is. The house, our children, everything goes so suddenly. I realized that quite so long ago, so I came back. I remember that lost look on your face that time in Reckongua. And I stole the birth certificate to tell Dogra about it, and hated him too… Then I kept coming back. I love you. It is as simple as that.'

I blushed. So he knew everything. Who was I hiding this secret from, then? If he had understood, maybe Maddy would too, one day.

'Keep the knife, it's yours,' he was saying. 'Remember I had given it to you all those years back when you wanted to see the hills in Reckongua? Something to remember me by.'

We sat by that riverbank, in the moonlight that made everything so much more unreal. He sat a step below, looking up and he told me what Maddy had said on the night of the award function. 'She thanked her parents, in a voice choked with emotion.'

I looked down at him, his face was in shadow and I heard his voice, quiet and insistent. 'She knew, like many of us knew.'

His shoulders heaved as he shrugged, 'How? Maybe Kerketta let slip one day, maybe… but who knows? The way children learn such things when they are taunted in school.'

And my daughter had looked for friends everywhere, had wanted to know what the perfect family was like, and all she was drawn to was unhappy, incomplete souls like herself; Reddy, and Mahesh. Or perhaps it was Jaspal who was her first love, and they always hurt us the most. 'In Bombay, it didn't matter, not one bit, and she had the looks. Every way, her mother's daughter.'

'I hope she doesn't know her mother's unhappiness.'

He grinned his rakish grin. 'But you weren't unhappy, you could never choose to be so. All the walks by the river, all that lovely dressing-up. You thought you had your secrets and this town had them too. This jungle,' and he jerked his head back, 'is dying, being looted and this town will change too, very soon, and will still have its secrets.'

He paused, letting my thoughts run their course and I didn't want to say anything. I wanted this moonlit night to be the last permanent feature of my life, with only the trees listening in. But he said after a while, ever so quietly for he didn't want to really, 'Need to be going. Leave some of the cake for me too. She does make them well.'

He was smiling as he got up, brushing the dust off his bottom, a patting sound that deliberately dispelled the magic of the night. I wanted to hold on to it, to him and he could so easily talk of the cakes someone else had baked. Something clutched at my heart. Jealousy, at my age…

'He was already dead, I believe that,' I thought he said, and my sins could be washed away in a voice so gentle as that.

'Didn't you realize that was why he did not listen to you that afternoon? That all your shouting, and pleading was of no avail, he was giving up already? What a waste... and there I was, always ready to cling to your every word.'

He smelt of the woods, of stale cigarettes as he bent forward, his face very close to mine. His lips were dry, cracked and old, and tasted of all the places he had been to. And I had been kissed for the first time since that long lost afternoon of December 1971, as war raged very close. He kissed my bloodied hands, hid his face in them and I closed my eyes, knowing this moment would pass and feeling redeemed in some measure. Was he telling me the truth this time?

I looked at his eyes when he raised his head finally. Eyes, warm and chocolatey in colour, just the way they had been when he had leaned close to me the evening I had first seen him. And then he was gone. Walking at a fast pace, quick steps that like brushstrokes erased my memory, past the riverfront houses, down the broken river steps and then he was lost in the mist.

I could not follow him, I held the knife feeling an excruciating pain in my legs. And I would never make a fool of myself hobbling after him.

I love you. I said in my quavering old woman's voice, using all my strength. He could not possibly hear me any more.

That was the last I saw him, the man who had loved me truly of all the rest. And if you, dear reader, should ask me what is the purpose of all this, I would say this isn't my story but about love. You never know who really loves you, and it's best that sometimes we never know.

As for Maddy, I hope she will believe me too and find love

in her own way. This isn't any story I wrote, but also the drama I created out of my terribly boring life. George Singh has left for Canada. I've told him to pass on this letter to her when he reaches Bombay. I don't trust the postal guys any more.

Where the walls of the old houses ended, and he was a small figure far away, he turned. I rose and watched him. And I thought he said too, I love you, before he waved one last time.

I walked into Dogra's room, I had seen the shadow on the wall. He did not hear me because I came in through the back, using Kerketta's key. I climbed the stairs, still I did not hear him shout down from the banisters. For all the noise I made, he would never deign to notice me.

He had to listen to me. He had to believe that Maddy was his daughter, our daughter. Born out of one crazy, love filled afternoon in 1971 as war threatened and there was fear everywhere. I had written to him but there had been no response. And on the riverbank, he had looked at me with downright contempt.

I gripped the knife firmly. I would not think of anything else. Arjuna had only looked at the bird before he shot that fatal arrow.

How dare he ignore me all these years? Was it my fault that afternoon? Had he not been responsible in any way? And Maddy was there, she existed. Maddy, his daughter, just as Asha was.

I stabbed him as he sat hunched over his table, already tired from the effort of writing his pamphlets, and from shouting at his daughter. I had offered to help him there too but he had ignored me. Ignored me as if I did not exist. His one withering glance, his silence could totally efface me out of existence. He looked at me once, his eyes narrowing in contempt, and he raised his voice loudly, yet weakly, 'Get out, you…' and he never finished.

The long knife went straight in and I pulled him back, hoping to see his face. I saw his bloodshot and helpless eyes and I pulled the knife out. I didn't see the shyness or even the love I had imagined seeing there, one afternoon. The knife went in again, almost of its own will. And I saw then, the hand clutching his heart. I let go of the knife, held his face, a face I had loved for so long. My hand was on his heart, and the warm blood ran over my hands, as he looked at me till the very end.

And it was done, easy as that. I forced myself to think it over, another day again as I sat by myself on that riverbank, watching the emptiness, hoping it would bring him back like before.

From Dogra's room, I took all the letters I had written. They were easy to find. I disturbed nothing else. I saw the vials and knew they were the medicines Kerketta had made for his bad heart. And I let myself out the way I had come. The dogs on the riverfront of course recognized me, and rose to greet me joyfully. They knew the smell of the rag picker but something about the smell of blood on me excited them and that was how I got bitten. I still walk with that pronounced limp.

I wish Soumen would come back, and for good too. But I know his story, and he does mine too, and maybe for a while he will stay away. I remember him, laughing as I told him, as we sat on the steps. 'There is nothing that you have against me, you know. You are implicated too, you know that, for hiding the weapon.'

He shrugged, 'It doesn't matter. I have always longed to be a partner in something.'

I remember it now and not before. Maybe one day the loneliness will get to him and he will return. I will hear his footsteps again. And me, I find it boring living the life of a leisurely lady, albeit an old one. There are too many people in the house now besides. If Soumen returns as I am sure he will one day soon, I should be ready. I had to look up Farah's for an appointment and my skin is still as good as before, never mind the long riverside walks, all taken in the hot afternoon.

The other day I told Asha that the rag-picker had returned. And she joked that there was more waste stuff now we could give her. I looked out of the window and pointed, she was there a while back, holding up a blouse, a gold threaded one.

Asha didn't catch on. Sometimes I envy her. But a part of me has got used to living another life, anonymous and forgotten, and I will return to the boulders one day soon. He will be there too.

Acknowledgements

For this book, I owe much to my parents, Chinmay and Uma Chakrabarty: my mother was my first storyteller and my father, my first provider of books. My siblings, Dhruba and Soma, know Brooks Town in their own way, and perhaps will let my version stay. Devyani and Melody were each other's playmates and so helped when this manuscript was in its last stages. I am especially grateful to Nandita Aggarwal and Rohan Chhetri for being with me all the way on this book and their ever helpful suggestions. There have been friends who have been with me while writing this book: Gauraang Pradhan, Leela Solomon at the *Economic and Political Weekly*. And those who have read parts of it at various stages: Ajit Sanzgiri and Divya Dubey. Maithreyi Krishnaraj, for the interest she has always had in my work; Kiran Nagarkar and Pankaj Mishra, for their early encouragement. And finally for Krishna Raj and Shama Futehally, two people I lost early but without their support, this journey would never have begun.